***It was Doug on the*** [...] ***metal chair in a n*** [...]

Annja's anxiety propelled [...] television as she turned u[...]

Not that Doug was speaki[...] legs were tied to the chair, leaving his hands free and his bare feet resting on what looked to be a wet concrete floor. The camera was close enough that Annja could tell his face was bloody and swollen. A thin line of dried blood ran down the side of his face. When he raised his head and looked at the camera, the one eye not swollen shut was filled with fear.

"Help me, Annja," he said, and his voice was little better than a croak. "I don't care what he asks you to do or who he asks you to do it to—I'll die here if you don't do what he wants."

The camera zoomed in on his face and then slipped down to his body and stopped on his right hand. That close, Annja could see that his last two fingers were bent at odd angles.

She could hear Doug saying, "No, no, I didn't do anything! Don't!" She steeled herself but she didn't turn away. Annja owed it to him to watch what he was having to endure.

A gloved hand reached into the camera frame. It was neither large nor small, so she couldn't tell if it was a man's or a woman's, though she suspected the former. Not because a woman couldn't be that cruel—she knew from experience that that certainly wasn't the case—but because her mystery caller who'd sent the DVD had claimed to be the one who had kidnapped Doug.

The individual took hold of Doug's middle finger and snapped it. Doug let out a shriek of pain and the screen went blank.

Watching the kidnapper inflict pain on Doug to coerce her into action filled Annja with a righteous fury.

He'd picked the wrong woman to tangle with.

**Titles in this series:**

# ROGUE Angel

### Alex Archer

## BENEATH STILL WATERS

A GOLD EAGLE BOOK FROM

# WORLDWIDE®

TORONTO • NEW YORK • LONDON
AMSTERDAM • PARIS • SYDNEY • HAMBURG
STOCKHOLM • ATHENS • TOKYO • MILAN
MADRID • WARSAW • BUDAPEST • AUCKLAND

First edition July 2015

ISBN-13: 978-0-373-62175-0

Beneath Still Waters

Special thanks and acknowledgment to
Joe Nassise for his contribution to this work.

**Printed in U.S.A.**

# The
# LEGEND

...THE ENGLISH COMMANDER TOOK
JOAN'S SWORD AND RAISED IT HIGH.

The broadsword, plain and unadorned,
gleamed in the firelight. He put the tip against
the ground and his foot at the center of the blade.
The broadsword shattered, fragments falling
into the mud. The crowd surged forward,
peasant and soldier, and snatched the shards
from the trampled mud. The commander tossed
the hilt deep into the crowd.
Smoke almost obscured Joan, but she continued
praying till the end, until finally the flames climbed
her body and she sagged against the restraints.

Joan of Arc died that fateful day in France,
but her legend and sword are reborn...

# 1

One last mission.

That's how they'd sold it to him. One final mission that would not only provide for their future security, but would put his name in the history books alongside those of Goering, Goebbels and Himmler, men who had gone above and beyond the call of duty in their aid and support of the Fatherland.

One final mission for the glory of the Third Reich.

Major Konrad Brandt had wanted to laugh in their faces.

He didn't give a damn about the history books, the Nazi Party, or even the survival of the Third Reich. All of it was meaningless in his eyes. All he cared about was getting out of Germany before everything fell completely into ruin. He knew that day wouldn't be long in coming, knew that time was running out, but his personal sense of duty to the oaths he had sworn, to serve and protect the Fatherland, had so far kept him from simply turning his back on his comrades and abandoning his post, no matter how insane matters had become. When they told him that this mission would take him beyond the borders of their lost and forsaken country without need of return, he knew his salvation had arrived and he'd practically fallen over himself to accept the responsibility.

Now, standing between two SS officers in the shadows outside the chalet that had been commandeered earlier in the week as a temporary headquarters for this mission, he wondered if he hadn't made a mistake.

*Too late to back out now, even if you did,* he thought.

He'd flown his Junkers Ju 88 into this makeshift camp in the woods outside Potsdam a week earlier, landing on a crude runway that had been plowed by tanks in the middle of a forest clearing. Once there, he found that the mission he'd been recruited for was "on hold" while they awaited the arrival of several important dignitaries.

No one, of course, could tell him who they were waiting for, just that they couldn't begin until they arrived. He'd been treated well, at least, given a bed in a room shared by several Wehrmacht officers and three decent meals a day, which was more than he'd expected. The army officers didn't pay him much attention—he was Luftwaffe, after all—but that was fine with him. He spent the days catching up on his sleep and thinking about what he was going to do once he was clear of this place.

EARLY THE NEXT morning the cavalcade that they'd been waiting for finally arrived. Brandt was on his way back from breakfast when he noticed the flurry of activity and hoped that meant that they could start getting things worked out within a few days, at least. Those in charge apparently weren't going to wait that long, however, for within fifteen minutes of his return there was a knock at his door. Opening it, he found a pair of Waffen SS thugs in their black uniforms and red party armbands standing outside in the hallway. The SS were the protective detail for the senior officials in the Nazi Party; their presence indicated that the dignitaries who had arrived the previous night were more than just senior army officers.

"Major Brandt?" said the man on the right, the taller and more senior of the two. "I am Major Adler. Come with us, please."

It was common knowledge that a person crossed one of Himmler's Shutzstaffel at his or her own peril, so Brandt did as he was told. The SS officers flanked him like an honor escort—*or a prisoner detail,* Brandt thought—and marched him across the camp to the building housing the dignitaries. They led him to a room on the second floor and then knocked on the door.

"Come," came a muffled call from the interior.

The senior SS officer inclined his head in the direction of the door. Taking his cue, Brandt opened the door and stepped into the room.

Whatever it had once been, the room clearly now served as a planning area. Maps hung on the walls, and another was laid out on a large table in the center of the room. There were no windows, and the only light came from a shaded lamp that stood at the edge of the table, highlighting the map but leaving much of the rest of the room in partial shadow.

Though he was half cloaked in shadow, there was no mistaking the identity of the man seated behind the table. When Brandt's brain caught up with what his eyes already knew, he snapped to attention and whipped out a near-perfect salute.

"Heil Hitler!"

The leader of the Third Reich waved in return and regarded his visitor for a moment. At last, he spoke.

"They tell me you are a good pilot. Is that true?"

Brandt thought about it for a moment and then shrugged. "I've survived so far. I don't know if that makes me a good pilot or just a lucky one."

The remark was flirting dangerously close to disaster, for to speak ill of the war was tantamount to treason in the eyes of many Party officials, but Brandt found that he just didn't care anymore. The Führer asked him a question; he gave a truthful answer. If that was a treasonous response, so be it.

Hitler watched him closely for several seconds and then laughed quietly. "Skilled or lucky, either one will do, I suppose."

He stood and leaned over the map. "We are here," he said, pointing.

Brandt stepped closer so that he could see.

"Your destination is here," Hitler continued, moving his finger to the southeast. "You will refuel here,

here and here. Crews are already in place, ready to service the aircraft in case you run into difficulty along the way."

*Difficulty. An interesting way to describe running headlong into a hornet's nest of Allied aircraft. But then again, according to headquarters, we are actually winning this war,* Brandt thought.

His feelings aside, he had to admit that the route had been well planned; the refueling stops were close to the range of his aircraft but not dangerously so and as a result he would have some extra fuel to maneuver with. Given that the Allies were pushing north out of Italy and Greece, he had no doubt that he was going to need it. It would have been safer to go northwest across territory controlled by the Soviets, given the state of their air force at present, but that would have meant refueling in enemy territory, which was clearly out of the question. No, southwest it would have to be, over the Alps and through Romania, then into Greece and Turkey. Once he was past the Turks, it would be smooth sailing from that point forward.

*You can do this,* he told himself. *A little skill, a little luck, and you'll be free of this place, this war, once and for all.*

"Any cargo?"

"Fifteen hundred pounds of supplies and this," Hitler said, passing him a leather satchel as he spoke. "You are to deliver both to General Giesler upon your arrival at your destination, is that understood?"

"Yes, my Führer."

The fifteen hundred pounds would bring the

weight of his loaded aircraft to just over thirty thousand pounds, but that was still a few thousand pounds below his maximum takeoff weight. It was no different from carrying a full complement of 500-pound bombs, really. It would cost him some speed and maneuverability in the air, but he was going to have to live with that.

"Will there be any fighter escorts to help me break the Allied lines?" Brandt asked.

"No," Hitler told him. "I believe a single aircraft has a greater chance of breaking through undetected than a full squadron. Crews are loading your plane now, and you will leave as soon as possible."

He came around the table to stand in front of Brandt, eye to eye.

"I cannot stress enough the importance of your mission, Major. It is not an exaggeration to say that the future of the Reich is in your hands. You must not fail or all we have worked for will be lost!"

For just a split second Brandt was tempted to speak the truth, that everyone but the madman in front of him already knew that they had lost, that it *had* all been in vain, but he squashed that notion before he could give voice to it and commit suicide by doing so. Instead, he simply clamped his heels together and threw out another salute.

"Heil Hitler!"

That seemed to satisfy the other man, who grunted an acknowledgment and turned away to study the map once more.

Brandt took that as a dismissal and headed for the

door, where he was met once again by his SS escorts, who walked him back to his quarters.

BRANDT STOOD AT the edge of the makeshift runway and watched with satisfaction as the mechanics swarmed over his aircraft, preparing it for the flight to come. With parts being in such scarce supply over the past few months, he was normally concerned about letting men unfamiliar to him near the plane, but given that he was on a mission for Hitler himself, he was confident that his beloved Junkers was getting the best care possible.

He and that aircraft had been together for the past four years, and he had begun to think of it more as a companion than a vehicle. They had seen each other through some hairy moments and even hairier missions, and the Junkers had become a talisman to him; as long as he was behind the controls of that aircraft, he'd live to fight another day. If he was going to survive the flight to come, he was going to need her to be in top shape.

The sound of an approaching train drew his attention, and he turned to watch a locomotive pull into the station a hundred yards away. No sooner had it stopped than a work team slipped out of one of the cars and quickly began unloading large wooden crates onto a waiting truck. The crates were heavy; it took four men to carry one of them. Brandt could see more of the same stacked in the car they were unloading, and he wondered just what they contained.

*Looks like you are going to find out*, he thought,

as the truck pulled away from the train and headed directly for the crew waiting by the bomb-bay doors underneath each wing.

Intrigued, Brandt wandered over.

As he drew closer, he could see black lettering stamped on the side of each box.

*Magyar Nemzeti Bank.*

He knew enough Hungarian to be able to translate.

Hungarian National Bank.

Hitler's words came back to him. *"The future of the Reich is in your hands."*

Now he understood. The fifteen hundred extra pounds of weight he would be carrying was most likely gold and silver bullion looted from the Hungarian national treasury and was no doubt designed to fund whatever operation General Giesler was putting together halfway around the world.

*If it is, you could buy your way to freedom with it*, a voice spoke up in the back of his mind. *Just fly right over Allied lines and deliver yourself, the plane and its cargo into their hands in exchange for your freedom.*

It wasn't a bad idea, provided the crates actually did contain treasure looted from the bank.

There was only one way to find out.

As Brandt approached, he called out to the crew chief. "Bring me a pry bar. I want to know what's in those crates before they're put aboard my aircraft."

The crew chief turned to comply, but a voice from inside the aircraft stopped him.

"I'm afraid that's not possible, Major."

Brandt looked up into the interior of his aircraft to find the same SS officer he'd dealt with earlier, Major Adler, looking down at him from inside the bay.

"The crates are to remain sealed. Orders." The officer smiled as he said it, as if he knew it was going to cause issues for Brandt and he was waiting for the inevitable confrontation.

Brandt wasn't going to give him one. He knew that he could always open one of the crates at the first refueling stop if need be, far from Major Adler's prying eyes, and if he discovered it to be the treasure he suspected it was, he could decide what to do with it from there. A fortune in gold and silver could set him up very nicely for the rest of his life in quite a few countries. He gave a smile of his own, trying to look reassuring in the process. "Of course, Major. Orders. Now the crew and I have a lot to do to get ready for takeoff, so if you wouldn't mind, please get out of my aircraft."

Another smile.

"I'm afraid I can't do that."

Brandt paused, a sudden suspicion forming. "And why not, Major?"

"Because I'm going with you, of course," Adler said.

# 2

Honestly, he should have seen it coming; he knew that. With a plane full of treasure and Hitler's personal papers in hand, he shouldn't have expected to make the trip alone. It would have been too easy to do exactly what he'd been thinking of doing, turning over the plane and its cargo to the Allies. An ordinary soldier wouldn't have worked as a guard, for he might have been convinced to abandon his post given the failing war effort, Brandt knew.

But an officer of the Waffen SS, the most fanatical of all Nazi units? That was the perfect choice. Brandt had no doubt that Adler would carry out his orders to the letter no matter what was happening on the home front, and nothing Brandt could say to him was going to change that. Especially since their orders had been hand delivered by Hitler.

*Best make the most of it,* he'd thought to himself and set out to do just that.

He spent the next half hour giving Adler a lecture on how to operate the rear-facing 13 mm machine guns in the rear cockpit. They didn't have ammunition to spare, so Adler was going to have to forego any practice, but it really wasn't all that difficult, just point and shoot. They had a much higher chance of survival with someone manning the guns if they were jumped by an Allied patrol, for the attack would most likely come from behind and any attempt Brandt made to outrun it would make his forward-facing 20 mm cannon next to useless.

While he was doing that, the crew loaded the crates into the aircraft and secured them so that they wouldn't slide around in the event he was forced to make any sudden maneuvers. He double-, then triple-checked their work once they were done; given their weight, even a single loose crate could be potentially disastrous if it came free in the midst of combat.

By the time the cargo was loaded, it was close to noon. Brandt would have been perfectly happy to wait to take off under the cover of darkness, but the higher-ups had other plans. As soon as they were loaded, the order came for them to get underway.

Brandt sighed. Even with the future of the Reich at stake, high command still wasn't thinking straight.

He climbed into the cockpit, stashing the satchel Hitler had given him under his seat, which was the only place big enough in the cockpit to hold it. He strapped himself in and began going through the pre-flight check, making sure that all of the instruments were working and the controls were responding properly before they left the mechanics behind for good. Behind him he could hear Adler testing the movement of the guns.

They took off moments later, with Brandt in the front of the cockpit in the pilot's seat and Adler in the rear manning the 13 mm machine guns, leaving the nose gunner–bombardier position empty. Brandt hoped they weren't going to regret that decision later.

The men's seats were literally back-to-back, so they could pass instructions and information to each other simply by shouting over their shoulders, but there was an internal intercom system available, as well. As Brandt took the plane into a vertical climb to give them some altitude, he heard Adler shout, "For the glory of the Reich!" but chose not to reply. He wasn't doing this for the Reich, after all. He just wanted to get out of Germany alive.

Once in the air, he turned the aircraft to the south and began to follow the route Hitler had shown him on the map, flying from Potsdam to Nuremberg before turning east to cross the Swiss Alps near Salzburg. Once over the Alps they would make their way through Austria and into Hungary, continuing from there down to Romania and then out over the Black Sea.

The extra weight from the cargo made the aircraft sluggish and slow to respond to Brandt's commands, just as he'd suspected it would. He made a few preliminary maneuvers, getting a feel for the way the aircraft responded so that he would know what he could and couldn't do in an emergency. The plane moved about the sky with all the finesse of a brick, which was going to make matters rather difficult if they encountered enemy aircraft, but there wasn't anything he could do about it at this point.

*It is what it is*, he thought stoically.

They had been in the air for just over an hour and had started crossing the Austrian Alps when things went south.

Brandt glanced at the topographical map in his lap, making certain that he knew exactly where he was in relation to the peaks below him, and when he looked up again a pair of American P51 Mustang attack fighters were diving out of the sun to his right. He never would have seen them if the second aircraft hadn't made the mistake of changing its angle of attack too early, allowing the sun to glint off the steel edge of the wings.

It wasn't much, but Brandt was a veteran pilot who had survived more than a hundred missions over the past few years, and that was more than most. Without hesitation he shoved the yoke forward and threw the Junkers into a desperate dive.

The Mustangs were faster and more maneuverable than his aircraft on a good day, never mind when it was loaded with crates of gold. His only hope of survival was to get down amid the mountain peaks and hope that the American pilots didn't have the nerve to follow.

Given what he'd heard about Mustang pilots, he didn't think that was very likely, but he wasn't about to sit back and let them blow him out of the sky either.

"Hang on!" he shouted to Adler as the plane turned over and headed toward the earth in a screaming dive.

Brandt had his hands full keeping control of the aircraft, so didn't dare look over his shoulder in an effort to locate the enemy planes. As it turned out, he didn't need to; the thunder of the guns from behind him as Adler opened up let him know that the Mustangs were following them down.

Bullets began stitching their way across the port wing in response, leaving half-dollar-sized holes in their wake, but thankfully they didn't appear to have damaged anything important as the plane kept flying. Brandt threw the aircraft into evasive maneuvers, twisting about the sky as he sought to escape his attackers. A narrow mountain pass loomed ahead of him and he aimed directly for it, pulling up out of the dive at the last second and soaring between the two peaks at dangerous speed.

Behind him, the Mustangs followed.

The next few moments were some of the most hair-raising he'd ever experienced in his career as a fighter pilot. He tossed his aircraft all over the sky, despite its heavy load, doing everything he could to throw the Americans off his tail. He clung to the mountains where and when he could, trying to get his pursuers to make a mistake as they twisted through the air, hoping against hope that one if not both of them would slam into the nearby peaks and leave him and his charge in peace to continue their mission.

It was wishful thinking and, like most wishes, didn't come true. The Mustangs stayed behind him the whole way, firing at his aircraft when the opportunity presented itself and content to stick with him when it didn't. Bit by bit their machine-gun fire began to whittle away at the frame of his aircraft.

At some point one of them was going to get lucky, hit the fuel tanks or aileron controls or even the ammunition that was stored aboard for the forward and aft machine guns, and it would be all over. There would be nothing left of him and Major Adler but a smear on the landscape.

He had to do something, but what?

The solution, when it came to him, was surprisingly simple and, dare he say it, rather elegant.

He'd spent all this time and fuel trying to get away from the Mustangs. What if he got in close instead? The only shots that had been fired had come from the rear of his aircraft, and he would bet that the pilots of the American aircraft were convinced by now that the forward weapons were inoperable. Add to that the fact that all he'd done was run, and it was a good bet that the Americans thought him little more than a sitting duck. They wouldn't expect him to suddenly turn and bring the battle to them. If he could catch even one of them napping, he could even up the odds a little.

It was worth a try.

He quickly explained to Adler what he was going to do.

"Are you insane?" the major cried on hearing the plan, to which Brandt replied that he might very well be. It didn't matter, though, because they were going to try it whether Adler liked it or not.

He kept running, waiting for the right moment.

It came sooner than he expected.

Ahead of him loomed another cluster of rising peaks, with a narrow pass between two of them. It was just the kind of terrain he'd been using for the past several minutes to try to shake his pursuers. If the American pilots were as good as he thought they were, they would be expecting him to make for that pass like a rabbit for its warren.

Brandt intended to disappoint them.

Instead of diving for the space between the peaks, Brandt pulled back on the stick, sending the Junkers into a steep climb as if he intended to loop the plane in a big circle to try to get behind the mountains. The maneuver might have been worthwhile if he'd been flying one of the newer fighters such as a Focke-Wulf or a Messerschmitt, but in an overloaded night bomber like the Junkers he might as well have been standing still.

Behind him, the faster and more agile Mustangs moved to intercept.

This was the crucial moment. If the Americans caught him before he managed to roll out again, he would be moving perpendicular to their line of travel and would present nearly the entire surface of his aircraft to their guns. He didn't want that to happen.

"Hold on!" he shouted as the plane reached the apex of its climb. He completed the classic Immelman Turn maneuver by rolling out at the top and rushing back in the direction he'd just come from.

One of the Mustangs was caught rushing toward him, trying to get into the very position he'd been worried about, and made the mistake of hesitating for a split second as he realized the two planes were now flying directly toward each other at impressive speeds.

Brandt didn't make the same error. He began firing as soon as the Junkers rolled out of its turn, slamming the Mustang with a barrage of fire from the Junkers's forward-facing 20 mm cannons. Tracers whipped between the two aircraft as the American sought to respond, but Brandt had been just a hair quicker off the mark and drilled the other aircraft with gunfire even as it began to take evasive action.

One second the Mustang was racing toward him, the next he was doing everything he could to get up and over the exploding cloud of debris that had once been an American aircraft.

Brandt let out a shout of triumph.

His exultation was premature, however. In focusing on the lead aircraft he'd lost sight of the second, and that came back to bite him as the American roared up from below. The pilot had anticipated Brandt's roll-out, diving and then swooping back up to come at the Junkers and its unprotected belly. Bullets ripped through the port engine, the wing and the cockpit as the Mustang flashed past. One of the bullets took a chunk out of Brandt's calf, and he gasped in pain; he could feel blood course down his leg and into his boot.

The enemy gunfire shredded the controls for the wing flaps and set the engine alight, causing the plane to yaw heavily to the left. Fortunately Adler's guns roared to life in that moment, catching the Mustang as it raced past and sending it spiraling out of control to crash into the nearest mountainside.

"I'm hit, I'm hit," Adler called, but Brandt couldn't do anything to help him because not only was he hit himself, but he had his hands full just trying to keep the plane aloft. He fought the controls, hands straining on the yoke, feet pumping the foot pedals in an effort to force the damaged hydraulics to work long enough to get the ailerons and flaps trimmed the way he needed them. At the same time, he maneuvered through the maze of snow-covered peaks, desperately trying to avoid ending up like their recently departed foes. He could hear Adler thrashing around in pain but had no choice but to block it out as he concentrated on keeping them both alive.

By the time he managed to get the aircraft level again, Adler had gone quiet and still. Brandt knew what that meant; Adler was either dead or, at the very least, too wounded to be of any help. For the first time Brandt noticed the freezing air flowing in through the holes in the cockpit floor and canopy, chilling him to the bone but helping to keep him from slipping into shock from his own injury. Shock was probably the least of his worries, for the plane was losing altitude fast and the rushing winds were fanning the flames in the port engine into a veritable bonfire. Brandt didn't know which would be worse, slamming into the side of a mountain or being blown to bits when the engine exploded. Right then, both seemed like a possibility.

He racked his brain for a solution to the problem facing him and came up with...*nothing*. All he could do was fight to keep the plane in the air and pray for a miracle.

Then he saw it.

A few miles ahead of him was the frozen surface of a long, narrow glacier.

If he could get to it, he could attempt a landing. He knew his chances weren't good. With a fully operational aircraft it would be a difficult feat. With the mangled wreck that he was flying it was going to be nearly impossible, but what other options did he have?

None.

*You can do this,* he told himself.

He was coming in too hot and too steep, so he needed to bleed off some of his airspeed and he needed to do it immediately. He dropped the flaps, feathered the engines and tipped the nose up slightly to create more resistance as the plane continued what could best be described as a controlled fall out of the sky.

The Junkers wanted to drag to the left, but Brandt fought the stick, doing everything he could to keep it lined up on the glistening surface of the glacier, now dead ahead of him.

*Come on, baby! Keep it in the air just a few more minutes!* he urged.

As Brandt drew inexorably closer, he hit the switch that controlled the landing gear, only to hear the steady drone of the alarm warning him that the hydraulics had failed.

He cursed a blue streak even as he reached over and began turning the crank that would lower the wheels by hand. By the time he was finished he was almost to the glacier and little more than five hundred feet in the air.

It was going to be close.

Brandt continued to push the aircraft on, demanding that it stay airborne for a few more seconds, just long enough to get him past the trees lining the shore and over the ice itself.

Fate took pity on him, for the aircraft did just that, sailing over the tree line with barely inches to spare and flying toward the ice in front of him.

*You're only getting one shot at this. Make it count,* he told himself.

Brandt kept the nose up as best he could as he came in, knowing to do anything less would be disastrous. He reached out and killed the engines as the wheels made first contact with the ice, the whole aircraft bouncing once, then twice, before settling down and racing toward the opposite end of the glacier.

Now Brandt had a new problem on his hands: how to stop the lumbering wreck before it crashed into the shore on the far side. He pumped the brakes while holding the yoke steady, but it was little more than throwing cupfuls of water on a raging forest fire. He was going to stop or he wasn't, and there was little he could do about it either way.

He was lucky that the glacier was several miles in length and he had plenty of room to run. Gradually the plane began to slow and finally it came to a skidding halt in the middle of the glacier.

Brandt leaned back against the seat and breathed a sigh of relief.

The sound of the ice cracking beneath the weight of the aircraft was a thunderous boom, and instantly he realized his mistake.

He hadn't set down on a glacier at all, but the frozen surface of a mountain lake!

With a lurch, the nose of the aircraft dropped several feet as the ice beneath the wheel struts gave way. Brandt shouted in fear and scrambled to open the cockpit canopy, knowing he had to get out of the aircraft before it slipped beneath the surface of the icy water or he was as good as dead.

He quickly unbuckled the safety belt holding him in his seat and grabbed the latch to eject the canopy, giving it a good yank.

Nothing happened.

He did it again, pulling harder this time, but it still wouldn't budge.

*The safety latch!*

Removing the safety was normally the job of the observer, as it was above the rear panel in that section of the compartment, which was why Brandt had nearly forgotten about it. He twisted in his seat and looked into the rear section of the compartment.

Adler was dead, just as he'd suspected. He was still buckled into his seat, however, which would make getting past him to the safety latch a little bit easier. Brandt began to squeeze around his own seat, preparing to do just that when there was another splintering crack and the plane lurched downward.

Except this time it kept going.

Water began filling the cockpit through the bullet holes in the canopy as the rest of the ice beneath the Junkers gave way. The crippled aircraft dropped into the icy waters of the lake, heading for the bottom.

Even then Brandt wasn't prepared to give up. He pulled himself back into his half of the compartment and climbed onto his seat, ignoring the pain from his injured leg as he began pounding at the glass above, desperately trying to break it. The cockpit glass was extra thick, both to withstand the pressure of the G-forces it would be subjected to in flight and to keep it from fragmenting when a bullet passed through it. Pounding on it was like railing against a tsunami and about as effective.

As the water reached his waist and his view of the surface above was eclipsed by floating blocks of ice, Brandt realized that he'd managed to escape the war after all.

Just not in the way that he'd intended.

# 3

With her heart pounding, Annja Creed stood balanced precariously on the edge of the cliff and stared at the gleaming water far below her.

She could hear the shouts of those following her up the tunnel through the rocks and knew that they would catch up to her soon. She didn't want to be here when they did. She had just a few minutes at best to decide what she was going to do.

*Not that I have all that many options*, she thought. She couldn't turn back; doing so would only bring her face-to-face with those coming up behind her, and there was no way she would be able to get through them in the narrow confines of the tunnel. Nor could she stay where she was, for the ledge was narrow and there would be no room for her once the others arrived. Their sheer numbers alone would force her over the edge.

She glanced over the side of the cliff again; it certainly seemed like a long way down.

Did she really want to do this?

The voices were closer now, so close that they had to be just around the last bend in the tunnel. She knew that she had run out of time.

Annja had to make a decision, and she had to make it now.

*Do or die,* she thought. *Paul did it. So can you.*

She glanced once more toward the water below her, crossed her fingers in the universal plea for good luck and, taking a deep breath, stepped off the edge just as the others emerged from the rocky tunnel.

Annja's stomach jumped into her throat as she plunged toward the water, but at the same time she felt the thrill of doing something she'd never done before rush through her frame. It wasn't every day that she leapt off a fifty-foot cliff into the ocean below, and she relished the feeling of being so alive in the midst of that moment, even as she dropped like a stone. As the surface of the water loomed nearer, she pulled her legs together, pointed her feet downward and pressed her hands flat against her bare thighs, tucking her arms against her torso. By the time she hit the water, she was perfectly aligned to strike the surface and she did so with barely a splash, cleaving the water and disappearing into its depths as if she was born to be there.

The crystal blue water was warm and inviting, and she felt invigorated by its touch. She let the fall carry her down until she began to slow, then with powerful kicks and strokes of her arms she headed back toward the sunlight above. When she broke the surface of the water she found her companion and new love interest, journalist and photographer Paul Krugmann, treading water nearby and waiting for her.

"Well?" he asked.

"We have to do that again!" she said, and his smile matched her own.

They were in Jamaica, cliff diving at the world-famous limestone cliffs on Negril's west side. They had had lunch at Rick's, a cliff-side café that gave them a good view of the divers nearby, and a short time later had decided to try the jump themselves. Neither was a stranger to taking risks. If the locals could handle it, so could they.

It turned out to be just as exciting and entertaining as they'd thought it would be. They made three more jumps together, each one as exhilarating as the last, before their dive "instructor" waved them aboard the waiting boat for the short ride back to their beachside resort on the other side of the island. Paul was in Jamaica on business, sent there to do a photo montage piece on the resort where they were staying. He'd asked her to join him, saying they'd make a holiday of it, and she'd agreed. It had sounded as if it would be fun, and that was something she was sorely in need of.

Annja had just gotten back from a trip to Europe on behalf of *Chasing History's Monsters*, the cable television show she co-hosted each week. The show focused on the point where history intersected with myth and legend, and had taken her all over the world as its status as a cult favorite among the intended audience grew. Annja wasn't as popular as the show's other host, Kristie Chatham—for she tended to be more serious, focusing on the historical and scientific issues behind each episode's central theme, never mind that Annja had fewer "surprise" wardrobe malfunctions while filming—but that was just fine with her. She'd worked too hard to build her reputation to throw it away for ratings and other such nonsense, much to the continued disappointment of her producer, Doug Morrell.

*Chasing History's Monsters* had Annja on the road quite a bit during any given year, but she could live with that. She made use of the time on location to pursue her other major passion, archaeology. Just as her reputation as a television host had grown over the past few years, so, too, had her success as an archaeologist.

She'd made some startling discoveries over the past few years, some so amazing that she had been forced to keep news of them to herself. Those that she could talk about had cemented her reputation as both an adventurer and a scholar. She'd developed a network of museum contacts the world over as a result and was often called in to assess the provenance and authenticity of items the museums had recently acquired or was intending to purchase. More than once she'd saved a museum director from falling victim to a clever forgery, and the good will she'd generated had come back to her twofold.

But all work and no play made Annja very cranky, especially given her other, more esoteric duties as bearer of Joan of Arc's sword, and she'd impulsively agreed to accompany Paul to the Caribbean.

She and Paul had been dating for the past six months or so, which might not be much for him but was the longest stretch of time for any relationship she could remember in, well, forever it seemed. So far, things had been light and easy, which was probably the very reason it had been going so well. Annja's job could take her away at a moment's notice for weeks at a time, something few of her former boyfriends understood or wanted to deal with, but Paul was different. He lived the same sort of life, traveling at the whim of the clients who paid for his journalistic services, so he wasn't the type who would begrudge her the time away when work came calling.

Annja glanced over at him as the boat chugged toward the resort, admiring his sun-bleached hair and rugged good looks. He had a strong but wiry build and was deeply tanned from spending so much of his time outdoors. He wasn't hard on the eyes, which didn't hurt any, and so far had been both thoughtful and considerate in their time together.

Who knew? Maybe she'd found one worth keeping this time around.

She laughed aloud at the thought and, hearing her, Paul looked over and grinned in return.

*Yep. So far, so good.*

The boat took them around the island and up to the long wooden dock that stretched into the bay in front of the resort. They disembarked with the rest of the passengers, followed the group down the length of the dock to the shore, and then headed up the beach toward the entrance to the hotel. Annja's long hair and slim, athletic, bikini-clad body caught the attention of more than a few of the men on the beach, but she barely noticed. She was used to people appreciating her for her beauty or simply recognizing her from the show, so being the focus of attention wasn't all that novel anymore. In fact, sometimes it could be a real pain in the butt.

They entered the lobby, the cool stone floor beneath their bare feet a welcome respite from the hot sun outside, and headed for the elevator. Once inside, Paul punched the buttons for the fourth and fifth floors, where their respective rooms were. Annja liked the fact that when planning the trip Paul hadn't automatically assumed they would share a room, even though they were romantically attached. It was one of the things she appreciated about him—his willingness to give her room and let her take things at her own pace.

As the numbers on the floor panel ticked upward, Paul turned to her and said, "An hour to rest and change and then dinner?"

"Sounds good to me."

The elevator stopped at his floor. As the doors opened he gave her a quick kiss and then stepped out into the hall as Annja continued upward.

Paul had gotten her an oversized corner suite with an incredible ocean view. After arriving, she stood in front of the window for a short while, simply admiring the scenery, and then turned and headed for the bathroom.

Annja slipped out of her bathing suit and stepped into the shower, washing the salt from her skin and hair before getting out and toweling herself dry. She had just started brushing out her long hair when her cell phone rang.

Thinking it was Paul, she snatched it up without looking at the number.

Answering it, she said, "Don't tell me you're canceling dinner..."

"Annja, get me out of here! He's a freakin' maniac and I can't..."

The connection was abruptly cut while the speaker was in midsentence, but she'd recognized the voice immediately. It would have been hard for her not to, for she'd heard it practically every day of her professional career for several years.

It had been the voice of her producer in New York and the man behind the runaway success of *Chasing History's Monsters*, Doug Morrell.

She pulled the phone away from her ear and stared at it, as if it might suddenly impart the necessary information for her to understand just what the heck was going on. She could feel her heart rate rising, the blood rushing through her veins in anticipation of what might come, and her hand itched to call her sword to her side.

She found it funny that her body reacted to the situation as if there was real danger when intellectually she recognized it for what it was—one of Doug's crazy little stunts to get her to call him while she was on vacation.

He'd called and left messages several times over the past few days, begging her to call him in New York, but so far she'd managed to ignore them. She was on vacation, after all, and there wasn't anything urgent enough on her current schedule to justify his pulling her away from that.

He, of course, thought differently. In his early twenties, Doug ate, slept and breathed the program and its success. Nothing was more important to him than its continued success, and he'd been known to chase her down in the far corners of the globe to get answers to tiny little questions that weren't important and could wait to be answered, if answering was necessary at all, when she returned from her time off.

This was no doubt one of his more esoteric attempts to get her attention.

Calling was one thing. Trying to scare her out of her wits with some crazy scheme was another.

She knew of one way to put an end to that, at least.

She checked her cell phone's call log and found the number that the call had come in from. She didn't recognize it as his cell number or his office phone, but that didn't mean anything; Doug could have used someone else's phone.

Ignoring the faint feather of unease that was starting to unfurl in her gut, Annja hit redial.

It rang once, twice and then was answered on the third ring.

Annja didn't give Doug a chance to say anything.

"Listen up, Doug, because I'm only going to say this once. I. Am. On. Vacation. I can deal with the decisions about the show when I return, which will only be in a few days, so chill out with the sick jokes! Understood?"

There was silence on the other end of the line, and then a voice said, "This isn't a joke."

It didn't sound like Doug.

The voice was too deep, too guttural. Doug also talked a mile a minute, and this guy was calm, rational, his speech seemed carefully measured even in so short a response.

*That's what he wants you to think*, she told herself, *but don't fall for it. It's Doug. It has to be.*

She knew that he could have disguised his voice quite easily with the help of a voice modulator purchased from any halfway-decent electronics store. In fact, she thought she heard the slight echo behind his words that indicated that such a device was being used.

The speaker wasn't finished.

"Do not attempt to trace this call. The signal has been scrambled through more countries than I can count. Just listen."

*Trace the call?*

"I have your friend Doug. If you do as I ask, he will be returned to his home in good health. On the other hand, if you don't do precisely what I ask, then you will never see him again. Rest assured, though, that if that happens, I will make certain that he suffers considerably before I kill him. Do we understand each other?"

Annja felt the hairs on the back of her neck and arms stand at attention as the threat was delivered calmly and succinctly.

It certainly sounded convincing.

"Cut the crap. I know it's you, Doug. You can't fool me."

The voice chuckled. "Apparently, I can, because this is not Doug."

The chuckle caused Annja's irritation, already smoldering, to grow into an open fire.

"You're not Doug, huh? Well, we'll see about that."

Annja pulled the phone away from her ear and hit the disconnect button. She waited a beat and then immediately dialed Doug's cell phone from memory.

The phone rang and rang and rang.

No answer.

That flicker of unease she'd felt earlier came back and began threading its way up her spine like a snake moving through tall grass.

Frowning, Annja tried again, this time calling Doug at his apartment in Brooklyn.

No answer there, either.

*Of course not, dummy,* she berated herself. *He's at the office, just as you thought. Try there.*

She did as her subconscious bid her, calling Doug's office line and cursing herself for not doing that in the first place.

The phone began ringing.

*Come on, come on, pick it up,* she urged.

His voice mail kicked in after the fifth ring.

Now Annja was starting to worry. Doug was almost never out of contact; he even took his cell phone into the bathroom with him. The fact that she couldn't reach him anywhere was starting to feel suspicious.

*He's just on the other line,* she told herself. *Give him a minute and call him back.*

She did so, and this time the phone was answered on the third ring.

"Doug! Thank heavens!"

But it wasn't him.

"Annja?" a female voice asked tentatively.

"Who's this?"

"Karen, Doug's assistant."

Of course. Now that he had an assistant he was apparently too important to answer his own phone.

"I need to speak to Doug, Karen. Is he in?"

"No. I haven't seen him since you left for vacation," she said.

*What? Three days? Maybe longer?*

"Do you know where he is?" Annja asked.

With a sudden feeling of dread, she knew what the answer was going to be before it even came out of Karen's mouth.

"No. That's why I'm so glad you called. I was hoping you could help me find him."

It was a bad sign that Karen didn't know where Doug was.

A really bad sign.

"I'm sorry. I've got to go," she told Karen, hanging up the phone before the other woman could say anything more and fighting the sense of panic that was quickly filling her as she frantically dialed the original number.

Just as before, it rang three times and then was answered.

"I'm listening," Annja told the person on the other end.

# 4

"Perhaps now you will take me seriously, yes?"

Annja did her best to hang on to her temper. When she got scared, she had a tendency to get irritated and if this guy really had Doug she didn't want to tick him off by blowing her cool.

"Where's Doug? What have you done to him?"

"Done? I haven't done anything," the person said. "Yet."

It was just one word, but it had the power to freeze her blood in her veins.

The kidnapper went on. "I have simply persuaded Mr. Morrell that it was in his best interests to get in touch with you to convey my desire to discuss a business arrangement. He had initially declined my request, but very quickly saw the error of his ways. I hear that you are on vacation. Are you enjoying Jamaica?"

Annja sensed that time was of the essence, and she had no interest in bantering with this guy. She ignored his question about Jamaica, choosing instead to demand, "Who are you and what do you want?"

"Morrell was right about your temper, I see," the man said, infuriating Annja even further. She didn't like the position she was in, with all of the control in the kidnapper's hands, but there was nothing she could do until she knew what he wanted. For now, she was going to have to grin and bear it, something she wasn't very good at doing.

Her right hand reached into thin air and plucked a broadsword seemingly out of nowhere. The blade had once belonged to Joan of Arc, had, in fact, been broken asunder on the day and hour of her execution. More than five hundred years later it had been miraculously re-formed in Annja's presence and she had become the blade's current bearer.

The sword could appear or disappear at her will, and when she wasn't using it, it rested in a mystical place just outside the bounds of reality that she called the otherwhere. It could not be taken from her against her will and over the years had seemed to impart some extra bit of strength, dexterity and speed to her physical movements when the situation demanded it. She had become an expert in its use and, quite literally, didn't go anywhere without it.

Having the blade in hand helped calm her and kept her from raging at the maniac who had snatched one of her friends. He didn't know it yet, whoever he was, but having her as an enemy was not a good thing.

"Let me worry about my temper," she told the man, "and you can tell me what it is that you want. Clearly there's something you need me to do, otherwise you wouldn't have gone through the hassle of kidnapping my television producer."

"You are as perceptive as your reputation suggests, Miss Creed. That bodes well for your ability to carry out my requests."

Annja didn't like the "s" on the end of that word, for it suggested the caller had multiple things for her to do in order to free Doug, but she kept her mouth shut and waited for him to continue.

"There is a package waiting for you at the front desk. Retrieve it but do not open it until you are back in your room. When you have examined what is inside, call me back at the number I'm giving you."

The caller recited a new phone number, and Annja quickly memorized it.

But she wasn't ready to be a pawn in someone else's game quite yet. At least, not a pawn that didn't attempt to retain a bit of its own free will.

"Why don't you just tell me now, and I'll grab the package later?"

It was the wrong thing to do.

There was silence on the end of the phone for a moment, followed by a shriek of pain that seemed to go on forever.

"Hello? Hello? Are you there? What are you doing to him?" she cried.

The voice returned. "When I give an order, I expect it to be carried out without negotiation or discussion. Each time that doesn't happen, Mr. Morrell will pay the price for your obstinacy. Is that clear?"

"Crystal," Annja replied through gritted teeth.

"Then what are you waiting for? Go get that package."

And with that, the line went dead.

Annja sent the sword back into the otherwhere and hurried out of her room, clutching the phone tightly in one hand. She didn't dare put it down just in case the stranger called again; she didn't know what he'd do to Doug if he called and she wasn't right there to answer it.

A group of tourists stood in front of the elevator so Annja hurried past it and took the stairs, rushing down them two at a time in her haste to get to the ground floor. She considered calling Paul and asking him to join her, but decided against doing so. There was no need to get him involved unless she had to, and she wasn't sure yet if that was the case. It might be safer for Paul if she kept him out of it completely.

There was an elderly couple at the registration desk when Annja got to the lobby, and she had to stifle the urge to push them aside and ask about the package. She stood behind them, impatiently shifting from foot to foot as she waited for them to finish getting the directions they needed. The registration clerk gave her a sympathetic smile over their heads as they examined the map and Annja tried to smile back, but she was afraid it looked more like a death's head rictus.

At last they were done and Annja stepped up to the counter.

"May I help you?" the clerk asked.

"My name is Annja Creed and I'm in room 402. I believe you have a package for me."

"Ah, yes, Miss Creed. One minute, please."

The clerk stepped into the back room, leaving Annja alone. A sense that she was being watched washed over her and she spun to look, but there was no one there.

*Keep it together, Creed,* she told herself.

The clerk returned carrying a thick manila envelope and handed it to her across the counter. Her name was written on the front with black magic marker.

"Were you on duty when this was delivered?" she asked the clerk.

He hesitated and then said, somewhat reluctantly, "Yes, miss."

"Did you see who delivered it?"

"No, miss." He looked down and then looked back up at her. "To be honest, I had stepped away for a quick smoke, and when I came in the envelope was lying on the counter. I looked around to see who might have left it, but there was no one about. I'm sorry."

"That's fine. No problem," she told him, while inwardly she was cursing at having lost her best chance of getting a lead on who might be behind this.

Not knowing what it might contain, she didn't feel comfortable opening the envelope in the lobby, so she'd wait until she got back to her room.

She was grateful the envelope didn't contain one of Doug's fingers or anything gruesome like that, just a folder with several pieces of paper inside and a DVD in a paper sleeve. She turned on the desk lamp and sat down, flipping through the pages briefly. They appeared to be military action reports of some kind.

That was enough for her; she didn't have time to read them all. She could do that later.

She picked up the DVD and slid it out of its case, then walked it over to the entertainment unit in the suite's living room. It took her a few minutes to work out which remote control worked which device, but once she figured it all out she fired up the television and then slipped the DVD into the player.

The screen remained blank long enough that Annja thought the player might not be properly connected to the television, but as she got up to check it, the screen suddenly brightened and an image appeared.

It was Doug.

He was tied to a metal chair in a nondescript room somewhere. His forearms were tied to the arms of the chair, his legs to the legs of the chair, leaving his hands free and his bare feet resting on what looked to be a wet concrete floor. The camera was close enough for Annja to see that his face was bloody and swollen, as if he'd been subjected to a thorough beating at some point in the past few hours. A thin line of dried blood ran from his cracked and swollen lips. When he raised his head and looked at the camera, the one eye that he could see out of was full of fear.

"Help me, Annja" he said, his voice little more than a croak coming from an obviously parched throat. It sounded as though he hadn't had any water for hours. "You have to help me. I don't care what he asks you to do or who he asks you to do it to. I'll die here if you don't do what he wants. Please, don't let that happen, Annja, please."

The camera zoomed in to show his face and then moved down to his body and stopped on his right hand. That close Annja could see that his last two fingers were broken and bent at odd angles.

She could hear Doug saying, "No, no, I didn't do anything, don't," in a breathy gasp. She steeled herself for what was coming but she didn't turn away, feeling as if she owed it to him to watch what was being done so that she could avenge him for all the wrongs he endured to coerce her into action.

A gloved hand reached into the camera frame. It was neither large nor small, so she couldn't really tell if it was a man's or a woman's, though she suspected the former. Not because a woman couldn't be that cruel—she knew from experience that that certainly wasn't the case—but because her mystery man had claimed to be the one who had kidnapped Doug, and she had yet to see anything that made her think this was anything more than a single nutjob at work. As she'd expected, the individual took hold of Doug's middle finger and without further ado snapped the bone. Doug let out a shriek of pain and the screen went blank.

Watching the kidnapper inflict pain on Doug for no other reason than to make her do his bidding filled her with a righteous fury. She vowed then and there to make him pay for what he had done.

He'd picked the wrong woman to tangle with.

Annja picked up the phone and entered the number the kidnapper had given to her.

It was answered almost immediately.

"You have the package?"

"Yes."

"You've seen the DVD?"

Annja gritted her teeth and then replied in the same clear tone, "Yes."

"You understand that I'm not kidding around?"

"Yes, I understand. Now get on with it. What do you want me to do?"

"In April 1945 a particular German aircraft went down somewhere in the Swiss Alps. I want you to find that aircraft and recover what is inside it. You have one week to do so."

*Find a plane lost in the Swiss Alps over fifty years ago? This guy was a total loon!* Annja counted to ten to be sure she had a hold of her anger.

"So help me, if you hurt him any more than you already have, I will hunt you to the ends of the earth."

The man on the other end of the phone chuckled. "You can certainly try, Miss Creed. In the meantime, I would start looking for that wreckage. One week. I will call you at exactly noon seven days from now. Keep your phone handy."

The kidnapper hung up.

# 5

When Paul knocked on her door fifteen minutes later, Annja was sitting cross-legged on the couch, engrossed in reading the after-action reports the kidnapper had supplied. At the sound of his knock, she shouted, "Go away!" in the direction of the door and just kept reading. When she looked up moments later to double-check something she'd read in a previous report, she found him standing there in the middle of the room, watching her.

"How did you get in here?" she demanded.

He held up a small square of plastic. "You gave me a key, remember?"

Annja grunted and went back to reading.

Paul walked over and picked up one of the sheets of paper. "What's going on?"

"Don't touch that!" she said, snatching it out of his hands.

Paul actually took a step back at the venom in her tone. The tension in the room felt like a physical presence.

"You're scaring me, Annja. What's going on?"

Annja ignored him, jotting down notes on the cover of the folder the pages had come in and moving on to the next page.

"Look at me!"

This time the sharpness in his tone caught her attention. She stopped what she was doing and looked over at him, actually seeing him for the first time.

"I don't know what's going on," he said gently, "but whatever it is, you aren't going to be helped by letting it get the better of you. Take a deep breath, calm down a minute and tell me what's got you so riled up."

Annja realized that he was right; she wasn't going to help Doug if she went at this haphazardly and in a panic. Yes, the clock was ticking but this is what she did. She found things that had been lost or hidden away, often for centuries. She was good at it, too. She could do this; she just needed to stay calm and to stay focused.

"I'm sorry, Paul," she began, then told him about the phone call, the package, everything.

He didn't believe her at first. He looked at the papers, checked her call logs, even watched the video, though he turned it off in a hurry when he saw Doug's bruised and battered face. That was all he apparently needed to understand it was real.

His first reaction was a reasonable one.

"We have to go to the police," he said, reaching for the phone.

Annja stretched out her hand and put it over his, stopping him.

"No," she said softly.

"No? What do you mean no? Your friend has been kidnapped, his life threatened. You need to let the police handle this thing so they can get him back safely!"

"But that's just it, Paul. They won't."

He stared at her as if she'd suddenly grown a third eye in the middle of her forehead. "What? How can you say that?" he asked, bewildered.

"Because it's true!"

*Easy there, Annja,* she told herself. *He's just trying to help.*

"Less than one in two victims in kidnapping for ransom cases are returned unharmed when the ransom is paid. I know. I looked it up. And as crazy as it sounds, that's what this is essentially. A kidnapping for ransom. Our kidnapper just happens to have a really unusual demand."

Paul looked at her, a puzzled expression on his face. "That's what I don't get. What does he really want? And why kidnap a television producer in order to get it? That doesn't make any sense."

"Actually it does, in a strange kind of way. He wants my expertise in finding lost artifacts but can't approach me outright because he knows that I would require him to follow the law and turn the wreckage and any human remains over to the German government as befits a casualty of war."

"What's wrong with that?"

"Anything found within the wreckage would have to be turned over, as well. That means he wouldn't get to keep whatever the plane was carrying, and that's what he wants. Not the plane but the cargo."

Paul frowned. "So knowing that you wouldn't help him steal the cargo if you did, indeed, find it, he decides to kidnap the producer of your show?"

"Not just my producer. Doug is my friend, one of the few I have. And I have a reputation for going to the ends of the earth for my friends."

Saying it aloud brought a lump to her throat and she realized that she was scared, afraid for Doug's safety. Whoever the kidnapper was, it was clear that he wasn't afraid to use physical violence to get what he wanted and of her friends, few though they may be, Doug was probably the one least likely to be able to deal with what was coming his way.

*Which is precisely why he was the one who was targeted,* she thought.

"But why hurt him like that? Why not just kidnap him and let you know that he was being held?"

"Motivation," Annja answered. "Specifically, mine. He's got a deadline for some reason, and he wants the plane found before that deadline expires. If I thought Doug wasn't in any immediate danger other than being held captive, I'd stall every second I could on the search for the plane to give the authorities time to find him. By backing up his threat with a show of force, the kidnapper is taking that option away from me. I have no doubt he will hurt Doug, perhaps even kill him, if I don't do what he wants.

"Which brings us to the second reason we can't go to the authorities," Annja continued. "Time. Reporting the abduction will take away precious hours, possibly even days, from my hunt for the aircraft, and I can't afford that."

"So what are you going to do?" Paul asked.

She looked up at him, surprised. "Find the bloody plane, of course. What else is there to do?"

"But you don't even know what plane you are looking for. And last time I checked, the Swiss Alps are pretty damn big."

"That's where these come in," she said, picking up the stacks of reports that she'd been going through.

"Mission reports from both the German Luftwaffe and the American Air Force for the month of April 1945. I don't know how he got them, but he did and that's all that matters. Somewhere in here is the clue I'm looking for that will tell me what I need to know—the identity of the plane I'm supposed to find."

Paul shrugged. "Well, if you're confident you'll find it, so am I. Pass some of those over here," he said as he sat down on the other end of the couch.

"What are you doing?" Annja asked.

"What does it look like I'm doing? Helping you, of course."

She stared at him, at a loss for words. She hadn't imagined...

Paul's expression softened. "You didn't think you were going to have to do all of this alone, did you?"

Annja gulped down a lump in her throat for the second time that evening, but this time it was for an entirely different reason. She'd been on her own so long that she'd just assumed...

Finding her voice, she said, "Actually, yeah, I did. This isn't your fight and you've got things to do."

Paul laughed. "Things to do? Are you nuts? A man's life is at stake here. I think that's a little more important than some stupid magazine article, don't you?"

She nodded, unable to speak. She thought she just might be falling in love with this man.

She passed him half the stack of reports and settled down to read.

The clock was ticking...

# 6

Annja found the information she sought nearly four hours later. Surprisingly, it was in a report from an American airman, Captain Dennis Mitchell, who survived the crash of his P51 Mustang in April 1945 and hid among the partisans at the Swiss border for three weeks before he was able to rejoin an Allied unit and relay the details of what had happened that day.

The report detailed an encounter between the pilot's combat air patrol in a pair of P51s and a lone German Junkers Ju 88. Mitchell described how his patrol had come upon the Junkers flying low and slow as it neared the Austrian border. Figuring they had an easy target, the two Mustang pilots had gone on the attack. To their surprise the pilot of the Junkers turned out to be better than average and managed to elude their guns for several long minutes as they chased him over the Alps.

Just when they thought they had him dead to rights, the Junkers pilot had turned the tables on them, suddenly growing claws and becoming the cat instead of the mouse. A head-to-head attack directed at Mitchell's aircraft had critically damaged it and he'd bailed out just seconds before it blew to pieces. While floating to the ground under his parachute, he'd witnessed the destruction of his wingman's aircraft, but also the fatal wounding of the Junkers. When last he saw it, the aircraft was flying southwest on a course that would take it deeper into the Alps, with smoke pouring from one engine and a full-fledged fire engulfing the other. He hadn't thought it would get very far in that state.

Mitchell had landed in a valley between two peaks and had stumbled upon a partisan group as it crossed the mountain. They'd sheltered him from the enemy as the country fell apart around them and when the opportunity arose had escorted him back to Allied lines. He discovered that Hitler had committed suicide the previous day and the war in Europe was effectively now all but over.

There was a page added to the original report that stated post-war recovery crews had managed to find the wreckage of the aircraft belonging to Mitchell's wingman, Lieutenant Nathan Hartwell, as well as his remains, which had been collected and shipped to the States for burial back home. The wreck had been in the mountains along the border near the Austrian city of Salzburg.

"I think I've got something here," she said to Paul and then showed him what she had found.

"What would a German aircraft be doing flying alone and heading south at that point in the war?"

Paul asked. "Didn't we basically control all of Germany at that point?"

Annja nodded. Her particular field of specialty was European history, concentrating on the Medieval and Renaissance periods, but she hadn't neglected her study of the modern era. "The last major battle between Germany and American and British Allied forces took place near Lippstadt in the first week of April. About the same time, Soviet forces broke the German lines in the east and marched all the way to Berlin, reaching it on the sixteenth of April. By that point, the war was all but over except for the surrendering."

Paul thought about that for a moment. "The Battle of Berlin started on the sixteenth when Soviet forces attacked the capital. Hitler committed suicide on April thirtieth. But back on the fourteenth of April we have a lone German aircraft making a run for the border, flying 'low and slow' as Captain Mitchell put it. Sounds to me like somebody loaded his personal stash of loot and tried to get out of Dodge before everything came crashing down. What do you think?"

Annja nodded. "I bet you're right. And what's the one currency accepted anywhere in the world?"

The two looked at each other.

"Gold," they said simultaneously. "Gold."

Paul clapped his hands together. "That's why the plane was flying so slowly when Mitchell's patrol happened upon it. It was loaded with what was probably a fortune in gold," he said excitedly.

"That would also explain why Doug's kidnapper is so interested in finding it."

Now that they knew what they were likely looking for, they could turn their attention to locating it, which wasn't going to be easy, Annja knew. They had a general location where the dogfight had taken place, but no idea how far the pilot had managed to fly the crippled aircraft or in which direction he had ultimately headed.

"We need a map," Annja said.

Five minutes later they had her laptop out and open on the table, a map of Germany displayed on the screen. The Alps stretched across the southernmost part of Germany, along the border it shared with Austria and Liechtenstein. They were about seventy-five miles wide and rose to heights of nearly 10,000 feet in the region around Salzburg, which was the general area that they were concerned with. The wreckage of the Junkers, if it had even survived this long, was somewhere in the midst of all that.

Paul summed it up nicely with a single word.

"Damn."

Annja had to agree. It was a lot of ground to cover, too much, in fact. They would barely scratch the surface in the week that they'd been allotted. A thorough investigation would take years, decades even.

There had to be a better way.

She sat back, considering the information they had found. Mitchell's report indicated that the Junkers had been moving in a southeasterly direction when he had last seen it. If they could pinpoint where Mitchell had been at the time, then they could at least come up with a theoretical flight path for the aircraft and could limit their search to that area. It would give them a much smaller area to cover.

*So how to accomplish that?* Annja wondered.

There was nothing in the report to suggest that Mitchell had known where he'd bailed out of his aircraft except in the most general of terms, and the wreckage of his P51 had never been found.

But they did have the next best thing...

Annja snatched up the report and flipped to the last page, reading the notes in the margins a second time. The wreckage of the second P51 Mustang involved in the incident, the one belonging to Lieutenant Hartwell, had been located back in 1946.

Annja knew that the Joint POW/MIA Accounting Command, the military unit that was in charge of recovering the remains of US servicemen and servicewomen worldwide, kept very precise records of the location of any bodies discovered on one of their missions. Unfortunately, JPMAC hadn't been formed until 2003. It was unlikely that they would have any information on the remains of a soldier recovered during World War II. But that line of thought made her consider another alternative.

The military never did anything without documenting it in triplicate. If a recovery team had been sent to Salzburg to bring home Lieutenant Hartwell's remains, then there was almost certainly a record of it somewhere. They just had to find out where.

The best place to look for that, Annja knew, would be Hartwell's service records.

The only problem with that was the fact that unless a person was next of kin, the military service records of former soldiers were sealed.

So how to get access to those?

"Earth to Annja, come in, Annja."

With a start she realized that Paul had been trying to get her attention for several minutes.

"Sorry, I was thinking."

"Yeah, I could see the smoke coming out of your ears," he said with a laugh. "Want to tell me what is so engrossing?"

"I know how we can get the fix we need on a general search area," she said, and told him about her idea. "So if we can somehow get access to Hartwell's service records," she went on, "we could probably track down more information about the mission to recover his remains, which in turn would get us a starting point for our own search."

"So what you are saying is that you need a source inside the national military records center to help you get Hartwell's records, which tends to be frowned upon since it's a wee bit illegal, never mind a federal crime," Paul said.

"Yep, that about sums it up," Annja said with a sigh. "Know anyone who would commit a felony for you?"

Paul smiled. "As a matter of fact, I do. Hand me your cell phone."

Half an hour later they were in the hotel's business

center watching as the pages of Lieutenant Nathan Hartwell's military service records came over the fax machine. Annja could scarcely believe it.

"You forget that I'm a senior correspondent for one of the biggest magazines in the world," Paul said with a laugh when he saw her expression. "Our network, the people we know, are our biggest assets. We couldn't do our jobs without them."

"And who might you know at the National Archives?" Annja asked, only half teasing.

Paul winked at her. "Sorry. A journalist never reveals a source."

Annja's curiosity was still poking at her, but she let it go. The fact that they had the records was more important than who they had gotten them from, wasn't it?

Of course it was. Besides, she didn't care if it was from a woman. Or that he'd probably had to call her at home to get the information given it was well after hours.

She kept telling herself that all the way back to her hotel room.

Once there, they began going through the file, looking for information on Hartwell's death and the recovery of his remains. Fortunately, they found what they needed. While the file only listed Salzburg as the location where Hartwell had been killed in action, it did note the name of the recovery mission and its commanding officer. That was all they needed; from there, it was just a question of making a series of phone calls to the record keepers at the National

Archives in the morning and having one of them dig up the information they were looking for.

The dinner hour had long come and gone, but the resort had twenty-four-hour room service. With nothing more to do until morning, they put the files away and relaxed for the first time all evening.

Even though they'd made good headway, Annja couldn't help but feel the minutes wasting away, each one bringing them that much closer to the deadline.

Tick, tock, tick, tock.

# 7

The next morning Annja, with the help of an archivist, was able to track down the file number of the recovery mission that had retrieved Lieutenant Hartwell's remains. Since information on that type of operation had been declassified decades ago, she was able to submit a request for information about the mission and sweet-talked the archivist into filling it right away. A few hours later an email arrived in her in-box containing the scanned file.

The longitude and latitude of the location where Hartwell's plane had come to rest, and where his remains had been recovered, was right there in black-and-white on page three.

While Annja was on the phone, Paul bought a series of digital topographical maps from a vendor online. He called them up on-screen, selected the one that covered the region the best and used the coordinates Annja supplied to pinpoint the location of the wreckage on the map. Given the damage to the Junkers that Mitchell had reported, both Annja and Paul agreed that it probably couldn't have flown more than another ten or twenty miles from its last known position, so he electronically drew a circle on the map with a radius of twenty miles.

"There it is," he said when he was finished. "There's our search area."

Annja stared at it with a mixture of excitement and dismay. The thrill of the hunt had caught up with her overnight, and she was feeling exactly as she usually did at the start of a new dig. Archaeology was her one true love, the thing that she came back to again and again. She relished that feeling it gave her of reaching back into the past and the sense of satisfaction she got when she located something previously thought to have been lost forever in the mists of time. She'd felt that way on her first dig at Hadrian's Wall years ago, and she still felt that way today. Finding an aircraft that had been missing since World War II was the type of challenge she normally would jump at.

Although, the life of one of her friends didn't normally hang in the balance, completely dependent upon her success, and that's where the dismay came in.

The deadline was the problem. Given enough time and materials, Annja knew that she could probably find the airplane. She didn't have any doubt about it. If it was there, she would find it. But with only seven days to do it—actually six, now—it was going to be nothing less than a Herculean task. They needed help; it was as simple as that.

Good thing she knew where she could get some.

Normally she'd be worried about the price tag that would come with that help, and she would carefully consider the pros and cons of picking up the phone and getting him involved, but she didn't have the luxury to worry about such things at this point. Time was too precious a resource to waste. Whatever the price, she was willing to pay it in order to rescue Doug.

Paul looked over at her. "I've got be honest, Annja. I don't know how we could search an area of that size even with an army at our disposal. An army that, I should point out, we don't have."

"Yeah, I know. I'm working on it."

With only a trace of reluctance, Annja picked up the phone and called Garin Braden.

"Hello, Annja," he said, when he answered the call. "To what do I owe this pleasant surprise?"

"I hate to say it, Garin, but I really need your help."

Garin laughed. "The mighty Miss Creed needs my help? You must be joking."

Annja gritted her teeth. "I'm serious, Garin. I really need your help."

"Well, in that case let me drop everything I am doing and rush to your aid."

His sarcastic tone made her wince, but she pushed on anyway. "Please, Garin. A friend's life is at stake and time is of the essence."

Garin Braden was over five hundred years old. When she thought about it, that sounded crazy even to her, but she couldn't deny the fact that it was true. Garin had been squire to a French knight named Roux, who in turn had been assigned to watch over Joan of Arc. Roux and his squire had failed in their mission, and when Joan's sword was broken in the moments before her execution, the lives of the two men had been mysteriously lengthened. Over the next few centuries Roux searched for the fragments of the blade, intending to bring them back together, while Garin fought to keep that from happening, convinced the fragmentation of the blade was the very thing that assured his extended life span.

Annja was aware Garin had since come to realize that his efforts had likely been wasted, as her custodianship of the blade so far had had no ill effect on him. In fact, he seemed to be growing quite fond of her. Annja had diligently resisted his efforts to flirt, despite her attraction to him. The fact that he was the perfect example of tall, dark and handsome, never mind ridiculously rich, constantly battled with her understanding that Garin cared first and foremost about himself. He was determined, ruthless and used to getting what he wanted, no matter what the effort or cost. It made him dangerous in more ways than one.

She knew it was in her best interest to stay as far away from him as she could and yet here she was, reaching out to him for help in her moment of need.

*Apparently my heart and my head aren't seeing eye to eye again,* she thought.

Knowing his nature, Annja expected Garin to ask what was in it for him and, frankly, she didn't have an answer. The last time she had asked for his help he'd insisted on taking her to dinner and she'd had no choice but to agree. She was afraid of what he would require this time around.

To her great surprise, he didn't do anything of the sort.

"What do you need?" he asked.

Given the nature of some of the expeditions she'd been on in the past, Annja had learned not to talk about them too much over an open telephone line, for you never knew who might be listening in. Instead she told him that she needed to find a certain object within a certain specified time frame and left it at that, knowing he would read between the lines and understand that she was after an artifact of one kind or another.

That was close enough for what she needed until she could see him.

Garin was silent at first and then asked, "Where are you now?"

"The Hotel Planita in Negril, Jamaica."

"Okay, stay there. I'll send a chopper for you."

Garin hung up before she could thank him. He always did like having the last word.

JUST UNDER THREE hours later, a massive AW101 VVIP AgustaWestland helicopter settled onto the hotel lawn, inviting stares from more than a few observers. Annja didn't blame them; this was the same helicopter used to transport the President of the United States under the designation Marine One, and just seeing it up close was pretty awe-inspiring. Given that it was one of Garin's helicopters, Annja had no doubt that the interior would be even more lavish than she could imagine.

She and Paul watched as the door opened and a set of steps unfolded from inside the aircraft. Seconds later a black man with a shaved head and a soul patch on his chin appeared in the doorway. He was wearing a sharply cut suit and dark sunglasses. He scanned the small crowd assembled on the other side of the lawn before his gaze settled on Annja and her companion. He gestured them forward without hesitation.

Annja crossed the lawn and climbed the stairs. "Hello, Griggs," she said, as she stepped aboard the aircraft.

Matthew Griggs, head of DragonTech Security and Garin Bradin's right-hand man, nodded to her. "Miss Creed," he said, with that lilting British Caribbean accent of his. "Please make yourself comfortable."

The interior of the helicopter resembled that of a private jet more than any helicopter Annja had ever been in, with mahogany fittings, lush leather seats and even thick carpet underfoot to help absorb the sound of the rotor blades.

Griggs turned just as Paul came up the steps. The DragonTech Security man interposed himself between Paul and the interior of the aircraft. "I'm sorry, sir," he said, "but this is a private flight."

"It's all right, Griggs. He's with me."

Griggs spoke over his shoulder to Annja without taking his eyes off Paul. "Is Mr. Braden aware of this?"

He wasn't, but Annja wasn't about to admit that to Griggs.

"Of course."

"Very well."

Once both guests were settled, Griggs said, "Help yourselves to the refreshments. We'll be in Miami in about three hours."

With that, he pulled in the stairs, secured the door and returned to the cockpit. Five minutes later they were airborne.

Glancing around the cabin, Paul gave a low whistle. "You said you were going to get us some help, but this is a bit more than I expected. Dare I ask who it belongs to?"

Annja didn't see any reason not to tell him, especially considering the fact that Paul was likely to be meeting him in a few hours.

"Garin Braden."

Paul started in surprise. "Garin Braden?"

"Yes."

"Garin Braden the industrialist?"

Annja would have been more prone to call him Garin Braden the scoundrel, but that was splitting hairs, in her view.

"Yes."

An uneasy expression crossed Paul's face.

Seeing it, Annja asked, "What's wrong?"

"Braden and I had a bit of a run-in at a press conference when I asked him some uncomfortable questions," Paul replied.

"When was this?"

"A year, maybe eighteen months ago." He shrugged, then waved it off. "I'm sure he's forgotten about it by now."

Annja wasn't so sure of that—Garin tended to carry a grudge longer than anyone she knew—but she agreed and left it alone for the time being. If it was an issue, they'd deal with it later. "Might as well relax," she told him. "We've got a few hours of flight time ahead of us, it seems."

While Paul wandered around, checking out the cabin, Annja pulled her laptop out of her backpack and fired it up. She connected to the flight's onboard Wi-Fi and began researching the Junkers aircraft and its capabilities. Getting a better sense of its strengths and weaknesses would allow her to better pinpoint how far it might have gone after being damaged in the dogfight with Captain Mitchell and his wingman, which in turn might allow them to narrow their search area.

*Or, if we're particularly unlucky, make it even bigger.*

She was thankful that there was a fair bit of information available.

The Junkers Ju 88 was a twin-engine multirole combat aircraft built by the German firm Junkers Flugzeugund Motorenwerke for use by the Luftwaffe in World War II. It had been intended to be a fast bomber that could outrun any Allied fighters that tried to chase it. According to most of the sources Annja checked, it had been moderately successful.

Despite being plagued by several problems in the later part of its development, the aircraft and its many variants were in constant production from 1939 to the end of the war in 1945. More than 160,000 were built, more than any other German twin-engine aircraft of the time period. It served successfully as a bomber, dive bomber, night fighter, heavy fighter and reconnaissance aircraft. They had seen heavy action during the Battle of Norway, the Battle of France and the Battle of Britain, as well as in various campaigns on the Eastern Front.

The Junkers had a top speed of 292 miles per hour, a ceiling of 29,000 feet, and a maximum range of 1,700 miles. It had been built to be flown by a crew of either three or four, though one man could manage it on his own if the rear-facing cockpit guns and the weapons bay under the nose were left unmanned. Annja's research told her that one of the key features of the Junkers aircraft was its ability to keep fighting even after taking heavy damage. That explained how the target aircraft had managed to stay aloft despite being savaged by the pair of P51s under Mitchell's command. That concerned her somewhat, as the Junkers's hardiness might mean it had managed to go even farther than they suspected after the destruction of the Mustangs.

All in all, it seemed like a pretty hardy aircraft. It made her wonder what the pilot's destination had been. Where had he been trying to go with all that gold, if that, indeed, had been what he'd been carrying?

She called up a map of Europe and the Middle East on her screen. She looked at it for several minutes, trying to work out reasonable routes in her head. With a possible range of 1,700 miles, the pilot certainly had his choice of destinations available to him. If he'd flown due south, he could have reached the deep deserts beyond Tripoli in Libya. Flying due west would have taken him nearly to Atyrau, Kazakhstan. An agent of the Reich might have found assistance in either location and could have flown on from there after refueling. While dangerous, both would have been safer than the route he had chosen; southeast through Austria and into the teeth of the Allied army marching north toward Berlin. It didn't make a lot of sense.

*Nothing made a lot of sense in those days,* she reminded herself. *The war was all but lost and the Reich was falling apart. The guy probably loaded up what he could and made a run for it. Stop trying to read more into it or you'll drive yourself nuts,* Annja thought.

With that warning ringing in her ears, she put the laptop away and sat back to enjoy the rest of the flight. She knew all too well that there would far too little time for rest in the days ahead.

# 8

Griggs's estimate had been right on the money; they landed at Miami International Airport just under three hours later. A black SUV with dark tinted windows was waiting for them next to the helipad. Griggs escorted them to the vehicle and then climbed in beside the driver. Annja assumed they would be taken to wherever Garin was staying, so she was surprised when the driver raced around several parked Airbuses and delivered them to a sleek business jet waiting for them on the other side of the terminal.

Annja was about to ask what was going on when she noticed the corporate logo of a gold dragon poised in midflight on the tail of the aircraft. It was the same one that had been on the tail rotor of the helicopter they'd just left behind.

*DragonTech Security.*

When the car stopped, Griggs escorted them up the steps and into the aircraft.

Garin Braden was waiting for them.

"Ah, Annja," he said, as a broad smile swept across his face. "So good to see you."

Garin was a big man, both physically and charismatically. He seemed to fill the room wherever he was. His dark hair was pulled back in a ponytail and his beard was immaculately groomed, as usual. This day he was dressed in a dark shirt and jeans, which was unusual for him. Annja was more used to seeing him in impeccably cut suits.

*Everybody needs a dress down day*, she thought with a smile.

Annja introduced Paul to him, noting that Garin held the other man's hand just a moment longer than normal.

Had he recognized Paul? she wondered.

Garin didn't say anything or acknowledge that the two had previously met, so Annja let it go. He ushered them into chairs opposite his own and got right down to business. "You said it was urgent. Tell me what is going on."

Annja laid it all out for him: Doug's kidnapping, the phone call, the package, the fact that the kidnapper knew she was in Jamaica, the demand that she find and recover the plane and its contents. The only thing she left out was the fact that she was romantically involved with Paul. She didn't need Garin critiquing her choice of companions, but she knew he would do so anyway. No sense in giving him more ammunition for the task.

When she was finished, Garin sat back and considered what she had said for several minutes. At last he asked, "Who knew that you were going to be in Jamaica?"

"Me or Paul?" Annja asked.

"The two of you together."

Annja frowned. "No more than a handful of people."

"Who, specifically?" Garin wanted to know.

Paul spoke up for the first time. "The editor who assigned me the story I was supposed to cover and his assistant, I'd guess. The secretary who booked my flights and hotel reservations. That's about it."

"Did they know Annja was going with you?"

Paul shook his head. "No."

"What about you, Annja?" Garin asked. "Who knew that you were going to Jamaica with Paul?"

"No one, really. He asked me to go last minute and I just packed up and went."

"You didn't tell any of your friends, people you hang out with?"

She didn't hang out with anyone regularly, and she could count her friends on the fingers of one hand, but Annja wasn't about to tell Garin that. He knew enough embarrassing things about her already without her adding to the pile. "I didn't tell anyone," she told him.

Garin wasn't going to leave it at that, though.

"Doug didn't know where you were going?" he pressed her.

Annja considered the question. "I don't think so. I told him that I was going to take a week's vacation, but I didn't tell him where."

"How about his secretary?"

She shook her head. "No, definitely not." Doug

didn't really have a secretary per se, just an intern, Karen, who served as his assistant. Annja knew that she hadn't discussed her travel plans with her. "Why? What's this about?" she asked.

"I'm just trying to figure out how the kidnapper knew that you were in Jamaica. If you and Paul are the only two who knew you were going to be there, I have to wonder if he's the man behind all this."

Annja was so stunned by the suggestion that she didn't know what to say.

Paul did though. "You can't be serious," he said crossly. Annja could hear the indignation in his voice. He hadn't liked the insinuation, not one bit, and it was clear from his tone that he wasn't going to put up with remarks of that caliber.

Annja didn't blame him.

Garin ignored him, speaking instead to Annja. "Seems pretty suspicious to me. *He* invited you to Jamaica. *He* booked the hotel. *He* knew what room you were in and even when you were there and when you weren't. He could easily have dropped off the package at the front desk with no one the wiser."

"Now wait just a minute—" Paul began, but Annja cut him off.

"Paul was with me the whole time we were in Jamaica. It's not like he could have flown back to the mainland and kidnapped Doug when I wasn't looking."

Garin was staring at Paul with suspicion as he said, "Aren't you the one who said Doug had been missing for a few days before you spoke to his assistant? For all you know, he could easily have kidnapped Doug and left him somewhere long before he met you for the flight to the Caribbean."

The frown that had blossomed on Annja's face at Garin's initial suggestion now deepened. "This isn't funny, Garin."

"I'm not trying to be funny. Tell me something. Was Paul in the room with you when the kidnapper called?"

"No, I was alone."

"So how do you know it wasn't him?"

Annja glared at Garin. "Knock it off. Right now," she said. "I don't have time for this kind of joke. Paul isn't the kidnapper and that's final. I fully vouch for him."

Garin sat back with the hint of a smile. "All right, if you say so."

He turned to Paul. "My apologies," he said.

It was the smile that did it. Garin had intentionally ruffled Paul's feathers, no doubt in payback for Paul's rudeness during the interview when they'd first met.

*The guy can sure hold on to a grudge,* she thought.

"So what is it that you want from me?" Garin asked, addressing Annja.

She leaned forward. "I don't have the resources I need to conduct the search. I was hoping you could supply equipment and manpower."

Garin nodded a couple of times, as if weighing what she'd said. Finally, he asked, "What's in it for me?"

Annja had been expecting that question, and there was only one answer that she could give him.

"Nothing except my thanks," she said.

Garin grunted in what sounded like amusement. His tone was light as he said, "Let me get this straight. You want me to spend millions of dollars to finance a massive search for a plane that's been missing for seventy years and might not even be in the location we're searching, never mind my time and attention, for nothing but a word of thanks from you?"

"Garin, look. Doug's life—"

He cut her off, his tone a bit more brusque than before. "Just answer the question. Yes or no? Is that what you expect?"

Paul bristled and Annja thought he was going to step in, so she glared at him to keep him quiet.

She caught Garin's gaze and said, "Yes, that's exactly what I expect."

She thought he'd argue, or bargain, or at the very least laugh at the idea. As long as she'd known him, Garin had done what was best for Garin. Expecting him to change now would be like asking water not to be wet.

To her surprise, a broad smile crossed Garin's face at her reply. Sure, I'll help you. I am at your service in every way."

Given the fox-in-the-henhouse look on his face, Annja knew she'd said or done something that was going to come back and bite her on the butt at some point, but she'd worry about that later.

# 9

They flew from Miami to Munich, Germany, in a little under ten hours. Already exhausted from everything that had gone on so far, Annja spent most of the flight sleeping in her seat. The few times that she opened her eyes or got up to use the restroom, she found Garin on the phone making arrangements for the work ahead. She found it oddly comforting to know that he was on top of things, and she began to think that maybe they could pull this off after all.

*Hang on, Doug,* she thought. *We're coming.*

Thanks to the time difference, it was just after 7:00 a.m. when they landed. An Immigration and Customs official met them on the plane and handled their visas and declarations paperwork, after which they transferred from the jet to another private helicopter. This one was much more utilitarian than the first. Gone were the plush leather seats and the mahogany interior. In their places were benches that could seat at least three people and riveted steel bulkheads. It was a working machine and it showed.

Duffel bags were waiting in the chopper's open

doorway, their names in black marker on the sides. Opening hers, Annja found cold weather gear and a few sets of clothing, all in the right sizes. The surprise must have shown on her face, for Garin winked at her and said, "You should let me shop for you more often."

Paul had clothes, as well, though his didn't fit quite as well as Annja's. The three of them quickly pulled on the boots, coats and gloves, and climbed aboard. Garin had a brief conversation with the pilot and then they were on their way, heading east toward the Austria border and the Alps.

Annja thought they would fly into Salzburg and then take ground transportation from there, so she was surprised when the pilot delivered them to a mountain camp on the German side of the Alps. Thanks to all of the time that she'd spent staring at the topographical map of the search area, Annja knew they were close to the spot where Captain Mitchell's plane had crashed. A semipermanent structure, the kind used for expedition work in out-of-the-way places, stood on a plateau at the edge of a valley. Two Sno-Cats were parked in front of it.

"Your people, I hope?" Annja said to Garin.

He nodded. "Yes, including one very special individual. You're going to like what he has to show you."

The helicopter set down a few dozen yards from the structure. Annja and her companions disembarked with Garin leading the way through the knee-deep snow and over to the structure.

Inside, they found a high-tech command center,

complete with oversized monitor screens mounted along one wall and three men seated at control stations in front of them. A fourth stood behind them, quietly giving instructions. He turned when he heard them enter and walked over to greet Garin.

"Annja, meet Reinhold Draynor, CEO and founder of GeoDent Industries" Garin said, introducing them.

"Pleased to meet you," the man said with a smile, as he shook hands with first Annja and then Paul. He was a short, stocky individual with black wire-frame glasses, thinning hair and what Annja would soon discover to be an infectious enthusiasm for his work.

"Good to meet you as well," she said. "Tell me, what's GeoDent Industries?"

"The answer to your prayers," Garin said, as he stepped over to observe the action on the screens.

Reinhold smiled. "I wouldn't go that far, but I do think we can help. GeoDent, short for Geo Identification, is a geophysical survey company. We use a set of sophisticated and proprietary tools to help find the location of subsurface deposits of various minerals, metals and other natural resources."

"So you can search for specific types of metals? Even through solid rock?" Annja asked. "How do you manage that?"

Reinhold stepped over to the command console and pointed at the screen mounted above it. The image on the screen was a wash of different colors laid over what seemed to be a topographical map.

"Subsurface deposits generate very distinct fields of electromagnetic radiation. By using drones capable of recording multispectral imaging and other key variables, we can measure the strength and intensity of those fields up to a depth of 5,000 meters, which in turn helps us identify pockets of everything from oil and natural gas to precious metals."

Annja felt her excitement growing. "What about nonprecious metals like iron or steel? Can it pick those up, too?"

"Absolutely."

Annja couldn't believe what she was hearing. Using this technology would make the search for the aircraft so much easier, provided they could get the drone to operate properly in the high winds of the Alps. She turned to find Garin watching her.

"You are a genius!" she told him. "I could almost kiss you."

He smiled and opened his arms. "Please do."

To her great surprise, she was actually tempted. Resisting the impulse, she flashed him a smile. "I said almost."

Garin waved his hand in a gesture that was meant to take in the whole command center. "When you told me about the project, I immediately thought of Reinhold. His technology is absolutely cutting-edge, so new that we haven't even announced it publicly yet. I figured this would be an excellent test run for him and his team."

"And we're looking forward to the task," Reinhold said. "I was just going to check on the preparations for the drone's flight. Care to join me?"

Annja, Paul and Garin followed the German scien-

tist as he went through the door at the far end of the
command room and entered another large room just
beyond where another team of men were currently
prepping the drone for flight.

The aerial vehicle looked very much like the well-
publicized Predator drones used by the US Air Force
and the CIA, but was probably a quarter of its size.
Looking at it, Annja guessed it was roughly ten feet
in length with a wingspan of something in the neigh-
borhood of fifteen feet. It had the same bulbous nose
as the Predator; in fact, Annja thought that this one
might be even more pronounced. It was still big, but
not the monstrosity that were the Predator and its ilk.

One crew member had the nose open and was
making adjustments to something—the imaging
equipment was Annja's guess—while a second was
fueling the bird from a long hose attached to a tank
in the far corner.

Reinhold continued with his explanation. "Once
we launch the drone, we'll direct it to make system-
atic passes over the target area, mapping it in grid-like
fashion similar to how you would handle a dig site,
Annja. A few hours after that the computer will be
finished crunching the data and will give us a three-
dimensional model of the search area complete with
its findings." He grinned. "If the aircraft is there, I'm
confident we will find it."

They returned to the control room, where Reinhold spent some time in conference with Annja, trying to identify the best section of the search area to
start with. In the end, they chose an area a few ki-

lometers wide by ten kilometers long moving southeast in a straight line from their current location. It matched the direction Captain Mitchell had reported last seeing the Junkers traveling, and it abutted a series of peaks that were, in Annja's view, too high for the damaged aircraft to have navigated over. They also identified two additional portions of the search area to try in case the first search was unsuccessful.

An hour after they had arrived they all stood in the control room watching the monitors. The oddly insectile-looking craft raced down the makeshift runway of hard-packed snow and took off into the cold mountain air with barely a sound. It was a clear day with little wind, for which Annja was deeply thankful. It would make the scanning much easier. Reinhold was quietly issuing commands to his team, and Annja was pleased to see that they worked like a well-oiled unit; these men knew their jobs and would perform to the best of their abilities. They sent the drone to the target altitude and got the search underway.

At that point, there was nothing to do but wait.

THE NEXT SEVERAL hours were particularly tense. Annja could feel the ticking of the clock, literally measuring the hours left in Doug's life if they didn't succeed, and the anxiety that generated had her on edge the whole time. More than once she considered alerting the authorities, but something stopped her. She couldn't have put her finger on precisely why, but she had the sneaking feeling that the kidnapper would know as soon as she got law enforcement involved, and she didn't dare risk Doug's life.

She passed the time playing cards with Paul in the breakroom, but her mind wasn't on what she was doing and he repeatedly trounced her. Eventually she gave up her seat to Garin, allowing Paul to have a bit of a challenge, and she sat staring at the wall, wondering if she was doing the right thing. By the time Reinhold stuck his head in the doorway and announced they might have something, she was about ready to crawl out of her skin. She jumped to her feet and followed the German scientist back to the control room, Garin and Paul at her heels.

At a word from Reinhold, the image from the drone's forward camera that was showing on the central screen was replaced by something much more complex.

Reinhold pointed at it. "What you're seeing here is a three-dimensional computer model we've built with the preliminary data sent back to us by the drone. We've isolated the various magnetic fields recorded by the drone's imaging equipment and assigned each of them a color. We then laid those colors over a topographic model of the rift valley itself."

The image in front of them was mostly gray, with a few blotches of dark red running throughout.

"The gray color represents the baseline material of the mountains, mostly granite, dolomite and shale," Reinhold said. He pointed to one of the veins of dark red running through it. "This dark color appears to be veins of hematite crystal, something the region is particularly known for. So far, nothing is surprising or out of the ordinary."

He nodded at the technician manning the controls and the imaging began to slip down the screen, revealing more of the valley, just as if the drone were flying over it. Everything looked similar to what they'd already seen, until they reached the far end. At that point, a blotch of blue color appeared.

"Initial measurements tell us that this anomaly is roughly fifty feet long by seventy feet wide and made mostly of a combination of iron, carbon and manganese. In other words, steel."

Reinhold looked at the trio with an expression of pride. "I would bet my professional reputation that this is your missing aircraft."

# 10

Excitement was high as the team put on its cold weather gear and got ready to go out to the crash site. The plan was to take the Sno-Cats—Annja and Paul in one, Garin and Reinhold in the other—and see what condition the wreckage was in. Once they knew that, they could make more detailed plans for how to get at whatever it was they were supposed to recover from it.

The Junkers Ju 88 had a length of 47 feet and a wingspan of 65 feet, which was roughly the same size as the anomaly Reinhold had picked up with his scanning equipment. That suggested the plane was actually intact, a rather surprising discovery but one Annja was excited about. Her research had told her that there were only two surviving Junker 88s in the world. Being able to add a third to that list would be quite a coup.

*At least something good might come of all this,* she thought.

At first, it was slow going. The terrain was a mixture of rocky ridgelines, boulder-strewn hills and long fields of glacial ice complete with crevasses large enough to swallow either of their vehicles whole. The Sno-Cats, however, were perfect for this kind of trek. The vehicle's four independent tracks moved up and down as well as side to side, allowing it to maneuver over, through, or around the various obstacles they encountered, while the high cab allowed excellent visibility. The fact that both vehicles were painted DayGlo orange would allow them to keep each other in sight, even if the weather should turn nasty before they got back to camp.

They had been underway for nearly half an hour when Paul broke Annja out of her reverie by saying, "I'm impressed."

"At what?"

"How quickly you managed to find this thing," he said. "It's been less than three days since you got that first phone call, you've flown halfway around the world and yet you've still managed to find the literal needle in the haystack."

"I did have a bit of help, you know."

"Yes, but still. You were the driving force behind this and that's impressive."

If it hadn't been for her skill in finding lost cities and artifacts, Doug wouldn't be in the position he was in, so she didn't much feel like celebrating her achievements at the moment and let it go at that.

After almost an hour of travel—in which they only advanced a few miles from their base camp—Draynor radioed that they were getting close to their destination.

Ten minutes later they came up over the last ridge
to find that the terrain flattened out ahead of them,
becoming a long, sloping valley with clear ground
directly ahead, allowing them to see a good distance
forward. Annja immediately began looking around,
searching for some sign of the wreckage or, better yet,
the aircraft itself sticking up out of the snow.

"Anything?" she asked Paul, who was doing the
same out his window on the right side of the vehicle.

"No, nothing."

*Where on earth is it?* she wondered.

The first Sno-Cat moved forward another half
mile, then began to slow before gradually coming to
a stop. Annja pulled up behind it and got out to see
what was going on.

"The GPS unit says we're less than a hundred
yards from the target," Reinhold said as she walked
over to where he was standing with Garin beside their
Sno-Cat.

"Less than one hundred yards?" Annja asked. "We
should be seeing something then, shouldn't we?"

Reinhold shrugged. "I'm not sure. If the plane
landed intact, then yes, we probably should. But if it
broke apart on impact…"

*Then it could be scattered in bits and pieces un-
derneath all this snow and we wouldn't know it.*

It wasn't a welcome thought, for Annja knew it
would make their job of recovering whatever it was
the kidnapper wanted from the wreckage that much
harder. Welcome or not, though, they had at least
come prepared to deal with the situation.

They pulled harnesses, ropes, a handheld GPS and a metal detector out of the back of the Sno-Cat. Annja and Reinhold each tugged on a harness and clipped into the ropes that Garin and Paul had prepared. If they encountered anything unexpected, like a snow-covered crevasse, the ropes would keep them from being dragged to their deaths before anyone had time to react.

Annja was well used to such precautions, but it was obvious Reinhold wasn't as comfortable. He fussed with the harness and double-checked the knot that secured the rope to it half a dozen times until Annja calmed him by reminding him that he wasn't going out there alone; she would be right next to him the entire time.

The GPS had already been programmed with the location of the anomaly from the scanned data. When they were ready, Reinhold activated the device and the two of them stepped forward, following the signal for nearly the length of a football field before Reinhold stopped and said quietly, "Right here."

Annja stepped up next to him and looked around. There was nothing to see but a flat stretch of snow in every direction.

"You're sure this is the right spot?" she asked.

Reinhold nodded. "Absolutely. According to the scan, the anomaly should be right here."

*So where was it?*

Annja turned in a slow circle, looking for something, anything, that might indicate a plane had crashed there fifty years before.

Nothing caught her eye.

She activated the metal detector and made a slow circuit around the spot where Reinhold was standing. When that didn't give her any hits, she moved outward about a yard and repeated the process. She kept doing that until she had made half a dozen revolutions around the point where Reinhold was standing.

The metal detector remained frustratingly silent.

"Anything?" Reinhold called.

"Nothing."

*Could the data have been wrong?* she asked herself. *Could the drone have picked up on something else entirely, something not related to their search?*

She stopped and turned in a slow circle, looking for she didn't know what. She had the nagging feeling that she was missing something, something obvious, but for the life of her she couldn't figure out what. She took in the flat stretch of land she was standing on, let her gaze roam to the sloping hills that rose from that flat surface on all sides. The valley reminded her a bit of a soup bowl. *A soup bowl?*

A sudden suspicion rushed over her.

She went down on one knee and began brushing aside the snow at her feet, digging with her gloved hand.

Annja could hear Reinhold calling to her, asking if she had found something, but it seemed to be coming from a long way off, because her attention was focused almost entirely on what she was doing.

She'd gone down about a foot when her hand struck something hard.

She began clearing away more of the snow as Reinhold hurried over to help her. In just a few moments the two of them managed to clear away a circular area about three feet in diameter, exposing a thick sheet of ice that ran in every direction.

Annja stared down at it, her heart beating madly in her chest as she realized why they hadn't found anything. The "ground" wasn't ground at all; they were standing on the surface of a frozen lake!

In her mind's eye she could picture the Junkers as it came though the pass behind them, fighting to stay aloft with at least one, maybe two, engines on fire and the wind whistling through the gaping holes in the fuselage from the Mustang's guns. It had been April, which meant the lake could just as easily have been frozen as not, but either way, the pilot had probably seen it as the best place to try to make a controlled landing. Given the size and shape of the anomaly seen on the data collected by the drone, Annja thought the pilot had pulled it off and brought the plane down relatively intact. Once he had, the plane had either broken through the ice or simply sunk to the bottom under its own weight once it filled with water.

Either way, she would bet it was right there on the bottom of the lake beneath the ice on which they stood.

Now they just had to figure out how to get down there to prove her theory.

# 11

Once back in the heated comfort of the command center, the group decided that the simplest course of action was to bring in some cold-water diving gear and send someone down to verify that the aircraft was where they expected it to be. It was going to take time to assemble the gear and have it flown to the site, which troubled Annja, but the truth of the matter was that there wasn't any way around it. They needed the gear if they were going to survive going into that freezing water for even a few minutes. Without it, they would freeze to death in moments.

Garin took care of the necessary arrangements, including footing the bill for all the gear, while Annja and Paul returned to the lake and used the plows on the fronts of the Sno-Cats to clear a fifteen-by-fifteen-foot area over the spot where the plane was supposed to be. Using a heating coil taken from the command center's emergency supplies and the power from one of the Sno-Cat batteries, they managed to melt a hole two-and-a-half feet in diameter most of the way through the ice. At that point they reverted to using hand axes to chop the rest of it away until they broke through.

Annja stared at the dark water at the bottom of the hole, knowing that in a few short hours she would be going into its depths, and felt none of the excitement she usually felt when on the verge of a discovery of this magnitude. The sense of accomplishment, of a job well done, was completely absent; Doug's kidnapping had tainted the whole operation for her.

*Stay focused. It will be over soon enough,* she told herself.

THE THUNDER OF rotors echoed off the mountain peaks two hours later, alerting Annja and her companions that the equipment they were waiting for had arrived.

Annja watched a large helicopter marked with the DragonTech logo touch down long enough for the men inside to unload several large crates of equipment from the rear cargo hold. It then lifted off again to make room for another aircraft, and another. Within an hour the quiet little camp had been transformed by a flurry of activity. Not only had Garin's men brought the necessary dive equipment, but they'd also brought generators, floodlights and a pair of prefab cold-weather shelters, one to serve as a base of operations for the dive itself and the other for the team to sleep in.

The crew got to work assembling the gear, setting up the lights and erecting the shelter next to the hole Annja and Paul had dug through the ice. Before long the surface of the lake was brightly lit and they were ready to proceed.

It was time to get back to the search.

Paul, Garin, Annja and Reinhold gathered inside the shelter.

"Are you sure you're up for this?" Paul asked Annja as she inspected the equipment that Garin's team had brought in. "We've been going all day. Shouldn't we do this after a decent night's rest?"

Annja shook her head. "We've wasted enough time as it is. We need to find that plane."

Paul moved in closer and took hold of her arm. "Annja, listen to me. You need to be at your absolute best to dive in water this cold. Wait and do it in the morning."

Annja pulled away, seriously annoyed with him for the first time. "I'm perfectly fine, Paul. I can handle this. If you don't want to be here, go wait in the tent, but I'm going down to that wreck and I'm doing it now."

Paul threw up his hands. "All right. We'll do it your way. Heaven forbid I try to talk some sense into you."

Annja knew that Paul's feelings were hurt, but she didn't have time for that right now. She put it aside and concentrated on what was in front of her. Paul was right about one thing; this *was* a dangerous dive.

The cold was her biggest enemy, but the wreck itself would be hazardous, too. Add to that the fact that she would be diving alone, since neither Paul nor Garin had cold-water diving experience, and the risk rose exponentially. She would need to keep her wits about her and be sure she didn't linger too long down at the wreck.

Garin and Reinhold went out to check on the setup of the guide wire she would be using for the dive, so Annja took advantage of the opportunity to strip down to her undergarments and begin pulling on her gear. She started with a polypropolene sheath that fit her like a glove and that was designed to wick away her body moisture while retaining her body heat. Over that she pulled on a layer of insulation made of Thinsulate, a microfiber known to have a high resistance to water and one that would retain its insulating properties even when wet. Her third and final layer of undergarment protection was a shell consisting of a one-piece jumpsuit.

Then and only then was she ready for her dry suit. Paul helped her put it on, making sure the neck seals and hood were properly adjusted to keep the water away from her skin, before helping her pull on the booties and three-fingered mitts. Fins came next, followed by a weight belt to help her counter the natural buoyancy of everything she was wearing.

Properly suited up at last, she slipped her arms through her tank straps and hefted the oxygen tank onto her back, securing it in place. Satisfied with the fit, she tested her regulator, ensuring that it was working properly, then grabbed her mask and headed outside.

The halogen floods pushed back the darkness and lit the place with their stark, white light. Under their glow the water inside the dive hole looked even darker than before, and at the sight of it Annja felt a brush of trepidation. She shook it off and walked over to the hole where Garin and Reinhold were waiting. A safety line had been anchored in the nearby ice, and Garin helped her clip the line to her belt. She would carry it with her down to the wreck so that she had a guide wire to follow back up when it came time for her to surface.

"Here, take this," Garin said, passing her a handheld dive light. "It's going to be pitch-black down there."

She clipped its tether to her suit, ensuring that she wouldn't lose it if she had to let go for some reason.

Annja went through a final check of her equipment for safety's sake and then, satisfied, sat at the edge of the hole with her feet in the water. She pulled her mask on and prepared to go into the water.

Garin crouched beside her. "You've got thirty minutes, no more," he said. "After that, we're pulling you out."

"Understood."

She gave him the thumbs up, put her regulator into her mouth and then pushed off the ice to drop into the dark water below.

Garin had been right; it *was* pitch-black. The thick cover of snow on the ice above, never mind the late hour, kept even the brilliant illumination cast by the halogen floodlights from reaching her. Hovering there with only the light in her hand to guide her, she felt as if she was all alone in the universe.

*Time's a-wasting,* her inner voice chided and she

listened to it, turning her face downward and kicking hard with her legs.

Down she went, deeper into the gloom.

Her dive light cut through the murk around her for a few feet before being swallowed up again, so she kept her pace slow and steady, moving downward a few feet at a time. At that rate it took her several minutes to descend the one hundred and twenty feet to the bottom of the lake.

She paused, orienting herself, and then pushed off again, cutting through the water like a seal with powerful kicks of her legs in the direction Reinhold's scan had suggested.

If the data were correct, the plane shouldn't be more than fifty feet ahead of her.

She was upon it suddenly, the dark shape seeming to materialize out of the gloom as if in response to her presence. Her dive light picked out the port engine first, jutting from the wing's leading edge, the propeller still intact and covered with hanging strands of algae that moved slightly in the water's current.

Annja moved a few feet to her left, bringing the rest of the aircraft into view. For a moment, all she could do was hang there in the water, staring in amazement at her discovery.

The plane was surprisingly intact, given that it had crashed into a lake and spent seventy years at the bottom. The cold water had limited the corrosion that the aircraft had suffered, and the damage that she could see appeared more the result of the dogfight with Captain Mitchell and his wingman rather than a crash landing, controlled or otherwise, into the waters of the lake.

The Junkers had come to rest upright on the bottom of the lake. The landing gear had either failed or broken off when the plane struck the bottom, for the gondola beneath the nose was resting on the lake bottom, canting the plane at a slight angle. The damage to the underside of the craft appeared to be quite minimal, however. It was almost as if the lake waters had risen around the aircraft rather than the aircraft having violently crashed into the water and sunk to the bottom.

*Perhaps it had landed on the ice, only to have the ice break away beneath it,* she thought.

It was an interesting puzzle and one Annja wished she had the time to figure out, but sadly that wasn't the case. She continued her inspection, conscious of the ticking clock marking not only the consumption of her air supply but the encroaching deadline for the project overall.

She kicked upward along the nose, and shone her light into the aircraft's cockpit.

A grinning face stared back at her from behind the glass.

Annja recoiled and nearly dropped her light, her heart pounding madly in her chest. She could feel herself sucking air out of her regulator at an accelerated pace as adrenaline flooded her system, and she forced herself to calm down and breathe easier so that she wouldn't hyperventilate.

When she was calmer, she approached the cockpit once more.

This time, prepared for what she would see, the grinning face behind the glass didn't startle her. She could see that it was actually the skull of the pilot, held in place atop its skeleton by the flight suit and hood that it wore. The skeleton wafted gently in the water. Annja followed the edge of the cockpit back a few feet so that she could look into the aft section. Another skeleton sat in that part of the cockpit, still strapped securely in its seat. At first she thought it was a navigator or gunner, one of the regular crew for a craft of this size, but then she caught sight of the twin lightning bolt insignias pinned to each side of the uniform collar that stuck up beneath the ill-fitting flight suit the corpse wore and realized that she was staring at a member of the Waffen SS.

*Curiouser and curiouser*, she thought.

Her research had told her that there were two ways into the aircraft—through the cockpit, where a hatch at the gunner's feet would allow access to the bomb bay in the underside of the fuselage, or through the gondola access hatch on the underside of the plane. Entering through the cockpit made her a bit uncomfortable since it would mean disturbing the dead. She'd do it if she had to, but first she'd try the gondola hatch.

She floated over to the other side of the fuselage to see if the plane's angle allowed better access from that position.

If anything, the gondola was buried in even more silt on this side.

*Perhaps I can find a hole in the fuselage?*

She left the cockpit behind and swam the length of the plane toward the tail. A cold chill passed over her at the sight of the Balkenkreuz, the black cross used as symbol of the various branches of the Germany military, still visible through the corrosion spreading across the aircraft's wings. Along with the swastika, that cross had become a symbol of the Third Reich known the world over and was not something that Annja looked on with any sense of fondness whatsoever.

As she neared the tail, she dipped over the side of the aircraft to take a look. She was surprised to find the entire plane intact; aside from a few bullet holes the fuselage was still in one piece.

It looked like it was going to be the cockpit after all.

A glance at her dive watch told her that she'd been down there for nearly fifteen minutes. It was time to move things along a bit quicker.

She swam above the aircraft and returned to the cockpit. The rear half of the reinforced glass that covered the pilot and gunner was designed to slide backward, opening the section above both seats. All she had to do was look on the outside of the cockpit for the hatch release lever used by the ground crews and she should be able to open it without too much difficulty.

Placing her hands along the lower seam where the

glass met the metal edge of the cockpit, she carefully slid them along until she found the narrow groove that housed the lever. Her thick diving gloves were almost too big to fit inside, but she was patient and managed to work them through the gap well enough to grasp the handle. When she was satisfied that she had a good grip on it, she turned her face away to protect it from potential debris and gave the handle a good yank.

Nothing happened.

She let it fall back into place and tried again.

And again.

The third time turned out to be the charm as the internal mechanism finally loosened enough to pop the latch securing the canopy, allowing it to open a few inches. Annja reached beneath the edge, got a good grip, then pushed it all the way back until it locked into place, providing an opening immediately above the pilot's and gunner's seats.

Annja slipped into the rear section of the cockpit, head downward, being as careful as she could not to disturb the skeleton. Her feet were sticking out of the open canopy above when she reached forward to access the hatch on the floor where the gunner's feet rested, but that was the only way she could reach it. The door had a handle on it that needed to be turned ninety degrees, and she was worried it might be stuck the way the canopy lever had been. But this one worked without a hitch. Once turned, the hatch fell forward, provided her with room to slip into the narrow access space below.

The short corridor—really just a gap between internal struts and the frame of the aircraft—allowed the gunner to reach the munitions storage compartment in the event that something went disastrously wrong, such as having an armed bomb get hung up on the rack. The gunner could assess the situation and attempt to manually release the weapon from inside the bay, removing the danger from the aircraft. The space was tiny; there was no other word for it. Annja was not a big person, but there was barely enough room for her and the added bulk of her suit and dive tank to slip along its length, her shoulders nearly touching the walls on either side as she went. She was grateful she didn't suffer from claustrophobia or the route would have been impossible for her to manage.

Reaching the other end, she shone her light into the starboard munitions bay and gasped at what she saw.

In the space where a 500-pound bomb would normally sit was a rectangular stack of gold bars at least three feet wide by two feet high!

# 12

She'd guessed what she would find, but guessing it and seeing it sitting there within arm's reach were two entirely different things, especially when you were talking about a fortune in gold.

She could see a few pieces of rotting wood along the base of the stack and realized that the gold had originally been inside a wooden crate that had slowly rotted away over the years. As the wood dissolved, the gold was slowly revealed until it stood there on its own, still perfectly aligned in the manner in which it had been packed.

Annja rolled over and shone her light into the port bay, only to discover the same thing: stacks of gold bars patiently waiting to be discovered by some lucky soul.

The stack in the port bay was closer to the access tunnel, and Annja was able to reach out and pluck one of the bars from the top of the stack. It was heavy, which somehow made it seem more real to her. When she brought it closer, she could see that there was an image of a crown atop a shield etched into the surface of the gold brick. She wasn't positive, but she thought it might be the Hungarian coat of arms.

If it was, that meant that she had located a small portion of the Hungarian national treasury that had gone missing during World War II at the hands of the Nazis.

It was a stunning find.

And one the world would probably never know about, for it was going directly into the hands of a criminal.

*No matter,* she thought. *Doug is the important thing. Save him and worry about recovering the gold later, if at all.*

She slipped the gold brick into the bag on her dive belt and was in the process of trying to maneuver herself around to head back the way she had come when the watch on her wrist vibrated.

Ten minutes of air remained.

It was time to head back to the surface. Turning, she began to pull herself back down the access tunnel in the direction that she'd come. It would take a minute or two to exit the aircraft and then a few more to follow the guide wire to the surface; she'd make it without difficulty.

Or so she thought.

The last thing she expected was to reach the end of the access tunnel and find another diver poking about in the front section of the cockpit.

His dive light was secured to the front portion of the canopy and pointing into the cockpit, illuminating the area well enough for her to see by.

At first she thought that Paul or Garin had dis-
obeyed her instructions and had come down with her
despite their lack of cold-water diving experience. But
then she noticed that the other diver was dressed in
a different model of dry suit than the one she wore,
which eliminated that theory. All of the gear Garin
had purchased had been of the same make and design.

That meant there was a stranger down there with
her.

Annja immediately doused her dive light, not
wanting to give away her position to the newcomer.
She also recognized right away that she couldn't remain where she was. Getting caught in the access
tunnel while her air ran out was not something she
intended to experience.

The skeletal remains of the pilot and gunner were
gone, apparently tossed out of the cockpit by the newcomer. Annja could see him crouched inside the front
section of the cockpit, most likely on the pilot's seat,
but she couldn't see what he was doing.

Knowing that every second she waited was another
second of air she wasted, Annja didn't hesitate. This
was probably going to be her only chance to get out.
She reached up, grabbed both sides of the opening to
the access tunnel and propelled herself forward with
a downward thrust of her arms so that she came floating out of the opening in one smooth motion.

Her sudden appearance, rising up out of the back
of the cockpit like a ghost, had to have shocked the
other diver, for he started in surprise and dropped
whatever it was that he'd been pulling on, giving her

the time she needed to get herself completely clear of the access door. She was close enough now to see that the other diver was a man, but she didn't have a clue who he might be.

Nor was the other diver going to give her the time to puzzle it out. He recovered from his surprise quickly and did the one thing Annja was hoping he wouldn't—he launched himself at her over the seats that separated them.

Annja was floating half in and half out of the rear section of the cockpit when the diver's bulk slammed into her. With nothing for her to brace against, she was forced backward until her tank slammed into the edge of the canopy behind her.

Her assailant raised an arm above his head, and Annja caught the glint of steel as the illumination from his diver's light reflected off the blade in his hand.

There was no doubt about his intentions at that point.

As the arm came down, Annja swung her own out to block it, striking the inside of the diver's forearm and forcing the knife off target to hit the canopy beside her.

She didn't wait for him to recover, but went on the offensive instead, slamming the palm of her other hand directly into his face mask.

Annja knew she didn't have a hope of breaking the glass of the mask, but that wasn't what she was after. She did it for the sheer shock value, using his own fear of losing the security of his equipment against him, and she smiled grimly when he recoiled from her as a result.

That opened up enough space between them for her to do what she really intended.

She reached into the otherwhere and grasped the hilt of her sword, drawing it forth into the real world just as the other diver was preparing to attack her with the knife once more. Instead of an helpless opponent, suddenly the tide was turned and her assailant found himself facing a woman armed with a blade that was four times longer than his own.

Annja watched the man's eyes widen in surprise at the appearance of the sword.

While she was still congratulating herself on her clever move, her assailant pushed off with his legs and twisted up and over the gunner's seat, putting himself in the front section of the cockpit with the seat now between them. He reached down, grabbed something off the pilot's seat beneath his feet, and then pushed off again out of the open hatch, kicking furiously in an attempt to get away from her.

Annja did the only thing she could think of; she threw herself forward, thrusting the sword ahead of her at the same time.

The resistance of the water slowed her strike considerably. As a result she only managed to slash the edge of the blade across the man's thigh instead of impaling him with it as she'd intended.

It might not have been what she'd planned, but it was enough.

The sudden pain across his leg made the other

diver release his grip on the object he'd retrieved from the plane. It dropped away from him toward the bottom of the lake.

Having lost what he'd come for and facing an opponent armed with a weapon much more versatile than his own, the other diver apparently decided that discretion was the better part of valor and headed off into the gloom.

Annja's dive watch was vibrating every few seconds now, the alarm telling her that she had less than five minutes to get to the surface. She could either chase after her assailant or recover whatever it was that he had dropped; she didn't have time to do both.

She chose the latter.

Holding her sword in one hand and flicking her dive light back on with the other, she slipped over the side of the aircraft, hunting for whatever it was that the other diver had dropped.

She moved the light across the lake bottom, searching for any object that looked out of place. At first she didn't see anything, but then she spotted a cloud of silt slowly dispersing a few feet away and she swam in that direction, hoping that it had been the falling object and not a fish that had disturbed the sediment.

Annja almost missed it, the leather of the satchel was the same dark color as the silt along the lake bottom, but fortunately the corroded buckle that held the front flap closed had enough shine left to reflect the beam from her dive light. She swam over, snatched it up, and then followed the guide wire all the way back to her original dive point. She released her sword back into the otherwhere as she went.

Time, unfortunately, had run out.

As she rose slowly toward the surface, one hand sliding along the guide wire, she could feel the air she was sucking out of her tank becoming thinner and thinner. The tank was down to its last meager sips of oxygen; she estimated that she had less than a minute of air left.

Annja, however, had no intention of drowning at the bottom of an Alpine lake.

She sucked in as much air as she could, grasped the guide wire, and then hit the quick release on the buckle that held her weight belt around her waist. Even as that dropped away and began its descent to the lake floor, Annja was doing the same with her dive tank, shrugging out of the harness and letting that fall away behind her, as well.

The sudden difference in buoyancy allowed her to swim upward at a much faster pace.

Annja kept her hand on the guide wire, not wanting to reach the surface only to find an unbroken layer of ice trapping her beneath it, and fought to hold on to her breath.

She could feel herself starting to get lightheaded and she struggled to force the dizziness back, knowing she was a goner if she blacked out now. She kicked furiously upward, straining to go faster with every second, knowing that her life and Doug's depended on her survival.

Above her, she could see the circle of light marking the dive hole.

*Just a little farther...*

Her head was pounding and her lungs were screaming at her to take in air, but she forced herself to ignore it all, focusing on the light above her to the exclusion of everything else.

*Come on, come on, almost there...*

She kicked with the last of her strength, her hands reaching upward for the light even as the dizziness she'd been trying to control finally swept over her, bringing with it a tide of darkness blacker than night.

She could feel her body going limp, could feel herself starting to drop back into the depths below, but there was nothing she could do about it, her air, and her strength with it, spent.

She'd been so close. Then, just as she'd been about to surrender to the blackness that longed to drag her down, a pair of hands shot through the circle of light above and grabbed her outstretched wrists.

She grasped the person's wrists with all she had left. Though she could feel herself being dragged upward, she succumbed to the darkness and knew no more...

# 13

Annja awoke to find herself bundled up in warm clothing and tucked into a sleeping bag in one of the prefab shelters. She luxuriated in the fact that she was still alive and then pushed herself up into a sitting position.

"Sleeping beauty awakens, I see."

She turned at the sound of Garin's voice and found him sitting in a camp chair on the other side of the room. "Hello, Garin."

"Cutting it a bit close, weren't you? If I hadn't seen your dive light coming up…"

Annja nodded. "It wasn't intentional, believe me. If I hadn't tussled with that other diver, I would have had…"

"Wait! What did you say? Another diver?"

"Yes. There was someone else down on the wreck with me. He would have surfaced just before I did."

Garin frowned. "No one came up out of that lake but you. I was standing by the dive hole the entire time."

"That's not possible, Garin. I'm telling you that

there was someone else down on the wreck with me. He's the one who discovered the satchel."

A cold thought ran over her.

"You did get the satchel, right?" she asked.

Garin nodded. "And the gold bar. Nice job on that, by the way."

Annja shrugged. She didn't see it as all that unusual; it was what she did, after all.

Garin frowned. "Tell me about this diver you saw."

Annja explained what happened, including the fact that she'd managed to injure the man, though she didn't know how severely.

"If no one came out of that hole before me…" she began.

"There has to be another way in," Garin finished for her.

Annja had been unconscious for about two hours, so the other diver was sure to have made his getaway by this point, but they organized a search anyway, just to be sure.

Annja, Garin and Paul boarded one of the supply helicopters and began searching the surface of the lake with the floodlight mounted beneath the aircraft while Garin's men fanned out along the shoreline, searching the area on foot.

Twenty minutes after they started, Garin took a radio call from one of the search teams. He listened to whatever the other man was saying for a moment and then leaned around the seat to speak to the pilot. The aircraft began making a sweeping turn to the right.

"Griggs found something on the far side of the lake," Garin told them. "We're going to take a look."

Ten minutes later the helicopter touched down and the three of them hurried out from under the still-whirling blades to where Griggs waited for them.

He led them to the shoreline where several flares had been arranged in a large rectangle, illuminating the area within.

A set of vehicle tracks started at the edge of a hole in the ice and disappeared out of sight in a straight line away from the lake and into the mountains.

*Could have been anything from a snowmobile to a Sno-Cat*, Annja thought.

"We also found this," Griggs said, leading them farther along the water's edge. A dry suit had been discarded a few yards away from the water. It was navy blue, which Annja thought might have been the color of the suit worn by the diver she'd encountered. The kicker was that when she picked it up and examined it, she found a long gash across one thigh.

Clearly, this was the dry suit her attacker had been wearing.

She said as much to the others.

"What do you think he was after?" Garin asked.

"Whatever is in that satchel, I guess," Annja replied.

Paul frowned. "Doesn't that seem kind of weird to you? You've got a plane full of gold bars, and this guy wants an old leather satchel?"

"It depends on what's in that satchel."

Annja glanced over at Garin, her eyebrows raised as if asking a question.

He shook his head. "We didn't open it. We figured you'd want to do that yourself."

*Darn right, I do*, she thought.

To the others she said, "I don't think we're going to answer the puzzle standing out here in the cold. Let's go back to base and take a look."

Both Garin and Paul agreed, but Garin wasn't quite ready to give up on the mysterious diver.

"Griggs, take a team and follow that trail," Garin instructed. "If you find anything worthwhile, get me on the radio."

"Yes, sir. Will do."

Leaving Griggs to organize the search, the others boarded the helicopter. Once back at the base, they gathered in the command center along with Reinhold to examine the satchel.

The bag was made of a dark leather of some kind, with a clasp in the shape of a silver swastika. The satchel didn't appear to have suffered any deterioration or significant water damage, which made Annja think it had been stored in some kind of waterproof container beneath the pilot's seat during the years it had been there. It had obviously gotten wet when it had been removed from its hiding place, but it had dried out fairly well in the intervening hours between then and now. Annja just hoped the water hadn't destroyed whatever was inside.

Using a digital camera she had brought along with her, Annja took several photographs of the front and back of the satchel, preserving a record of its condition for later study. When she was satisfied, she put the camera down and turned her attention to opening the bag.

Like the leather of the satchel itself, the clasp was in excellent condition and opened without difficulty on the first try. Looking inside, Annja saw that the bag contained a smaller package sealed in some kind of dark, plastic-looking material.

She reached inside and drew it out.

The plastic was actually a sealed bag made of stiffened rubber. Annja realized that it was what would have passed for waterproof packaging during the war years and that it was most likely a document case of some kind.

*Probably the pilot's map case,* she thought.

She used the camera to take several more pictures, despite Garin's exaggerated sighs of impatience. Without looking at him, she said, "I'm going to do this right or not at all. If you'd rather, you can wait outside in the cold."

Garin didn't go anywhere, but at least he stopped sighing.

Annja counted that as a victory.

When she had finished her documentation, she picked up the bag, broke the seal and looked inside.

A sheaf of papers stared back at her. She could see the official stamp of the Third Reich at the top of each page.

*Now things are getting interesting. One thing is for certain—this is no ordinary map case.*

Moving very carefully, conscious of both the age and the possibility of water damage from the damp satchel to the papers themselves, she reached in and drew the stack out of the bag.

She knew just from the feel of them that they were intact and undamaged despite being underwater for so long. From her view, the guy who devised the water-proof bag from which they'd been removed deserved a medal; even today's containers would have had a hard time providing as much protection. She laid out the pages one after another on the table in front of her.

They were yellowed with age, and fragile as a re-sult, but still easily readable.

There was only one problem.

They were in German.

Annja's German was rusty, but they didn't have to rely on her translation skills.

"Garin, would you be so kind?"

"Of course," he said, walking around to her side of the table to get a better view. He leaned over the page for a moment, scanned it, then gave a low whis-tle. Before anyone could ask what he meant, he began translating aloud.

Martin,
As I write this, the Soviet attack on our beloved capital has begun. I have begun making prepa-rations to leave the city behind and move the Party to the new Führerhauptquartiere on Wolf Island. I shall be there within two weeks. I have

already sent the bulk of the treasury ahead of me to fund the next phase of our operations.

I know the existence of this new Führerhauptquartiere is most likely news to you. I'm sorry I could not take you into my confidence before this, but the eyes that are upon us are many and it is difficult to know who to trust at this late hour. Your recent exploits have assured me that you are still firmly on the side of the Reich and so I am passing this knowledge on to you. All you need to locate the island is contained herein.

This courier is carrying the funds needed to finish the final preparations. Major Adler, who accompanies them, can be trusted fully to act on behalf of the Reich in all things. Use him as you see fit to assist you in this endeavor.

I shall join you shortly.

Long live the Reich!

Adolf Hitler

Silence reigned for a moment after Garin had finished reading and then everyone tried to talk at once. Annja brought her fingers to her lips and whistled sharply, cutting them off in midsentence.

"All right, settle down. Let's not lose our cool at this point, okay?"

The others nodded, but the excitement in the room remained high.

Annja turned to Garin. "Is there anything else?"

"There is a series of symbols below the signature, but that's all."

"How about the other pages?"

Garin took a few moments, examining each one. Annja could see that Paul and Reinhold were practically bursting with questions, but she held up a finger, indicating they should wait until she received her answer.

At last Garin said, "As far as I can tell, these are the cargo manifests for several freighters carrying goods on behalf of the Führer. Construction supplies, arms and equipment, even furniture are listed on the various pages, complete with number and weight of each of the items."

"Is there a destination listed?"

Garin shook his head. "No."

A glance at Paul told her he could barely contain his excitement, so she nodded in his direction.

"I'm sorry," he began, "but what's a *Führerhauptquartiere*?"

Reinhold answered first. "The direct translation is Führer Headquarters. It is the name commonly given to the various headquarters used by Adolf Hitler during World War II."

"Like the Führer Bunker?"

Reinhold nodded. "Yes. The *Wolfsshanze*, or Wolf's Lair, and *Berghold*, the Eagle's Nest, are two others. There were at least half a dozen, if not more."

"And now, apparently, we've discovered another," Annja said. She turned to Garin and Reinhold, both German citizens despite the centuries that separated them. "Have either of you ever heard of this Wolf Island?"

They both shook their heads.

Reinhold leaned over the table, staring at the letter. "It's addressed to Martin. Could that be Martin Bormann?"

"That would be my guess," Annja replied. She glanced at Garin, who agreed that Bormann was the most likely recipient in his view, as well.

Martin Bormann had been a prominent official in the Nazi Party, having served as both the Party Chancellery, and as Hitler's private secretary for many years. He had remained loyal to Hitler up to the very end and for years had been thought to have escaped to parts unknown after Hitler's suicide.

More recent historical works stated that he had, in fact, committed suicide on a bridge near Lehrter Station, the main railway connecting Berlin to Hamburg, in order to avoid capture by the Russians during the fall of Berlin, just days after his Führer had taken his own life.

Now here was this letter, seemingly written in Hitler's own hand, suggesting that Bormann had actually been somewhere else during the time in question.

*Could it be true?* Annja wondered. *Could the rumors of Bormann's survival and the plan to create a Fourth Reich out of the ashes of the Third actually have some substance to them?*

It was the kind of information that could rewrite history, and she felt the call of the mystery as an almost physical force. It was exactly the kind of intriguing puzzle that she would normally jump to investigate.

But she couldn't.

At least, not yet.

*Right now our priority is salvaging the gold from the plane and trading it for Doug's life,* she reminded herself. *Nothing else matters until that task is complete.*

"As interesting as all of this is," Annja said to the others, "none of it helps us free Doug from the kidnapper's control. As much as I hate to do it, we need to table any further discussion of this topic until after we've rescued Doug."

To her satisfaction, no one disagreed.

# 14

"What, exactly, are you expected to do?" Reinhold asked, reminding Annja that he hadn't been there from the beginning and had only heard a few of the pertinent details.

She quickly filled him in.

Reinhold listened to her explanation and then said, "The kidnapper demanded that you find the aircraft. You've done so. Isn't that enough?"

*Oh, if only it were that easy*, Annja thought.

Yes, the kidnapper had ordered her to find the aircraft, no doubt so he could recover the gold before anyone else. Annja had no doubt that he hadn't expected the airplane to be at the bottom of an Alpine lake; she certainly hadn't, so why should he?

That was where things got complicated. She could leave the plane—and the gold it contained—right where it was and hope for the best, or she could do what she could to recover the gold in the time they still had available to them in the hopes that the kidnapper would see that as going above and beyond the call of duty and treat Doug commensurately.

While she wished she could say that the kidnapper had been reasonable in his demands so far, that certainly wasn't the case. Expecting her to find the location of an aircraft that had gone missing seventy years earlier at the end of the biggest war the world had ever seen, and to do it in seven days, was about as far from possible as she could imagine. She had little doubt that the only way she was getting Doug back safe and sound was if she had that gold stacked up and ready for delivery by the time she made the phone call two days from now.

In answer to Reinhold's question, she said, "No, I don't think it is, actually. The kidnapper is going to want to take control of that gold as quickly as possible. Bringing it up from the bottom of the lake is going to take some effort and increase his risk of exposure. That's not something he's going to be happy about."

She turned so she could speak to all of them at once. "We need to retrieve the gold from the lake in the time we have left if we hope to see Doug released unharmed."

Garin shook his head. "I don't know how you're going to manage that, Annja. There's no way you're going to be able to carry up more than a few bars from the wreck at a time. Not with what they weigh. If there are as many bars as your description suggests, it is going to take us weeks to bring them all up with only a single diver."

"We're not going to use divers to carry them up. In fact, we're not going to carry them up at all."

"Then how do you expect to deliver them to the kidnapper?" Paul asked.

Annja looked at the three men standing before her and said, "We're not going to bring up the gold. We're going to bring up the entire aircraft."

The resulting silence at her announcement was finally broken by a cynical laugh from Garin. "That plane has to weigh twenty, maybe twenty-five thousand pounds and that's before you add the weight of the gold. How on earth do you expect to lift that off the bottom of that lake?"

"With half a dozen float bags and your helicopters, of course," she replied, smiling.

The idea was relatively simple, she explained. They would have one of Garin's helicopters bring in several float bags, the kind used in underwater salvage operations to help right sunken ships or bring smaller vessels back up to the surface. When packaged for deployment the bags were about three feet long and two feet wide, making them easy to transport. When they were activated, however, they expanded into cylinders nine feet in length.

The group would break up the ice to provide an area of open water. They would then secure several of the bags to the underside of the aircraft, activate them simultaneously, and float the wreckage right up to the surface of the lake. From there they would attach cables to the aircraft and use a pair of Garin's helicopters to either tow it to shore or lift it out of the water entirely, depending on the condition of the plane once they got it to the surface.

"How do you know it isn't going to break into a hundred pieces when you activate the floats?" Paul asked.

Annja had to admit that she didn't, not for certain. "I'm willing to take that chance. From what I could see the aircraft was pretty intact. I don't think it crashed at all."

"Then how did it get down there?" Reinhold wanted to know.

"The pilot probably made a controlled landing on the ice, perhaps thinking it was a flat stretch of ground and not realizing what it actually was. Before he could evacuate the aircraft, the ice must have cracked open, sending the plane to the bottom of the lake with the pilot still in it."

It was a reasonable explanation for the condition of the plane and it matched the details as they knew them. Besides, it just felt right to her and she'd learned to trust her gut.

If the plane had made a controlled landing, the frame would still be structurally sound and they shouldn't have any problem at all bringing it back up to the surface.

Or so she hoped.

After a bit of discussion the others came around to her way of thinking and it was decided that they would make the attempt late the next afternoon, once the necessary gear had been flown in from Munich.

With a plan in place, it was time to call it a day. Annja was exhausted after all she'd been through and she was asleep within seconds of her head hitting the pillow.

THE THUNDER OF helicopters woke her up just after nine the next morning. She got dressed and stepped out of the shelter in time to watch two big AgustaWestland helicopters, like the one that had carried them from Jamaica, land nearby. Along with the floatation bags, the helicopters were carrying a team of four divers with experience in the kind of underwater salvage work she needed. Annja was pleased that she wouldn't have to figure out how to place the floatation bags where they would do the most good, but concerned that there were now four strangers who knew what they were doing. Word could spread rather quickly, as the presence of their mystery diver indicated, and the more people involved the easier it would be for the truth to leak.

Her concerns, however, were put to rest when Garin explained that the divers were part of his personal security force and could be trusted to keep their mouths shut about what they did and saw during the operation. They were here to do their jobs and that was it; nothing else mattered to them. Garin paid them quite handsomely to insure that.

By early afternoon small thermite charges had been used to break up the ice on the surface of the lake, and the divers had taken the floatation bags to the bottom and securely attached them to the wreckage of the aircraft in the appropriate locations. Once that was complete, the team was ready to make its first try at bringing the aircraft to the surface.

Because Griggs's attempt to follow the mystery diver's tracks back to their place of origin had failed,

Garin made sure to post several other members of his armed security team at various points around the lake, just in case someone tried to interfere with their attempt to recover the aircraft.

Satisfied that they had done all they could to ensure a successful conclusion to their salvage operation, Annja gave the order for the floatation bags to be deployed.

For a moment, nothing happened.

Then, slowly at first but with increasingly greater frequency and agitation, the surface of the lake began to bubble and churn as the mass of the aircraft began pushing up from below.

The tail of the plane broke the surface first, followed quickly by the glass of the canopy up front. Soon the entire aircraft was sitting on the surface of the lake, visible in the midday sun for the first time in seventy years. Cheers broke out all around the lake as those on site—both workers and security   felt the thrill of victory at the recovery mission's success even if they didn't know what it was all for.

Annja wasn't ready to cheer quite yet; they still needed to lift the plane out of the lake and onto dry land, but she did indulge in a smile that her on-the-fly idea had actually worked. She hadn't let it show, but she'd been nervous as heck that the whole thing would just fall apart when the floatation devices began their push for the surface.

*Hopefully the second step will go as smoothly as the first.*

Even as she thought it, the helicopters were mov-

ing in and positioning themselves over the wreck.
Cables were lowered to the four divers in the water,
who secured them to the chains holding the floatation devices to the aircraft. This way there wouldn't
be any direct pressure on the plane's fuselage, which
she hoped would increase their chances of getting the
plane out of the lake intact.

When the divers were finished securing the cables, they swam away from the wreckage so that they
wouldn't be hit by any falling debris should things go
awry. When the lead diver gave her the signal, Annja
brought the handheld to her mouth, depressed the talk
button and said, "You are go for lift."

She crossed the fingers of her other hand even as
the words were leaving her mouth.

After that, there was nothing to do but watch and
hope.

The helicopters began a steady lift, moving in tight
formation and in unison with each other to keep the
force being applied to the aircraft's frame as even
as possible. The wreckage creaked and groaned, as
if protesting being taken from its watery grave, but
nevertheless it began to rise slowly into the air, water
streaming off it at every angle.

Foot by foot the aircraft rose above the water and
took to the air once more, perhaps for the final time.

The helicopters carried the Junkers away from the
lake and set it down in the snow on the far side of
the camp, where another team of Garin's men were
waiting to release the tow cables and free the chop-
pers of their burden.

Annja's radio crackled to life. "Big bird to base. Mission accomplished."

She had done the impossible! *Now* she felt like cheering.

# 15

After posting guards around the aircraft, the team returned to the command center. It was one o'clock in the afternoon in Germany, which made it three in the morning back in the States, at least, on the east coast, but Annja didn't care. She pulled out her cell phone and punched in the number the kidnapper had given her.

The phone rang several times before it was picked up.

"Hello?" Annja said.

A series of clicks echoed down the line before the kidnapper's voice sounded in her ear.

"Have you found the aircraft?" he asked.

"I have. You can pick up the gold anytime you want."

His voice sounded a little different this time, as if there was an accent hiding under his excellent English. She wondered if it had been there the last time they'd spoken or if it was just an artifact of the quality of the connection between them.

"Gold?" the voice asked. "You believe it is the gold that I'm after?"

Annja's blood ran cold. Something was wrong, and she was suddenly afraid that she knew what it was.

Still, there was no sense in admitting defeat at this point. She'd play the game as long as she could, hoping the kidnapper might give something away during the course of their conversation that would help to locate Doug.

Annja plunged ahead. "I do, yes. The original crates have rotted away, so I'd suggest that you bring new ones with you when you come to pick it up. Now let me speak to Doug."

"You can speak to Doug when you have completed the task I set out for you."

*Here it comes*, she thought.

"You asked me to find the plane. I've done that. Our deal is over."

The others were watching her and knew that something had gone wrong. Paul got up and started toward her, but she waved him off, not wanting the distraction at the time when she needed to concentrate most.

"If you found the plane, then you obviously found the letter as well."

"What letter?" Annja asked.

There was a pause and then in the background Annja heard a man begin to scream.

And he kept screaming.

"Hello?" Annja shouted into the phone. "Are you there? Stop it!"

The scream cut off abruptly and the kidnapper's

voice came back over the line. "Your friend does not tolerate pain very well."

"Stop," Annja said, her heart sinking in her chest. "Just stop. Please. Yes, I found the letter."

With an air of satisfaction, the kidnapper asked, "Did you read it?"

"Yes."

"Good. Then there is no need to explain myself. The real target is *Insel Wolf*."

*Wolf Island? He can't be serious*.

"We don't even know if that's real," she protested.

"Oh, it's real all right. And you're going to find it for me, just like you found that aircraft. Or else I'll start mailing pieces of your friend here to that lovely little apartment you have in Brooklyn."

Annja had to bite back the anger that threatened to overwhelm her at the kidnapper's words. One thing was for certain; when she caught up to him, she was going to ensure that he couldn't do anything like this to anyone else ever again.

"And when I find your mystery island, what then?"

"Then I will release Mr. Morrell on the street corner of your choice in downtown Manhattan, alive and…well, reasonably unharmed. You have another week, no more. Find that island!"

"Wait!" Annja cried.

Too late. The line had been cut.

She hit redial and waited for the phone to be picked up on the other end, but it just rang and rang. After a few moments of listening to it, she hung up in disgust.

She looked up at the others, who had been watching her closely during the call. Obviously, they knew something wasn't right.

"He doesn't want the gold," she said. "He wants the island."

Reinhold shook his head in disbelief. "This guy must think you're some kind of genius. What are you going to do?"

Genius or not, she didn't think she had much choice.

"Find it, of course."

"But we don't even know where to begin," Paul said dejectedly.

He was wrong on that score.

"Yes, we do," she told him. "We just don't know what it means yet."

"The symbols on the letter," Garin said quietly.

"Exactly. I'm guessing the symbols are some kind of coded message, revealing the location of the island. Hitler did say that everything Martin needed in order to follow his instructions was in the letter."

"You can't be sure of that," Reinhold said.

"But I am. Have to be, for Doug's sake. Hitler himself stated that Martin, the letter's recipient, didn't know the location of the new headquarters, yet he asked him to complete the preparations for his arrival two weeks later and that everything he needed to carry out his orders was contained right there in his letter.

"If the coded message doesn't give the location of Wolf Island, then at the very least, it will tell us how to find it."

Annja was confident she knew what the code was hiding. What she wasn't so confident about was her ability to crack it, especially in the time frame given.

Still, she had no choice but to try.

Figuring four heads were better than one, Annja copied the symbols at the bottom of the letter onto individual pieces of paper and then handed one each to Paul, Garin and Reinhold, keeping one page for herself. She packed the original documents back into their waterproof container and slid the container inside the satchel. They'd been stored like that for decades without any damage, so she figured another few hours wouldn't hurt. When she had the chance, she'd turn it over to the proper authorities, but for now she'd just keep it protected and close. Satisfied, she took her copy of the symbols and her laptop and settled down in a corner to see if she could break the code.

Her work in archaeology had introduced her to a fair number of different types of codes, and she was expecting to make short work of this one.

Things began to go wrong right from the start, however.

Looking at the symbols, she immediately discovered that none of them were familiar to her. Some looked like Hebrew characters. Some like Teutonic runes. Others like Japanese kanji. It was almost as if the code maker had taken symbols from a variety of cultures and slapped them together to create a new kind of alphabet.

She spent an hour trying to separate the ones that were familiar from those that were not, only to find that even the familiar characters had subtle differences to them that made her unable to classify them with definitively.

When that didn't work, she decided to approach the cipher as if it were a simple substitution code. By assigning a letter to each symbol based on its frequency of appearance, she could begin to identify certain repetitive symbols and the English letters associated with them. For instance, E was the most common letter of the German alphabet, so she looked for the symbol used most frequently and assigned the letter E to it. N was the second most common, so she found the second most common symbol and assigned the letter N to that. With enough correct letters, the code breaker could then make some educated guesses about the other symbols. If a three-letter word started with the symbol that corresponded to T and ended with the symbol that corresponded to E, it was a fair guess that the middle symbol was most likely H. And so on.

Unfortunately, after making several such substitutions it became obvious that the message wasn't long enough to get a good handle on it following that process. There simply weren't enough letters or variations therein for it to work.

She decided to try the Caesar cipher after that. Used by a Roman emperor, the Caesar cipher was actually multiple substitution codes in one. To use it, Annja assembled two wheels, one inside the other. She wrote the German alphabet on the outside of each wheel. By turning the inner wheel and aligning a letter on that one with a letter on the outside wheel, a substitution code was formed. This method provided twenty-six different possibilities and Annja took the time to work through them all, assigning the most frequent as the letter E and then using the code to assign values to the other symbols based on frequency.

When she had exhausted her own knowledge, she used the satellite uplink in the command center to connect to the internet and spent several hours researching everything she could on Nazi codes from World War II. She learned more than she ever wanted to about Enigma, *Reservehandverfahren*, *Geheimfernschreiber* and other German codes, but none were any use in cracking the one in front of her.

Long after the sun had set, Annja finally put her pen down in disgust. She'd been at it for hours and was no further than when she'd started. She knew the others had given up hours ago, but she'd stubbornly continued, believing that at some point she'd find the key. Now she sat, surrounded by her notes and sketches, her various attempts to solve the puzzle, and realized with a growing sense of despair that she might never solve this one.

The door on the other side of the room opened and Garin stepped inside. "Any luck?"

Annja shook her head. "At this point I'm convinced it is some kind of high-level German code that was only used by a handful of select individuals. If the Allies knew anything about it, during the war or after, it was never made public knowledge."

She pounded the table once in frustration. "I don't even know where to go from here, Garin."

He looked at the floor as if contemplating something, and then glanced up at her. "I may know some-one who can help us with it."

Annja had known him long enough to recognize the tone of voice he was using. "And?" she asked, knowing that there was more, that there was something Garin wasn't telling her.

"I hesitate to get him involved because he is a… well…let's just say that he's a less-than-savory character."

Now that was rich. Garin judging someone else's morality. This from the man who had no qualms about industrial espionage or the theft of priceless artifacts and who thought more about what he was having for dinner each night than he did about taking someone's life.

*If Garin thinks the guy is unsavory, he must have crawled out of a dark cesspool somewhere.*

She didn't care.

She needed to solve the cipher in order to rescue Doug, and so far all of her efforts had been for naught. Even worse, she was out of ideas.

If she was going to solve it, she was going to need some help and right about now it didn't matter at all where it came from.

She said as much to Garin.

"All right," he told her. "I'll make the arrangements. He won't come to us so we're going to have to go to him. Thankfully, he's close."

"How close?"

Garin smiled. "This time tomorrow we'll be out of the cold and dining in Paris."

# 16

After leaving Griggs in charge of removing the gold and shipping it to Garin's headquarters in Munich for safekeeping, Annja, Paul and Garin boarded the DragonTech Security executive helicopter for the flight to Paris.

Annja was glad to be going. She knew it wouldn't be long before word of what they were doing in the Alps reached the press. There had already been a few flyovers by the curious, who no doubt had seen the resurrected bomber sitting in the snow, and she didn't want to be associated with the project in any way in case that scared the kidnapper into doing something rash. She knew Griggs would discourage anyone who was overly curious, but she was still glad that at least for now it was Garin's company, DragonTech, that was the public face of the operation.

They landed in Paris as the sun was setting. To Annja's surprise, Garin didn't have a car waiting. Instead, she and Paul followed him as he walked out the front doors of the terminal and got in line for a cab. In all the time she'd known him, Annja couldn't remember a time he'd taken a cab by choice.

"Slumming, are we?" she asked, a mischievous smile on her face.

Garin glanced at her and said, "Trust me. You'll appreciate it in a bit. We want as much anonymity as possible for where we're going."

On that ominous note, they piled into a taxi and headed out. Under Garin's direction, the cabbie took them to the Les Halles area in the 2nd Arrondissement and let them out on a corner down the street from the mall entrance. Garin said that they would walk from there. Annja had spent a considerable bit of time in Paris over the past few years—her friend and sometime mentor Roux lived nearby—but the neighborhoods she frequented were a bit more upscale than this.

Once the site of Paris's central food market, the place was now home to a giant underground mall that was in the midst of a badly needed makeover, the area had unfortunately become a haven for pickpockets, drug dealers and those with a penchant for petty crime.

The three of them got their fair share of glances as they got out of the taxi, but the predators had to have sensed that they were far from prey and left them alone. Garin led them east several blocks, until they reached Rue St. Denis, where they turned left.

One of Paris's red light districts, this area was even seedier than the one they'd just left.

GARIN LED THEM to a door at the end of an alley. There were no markings on it, nothing to indicate that it was any different from any of the other doors that they passed along the way.

He raised a hand to knock and then hesitated. Turning to Paul and Annja, he said, "The man we are here to see knows me as an American collector of unusual artifacts. No matter what you see or hear in there, keep your thoughts and opinions to yourself. Doing anything less can put us in considerable danger. Understood?"

They nodded in agreement.

Turning back to the door, Garin pounded on it with his fist. After a moment a small panel slid open, allowing whoever was on the inside to look them over. Garin said something in German in a low voice to whoever was on the other side, which apparently satisfied him, for the lock clicked and the door swung open.

Annja followed Garin inside, with Paul at her heels.

Three muscular men in dark suits were waiting for them. Annja noticed that each had the telltale bulge under his suit coat that said he was armed, most likely a handgun in a shoulder holster.

All three were blond and blue-eyed.

*It's a coincidence*, Annja told herself. *It doesn't mean anything.*

But given the nature of what they needed help with, Annja didn't quite believe it was a fluke.

The guard gestured for Garin to step forward, but

didn't search him. Apparently Garin was known to these people.

*Interesting*, Annja thought.

The guard waved Paul forward, saying, "Arms out."

Paul did as he was told, standing there with his arms out to the sides while the guard patted him down quickly.

Annja noted that it was done rather sloppily; she wouldn't have relied on these men to protect anything important.

The guard was leering when she stepped forward, but she met his gaze with a hard stare of her own, letting him know nonverbally that she wasn't to be trifled with any more than her companions. He had to have gotten the message, for the smug expression dropped off his face and his hands didn't wander any more than necessary during the pat-down.

*Score one for the good guys*, Annja thought. While she was pleased with her moral victory, she took even greater solace in the knowledge that they could search her all they wanted, but she would still have a weapon within arm's reach that they would never find.

*And if this is the viper's nest I think it is, I'm going to be glad I have it handy.*

Satisfied that they were unarmed, the guard took a cell phone out of his pocket, placed a call and said a few words in German to whoever answered. Finished, he turned and led them down the hall to another door, which, when opened, revealed a staircase leading downward. The thundering crash of heavy metal music rose to greet them.

"There's a door at the back of the club," the guard said, indicating with an outstretched hand that they should proceed down the stairs.

Below, the party was in full swing. The underground club was large and rectangular in shape, with a mirrored bar to the left, a raised DJ booth to the right and a dance floor in between. Strobe lights flashed overhead, making everyone seem to be moving in fits and starts like puppets on strings. The bartender was another blond, blue-eyed Aryan and given the oversized Nazi flag hanging from the DJ booth, it wasn't all that hard to figure out that the clientele consisted of neo-Nazi extremists and those who wanted to curry favor with them. The pounding pulse of the music was even louder down there than it had been on the stairs, making it nearly impossible for Annja, Garin and Paul to speak to one another. Garin didn't even try; he turned toward the dance floor and began carving a path with his broad shoulders through the writhing bodies of the dancers, heading for the office in the back. Annja followed in his wake, with Paul bringing up the rear.

Another set of guards stood in front of the door to the office on the far side of the room. They saw Garin coming and opened the door, ushering the three of them into the room beyond.

When the door was pulled closed behind them, the sound of music was mercifully cut off. Annja didn't

think she'd ever been more thankful for soundproof-
ing in her entire life.

Annja took a look around and almost immediately
wished she hadn't.

The room was practically a shrine to the Nazi
Party circa 1945. A framed portrait of Adolf Hitler
hung on the wall in the position of honor behind the
desk, a Nazi flag on a stand on either side. Memora-
bilia covered the walls: battle flags and photographs
and a number of combat medals from a variety of
units. Annja leaned in to take a closer look at one of
the photographs and recoiled in horror when she recognized it as an image of the famed entrance gate to
the Auschwitz death camp, the slogan *Arbeit Macht
Frei*, Work Makes One Free, clearly visible above
the gate.

It took all of her effort to keep her expression neu-
tral as she turned from the photo and looked toward
the man they had come to see.

He was blue-eyed and blond like the guards, but
nowhere near as imposing a figure with his soft body
and thinning hair. He tried to offset these traits with
his wardrobe; if Annja wasn't mistaken, he was wearing a full Waffen SS colonel's uniform, minus the
hat, which was sitting on the corner of his desk, the
Werhmacht eagle and Death's Head insignias facing
his guests and polished to a high shine. Annja wanted
to be sick, but refused to give him the satisfaction.

Their host was not alone. Several of his follow-
ers lounged on chairs and sofas spread throughout

the room, and Annja felt their attention like a physical thing.

The man they had apparently come to see smiled across the room at them. "Mr. Albrecht!" he said to Garin. "Good to see you again! I see you've brought guests. Come, come."

He snapped his fingers and two of his flunkies brought chairs for the three of them to sit on, placing them in front of the desk.

Annja took note of the way the chairs were arranged and of how they were at a lower height than the one their host was sitting in, making them seem like penitents before a throne, and thought, *What a petty little man.*

Garin pretended not to notice the arrangement, stepping forward and extending his hand to shake the club owner's as if they were old friends before taking the middle seat. Paul settled into the one on his left and Annja into the one on his right.

"Aren't you going to introduce me to your companions?" their host said teasingly.

"Ah, forgive me, of course," Garin replied in a near-perfect Texas accent.

"Paul, Annja…this is Hans Stuggart."

Annja nodded and smiled, despite the fact that for all his pleasantness, Stuggart was giving her a case of the major creeps.

"Hans's father served the Fatherland in the war and Hans has done what he can to maintain his father's ideals. I believe he is the perfect man to help us with our task."

Smiles all around.

"What can I do for you, Klaus?" Stuggart said, leaning back in his chair and steepling his fingers, like a schoolmaster listening to the conclusions of those less intelligent than he.

"The three of us were going through the papers in a private collection, cataloging it for the client, when we came upon something written in a kind of code that we've not seen before.

"Remembering your fondness for this sort of thing, I thought we'd ask for your assistance in identifying it."

Stuggart frowned, clearly feeling the task was beneath him. "German military codes are well-documented. I'm sure you can find someone—"

Garin interrupted. "Based on other evidence at our disposal, we have reason to believe that this particular code was used between the Führer and only his most trusted associates."

That piqued Hans's interest; Annja could see it in his eyes.

"You've brought it with you?"

Garin nodded. Reaching into his pocket, he pulled out a piece of paper and passed it over to Stuggart. As he did so, Annja got enough of a glimpse of it to know that it was just a small portion of the actual coded message they had found in Hitler's letter.

Inwardly, she breathed a sigh of relief.

Stuggart glanced at the paper after taking it from Garin and then, sitting up straighter, looked at it again, this time with much more focus and intensity.

His excitement was obvious. As the others looked on, Stuggart pulled a pad of paper from elsewhere on the desktop and began writing something on it in earnest, then he made a note on the paper itself.

Annja looked over at the other two with a raised eyebrow and then back at Stuggart, who was now muttering to himself as he continued making notes.

After a few minutes Stuggart stopped, took a deep breath and looked up at Garin.

"May I ask where you acquired this?"

"As I said, we were cataloging—"

"I know that!" Stuggart snapped. "Whose collection and what else was contained with it?"

It was as if a curtain of steel dropped over Garin's face. He sat back, expressionless, and simply stared at their host without saying anything.

Far greater men had withered under that stare, Annja knew, and it didn't take Stuggart long to feel the menace now emanating from Garin.

He smoothed his tie and put on a gracious face once more.

"Klaus," he said, in an obsequious tone, "please forgive me. I let my excitement get the better of me."

Garin's brow furrowed in indecision. "Perhaps we should be going…"

"I won't hear of it," Stuggart said firmly. "I have offended you and for that I apologize. It will not happen again, I promise you. As chance would have it, I do know something of this code. May I share that with you?"

Annja looked on as Garin played the man like a

fiddle, appearing to be thinking about it a second time and then agreeing in the interests of maintaining their relationship.

"If I'm not mistaken, and I don't believe that I am, what you have here is a fragment of a message using one of the *Innenkreis* codes."

Paul spoke up for the first time. "Innenkreis?"

Stuggart glanced in his direction and frowned. "You look German. What's your surname?"

"Krugmann."

"With an Aryan name like that I would think you would speak your native tongue."

Paul opened his mouth to say something, but Annja jumped in so as to distract Stuggart's attention away from him. She and Garin might be used to this kind of subterfuge, but she doubted that Paul was.

"It means inner circle, doesn't it?"

Stuggart turned his pale blue eyes on her. "Yes, that's correct."

"Whose inner circle?" she asked.

She knew the answer, but figured she might as well play to the man's ego.

It seemed to do the trick. Their host looked smug as he said, "Hitler's."

*Thank you, Captain Obvious.*

Stuggart went on. "It has been rumored for many years that the Fürher developed a set of codes that were specifically designed for the men in his inner circle, those he trusted beyond all others. Each code was unique to its owner, so that no one other than that individual could read it. Himmler, Goebbels,

Brandt, Bormann, Hewel—they all had codes assigned to them.

"The Führer blended his love of the esoteric into the functionality of the codes, making use of magical symbolism, ancient texts and runic characters, which was one of the reasons that the codes were supposedly so difficult to crack."

"You say supposedly," Garin remarked, leaving the question open.

Stuggart nodded. "As I said, for many years the codes were just rumor, nothing more. Then a fragment of a letter using such a code turned up in an auction of wartime papers in East Berlin in 1979. Later analysis showed that it was the code assigned to Himmler."

Annja put two and two together. "You were the specialist who broke the code, weren't you?"

Stuggart nodded.

Annja wasn't fooled by his air of humility; it was as fake as a three-dollar bill. But if he could help her break this code…

Their host directed their attention to the code fragment in front of them. "Himmler's code combined the letters of two different alphabets—in that case ancient Greek and Coptic—to create a third and it was in this language that all correspondence was written."

"Similar to the way the Americans used Navajo code talkers," Paul piped in.

"Correct. This code seems to do the same." He pointed to the third symbol from the left. "Take this character, for instance. This would appear to be a combination of the old Nordic rune for Y, this rake-looking section here, with the Enochian letter for M, which is this B-like portion here."

Annja could feel her pulse quickening. Now that she knew what to look for, she could see the individual letters and how they were combined to create the third, new symbol.

"And these here, the Enochian P with the Norse F perhaps."

"What's Enochian?" Paul and Garin asked, almost simultaneously.

Without looking up, Stuggart replied, "The language of the angels."

At their looks of disbelief, Annja filled in a bit more detail. "In the late sixteen hundreds, a mystic by the name of John Dee claimed that the language of the heavens had been revealed to him by a group of angels. In concert with his partner, a spiritual medium named Edward Kelley, Dee wrote down the alphabet that made up this so-called language and named it Enochian, after the Book of Enoch, a protocanonical text."

Stuggart worked in silence for a few moments and then looked up.

"Is there more?" he asked Garin.

"More what?"

"More of this coded message."

Garin shook his head. "No, that's all we've found to date."

Stuggart stared at him as if judging whether or not

he was telling the truth. Garin met his gaze with a calm look of his own that gave nothing away.

"That's...unfortunate," Stuggart said at last.

Annja slid forward to the edge of her seat, readying herself in case Stuggart decided to stop being the gracious host and tried to muscle a bit more information out of them with the help of his flunkies. "Unfortunate? Why's that?" she asked.

"It seems that this is an incomplete sample. While it would appear to make use of both Norse runes and Enochian script, the resulting translation is utter gibberish. It doesn't actually say anything."

"So how would a larger sample help?" Paul wanted to know.

"It would tell us if there was a third language mixed in with the others, for one."

"That seems rather complicated, doesn't it?"

Stuggart laughed. "Maybe for you, but the Führer was a genius."

*A genius? No,* Annja thought. *A megalomaniac with delusions of grandeur and an inflated sense of self-worth? Yes.*

"So you're saying that you can't decipher this?" Garin's tone had decidedly cooled, but Stuggart didn't seem to pick up on it.

"Not without the rest of the document," their host replied. "Go back and search those archives again. I'm sure it's there somewhere. When you find it, bring it back here and I'll be happy to crack it wide open for you. Without it, well, my hands are tied."

Annja didn't believe him for a second. He'd crack

the code, she had no doubt about that. But he didn't seem like the kind of individual who would simply do so out of the kindness of his heart, regardless of his past relationship with Garin.

*That's another thing*, she thought. *What the heck has Garin been doing associating with the likes of this fool?*

She considered asking him when they were alone later, but ultimately decided against it. She knew Garin had his share of shady business dealings; perhaps it was better that she didn't know the details.

Stuggart rose, signaling the end of their meeting and the others got reluctantly to their feet. Annja reached across the desk and took back the piece of paper with the fragment of the code on it. Stuggart gave her a dirty look, but she simply smiled in return.

If he thought they were leaving a sample of the code in his hands...

He still had his notes, but without the original she didn't think they would be all that helpful. If he did manage to figure it out later, using what he had at his disposal, he would still need the rest of the message to do anything with it, so she decided not to push things.

"Thank you for your help, Hans," Garin said, leaning across the desk to shake the man's hand again. "If we find anything else, you'll be the first to know."

The man smiled graciously. "A pleasure as always, Klaus. Please, enjoy the club while you are here. On the house."

Garin said they might just do that and then the the

three of them were escorted out by a pair of Stuggart's thugs.

Annja could feel the club owner's stare even after the door had closed behind them.

# 17

"All right, so now what?" Paul asked.

The three of them were seated at an outdoor table in front of a quaint little Parisian café in the shadow of the Eiffel Tower. They'd gone straight there from Stuggart's underground club, needing a change of scenery to help them forget about the place as quickly as possible.

"We keep trying," Annja answered while looking over the menu. It had been hours since she'd eaten and even the distaste she felt for Stuggart and his cronies couldn't quite dampen her appetite.

Besides, fueling up now, she knew, was simply smart tactics. Who knew what lay ahead of them?

"That's all well and good, but it seems like we're at a dead end. Where do we go from here?" Paul asked.

Annja wasn't sure. Her initial wave of excitement at seeing how the separate alphabets were combined into one had swiftly passed when Stuggart revealed that the knowledge didn't really help them. The translated "text" wasn't text at all but gibberish.

She supposed she could consult some of her friends

in academia, experts in ancient languages and the like, to see if they might have any suggestions, but that would take time, and time wasn't a commodity they had a lot of. Even sitting there and eating felt like a betrayal. Here she was, enjoying a late dinner beneath the lights of the Eiffel Tower, and somewhere on the other side of the Atlantic her friend was spending another evening in captivity. She wanted to be doing something, wanted to feel as though they were making headway, but she didn't know where to turn.

Paul was right. Now what?

She didn't know.

The server came with their meals and they dug in. As hungry as she was, Annja finished before the other two, so while she waited she decided to once again tackle the puzzle in front of them.

She dug out the scrap of paper Garin had given to Stuggart and stared at what the man had written there. There were four groups of symbols that Stuggart had broken down into their component parts, one from each of the two ancient alphabets. He had written the corresponding English letters beneath them and when viewed that way they certainly didn't say anything recognizable.

But then an idea hit her.

What if there was more than one code? What if you had to solve the first layer in order to get the key to solving the second?

She stared at the collection of symbols, both the first set and the translated English letters beneath, looking for some connection between them. She didn't see anything off the top of her head, but she didn't have either the Norse runic alphabet or the Enochian alphabet in front of her for reference.

That, she could fix.

"Paul, give me your phone," she said, as she pulled her own out of her pocket.

A quick internet search brought up a picture of the runes of the Old Norse alphabet on her phone. A similar search brought up an image of the letters in the Enochian alphabet on Paul's. She began checking letters against symbols, looking for a pattern.

"You've got something, haven't you?" Garin asked.

Annja nodded, but didn't look away from the information in front of her. It was there, she knew it was, she could feel it in her bones. Right there in front of her, waiting to be…

"I've got it!" she shouted, and then ducked in embarrassment when she realized everyone nearby was now staring in her direction thanks to her outburst.

Bemused, Garin leaned closer. "What, exactly, is it that you have?"

"I've cracked the code."

"You're kidding," Paul said.

But she wasn't. She had, indeed, solved it.

"It's not one code, but two, nestled inside each other." She moved the piece of paper and the cell phones so the other two could see them.

"The first code is the combination of the Nordic runes and the Enochian letters, just as Stuggart showed us. But, again as he pointed out, that doesn't get us anything but gibberish. The words those letters form don't make any sense.

"The reason that they don't make any sense is that they are not the message itself, but simply the key to deciphering the message. The Enochian letters and their position in the alphabet tell us which Caesar cipher to use for each letter combination.

"Decoding each paired combination, we get the third and final layer, which is the actual message."

"So what does it say?" Paul asked.

Annja picked up her pen and wrote it out for them.

"One twenty leagues east of the Phoenix, ninety-four leagues southwest of Christmas."

They all stared at it for a few minutes.

Finally, Garin broke the silence. "Isn't this the part where you excitedly tell us you know exactly what that's referring to?"

*I wish,* Annja thought. But she'd gotten this far…

She began walking through it aloud, trying to work it out in the process.

"All right, let's think about this. A league is a unit of measuring distance, right?"

Paul nodded. "Roughly three miles," he said.

"But it is used more in relation to boating than anything else, which makes it nautical miles instead. That means a distance of three and a half miles instead of three."

Garin quickly did the math. "So the place we're looking for is 420 miles east of Phoenix and 329 miles southwest of Christmas."

"Southwest of Christmas? What on earth does that mean? Could it be another code?" Paul asked.

Annja didn't know. "We need an internet café, someplace we can do some research on something other than our cell phones."

"I know a place a couple of blocks from here," Garin said. He put a stack of euros on the table to cover the cost of their meal and then rose. She and Paul followed suit.

Turning, Annja saw him first.

He was about as big as the men who had been guarding the entrance to the club, but this man moved with the litheness of a panther on the prowl, light on his feet and totally confident in his ability to bring down whatever game he was hunting. With him were two other men of similar ilk, one walking on either side as if they were a presidential entourage. They walked with their bodies angled slightly toward Annja and her companions, their right hands down and half hidden behind their legs.

Annja had no doubt that they were carrying weapons in their hands.

"Down!" she shouted, even as the man in the lead caught sight of her and brought his arm up in their direction.

Garin didn't hesitate, throwing himself to the ground at Annja's command. Paul was a little slower off the mark, but Annja took care of that by tackling him in the seconds before the newcomers opened fire.

Gunshots filled the night air, the three men using their pistols to fire indiscriminately in the direction of Annja and her companions. Several other late-night diners were struck in the process, collapsing wounded into their seats or onto the ground beneath their tables. People were screaming and trying to get away as the gunmen fired on anything and anyone that moved.

It was utter chaos.

Annja rolled off Paul and pointed toward an over-turned table nearby. "Get behind that and stay low!" she told him. Having done what she could for him, she decided it was time for her to move as well. She had a better chance at staying alive if she could keep them guessing where she was. Annja was closer to the street than anything else so she rolled in that direction, stopping behind a parked car and putting a few thousand pounds of plastic and steel between her and the approaching gunmen.

She glanced about quickly, trying to assess the situation.

Like Paul, Garin was crouched behind a table a few feet away, an automatic pistol now in his hands. She'd expected him to be armed—he usually was—so she was pleased to see that she'd been right. Between the two of them they at least had a fighting chance.

To her surprise, when she looked back at Paul she found that he, too, was armed. He'd produced a snub-nosed pistol from somewhere on his person when she wasn't looking and was preparing to fire back at their attackers as well. Evidently the guards at the club were even more sloppy than she had imagined.

Bullets slammed into the car in front of her, but Annja ignored them. She was safe enough for the time being; she still had a few seconds before the attackers would be upon them.

Reaching into the otherwhere, Annja drew forth her sword. She could practically hear it sing with anticipation as it emerged, fully formed, into her grasp. The sword had seen her through many a tight spot and she had no doubt that it would do the same here.

No way was she letting a bunch of two-bit Nazi thugs take her out. Not here and not now.

She turned and began to duckwalk to the rear of the car, knowing the gunmen would be moving forward while firing, trying to keep Annja and her companions pinned down so that they could be finished off with ease. If she could move in behind them while Garin and Paul kept them occupied, she would be in a position to launch a surprise attack from the rear.

There was a pause in the gunfire as the attackers stopped to reload. Annja peeked up over the edge of the car's window just in time to see one of the thugs take a bullet to the throat and fall backward in a spray of blood.

*One down, two to go.*

The shot had to have come from Garin because the two remaining gunmen suddenly concentrated their fire on the table he was hiding behind. Bits of wood went flying each time a bullet struck its target, which was often. Annja hoped he was all right as she moved around the rear of the vehicle and peeked out the other side.

She could see the injured man in the street, but that was all. The other two had advanced far enough that they were either in line with the car or had passed beyond.

Now was her chance.

Annja rose to a crouch and rushed forward along the opposite side of the car, moving back toward where she'd started, but on the opposite side of the car.

As she drew closer to the hood, she was able to see around the front of the car. One of the gunmen stood a few feet away, firing repeatedly at either Garin or Paul. Perhaps both.

The sound of his shots would cover her footsteps, Annja knew, and there didn't seem to be any return fire coming this way for her to worry about. She took advantage of the moment and rushed ahead, rising from behind the front end of the vehicle at the last second, her sword already in hand and in motion as she struck out at the attacker.

The gunman caught sight of her and tried to turn, shouting out a warning as he did so, but he'd been startled by her sudden appearance and was slow to respond. He hadn't even completed half the turn, was still trying to bring his gun to bear on her, when the sword tore into him like a razor, cleaving him in two.

Annja let the momentum of the strike carry her around full circle, completing her turn so that she was facing the second man, who had been standing a few feet in front of the first.

Unfortunately for her, he'd heard his buddy's cry of surprise and had turned in response to it. Now he was staring directly at her, gun in hand.

Five feet separated them.

Five feet that might as well have been five miles, for there was no way she was going to be able to cross that distance before he could pull the trigger.

Annja braced herself for what was to come.

# 18

A shot rang out.

Annja jumped, releasing the sword, amazed that she wasn't dead. She glanced down at herself—didn't see any red stain blossoming across her shirt, didn't feel any pain—then looked back up at the gunman.

She was just in time to watch him crumple to the ground, a bullet having pierced his back and found his heart with unerring accuracy.

The man was dead before he even hit the pavement.

Annja found herself staring across the distance at Paul, who stood with his arm outstretched, the gun in his hand still pointed in her general direction and his expression unreadable.

For just an instant Annja felt a cold chill wash over her at the sight of him standing there, the muzzle of his gun looming large in her view as she stared down its barrel. Then he lowered his arm and rushed forward to wrap her in his arms.

"Are you all right?" he asked.

"Yes, yes, I'm fine," she told him, having recovered from her momentary shock at finding herself still alive. "Put your gun away. We're fine now. Where's Garin?"

"He's over…" Paul began, doing as he was told. Then he caught sight of the remains of the man she'd killed with her sword. The rest of what he'd been about to say apparently vanished from his thoughts. "What on earth happened to him?"

Annja ignored the question. If he hadn't seen her with the sword, she certainly wasn't going to tell him about it, not now at least.

*Maybe after all this craziness passes,* she thought, and then caught her breath as she realized she was honestly contemplating sharing her most closely guarded secret with someone other than Garin and Roux.

*I'm not ready for that kind of commitment, am I?*

She shook the thought away; now was definitely not the time to wonder about such things.

She could see Garin moving among the tables, checking on the bodies that were lying unmoving among the ravaged tables and chairs. The gunmen hadn't cared who they killed provided they also hit their targets and the evidence was all around them. It made Annja's heart ache for their loss.

The police were no doubt on their way; a gun battle didn't rage in the middle of Paris without someone calling the cops. In fact, she thought she could hear sirens approaching in the distance.

They had a few moments, no more.

Knowing Garin would do what he could for the

wounded, Annja bent and searched the man that Paul had shot, the leader of the attack. She rolled him over and looked at his face, but he wasn't anyone she recognized. She checked his pockets, both his coat and his pants, looking for a wallet or something that could identify him. She came up empty.

The sirens were definitely getting closer and Annja knew they had to go. She didn't like leaving the scene of a tragedy like this, but if they were detained, even for just a few days, that could spell doom for Doug. They had to get away and out of the country as soon as possible; it was the only way they were going to remain free long enough to help her friend.

Garin was suddenly there at her side. "Anything?" he asked.

"Nothing. He's clean."

"Maybe, maybe not." Garin reached down, tore the man's shirt open and pulled one side down off his shoulder, revealing a tattoo.

It was a Nazi swastika.

"We have something Stuggart wants," he said.

Neither of them had any doubt just what that something was.

"If we're going to go, we need to do it now, folks," Paul said.

He was right; the police were about to arrive.

They stood and began to walk from the scene as quickly as they could without drawing any more attention to themselves. They knew they'd been seen; half a dozen people were probably taking their picture with their cell phones right this very minute, but it would still take time for the police to identify them. Between now and then they needed to get to the airport and get out of France as quickly as possible.

The research would have to wait.

Garin led the way, taking random turns at each intersection to throw anyone who might be following them off their track. Once they had gotten ten or so blocks away from the café, he flagged down a cab and told the driver to take them straight to the airport.

It wasn't long before Annja and her two companions were back aboard the DragonTech helicopter en route to Munich.

It was nearly midnight by the time they arrived at one of the town houses Garin maintained in the city. Despite the late hour, the three of them gathered in the den to continue their attempt to make some sense out of Hitler's secret message.

Garin's computer system, with its multiple monitors and touch screens, made Annja feel as if she was sitting in the command console of an alien spaceship, but after a few minutes she got the hang of it. She fired up a web browser on each screen, went to the search engine and typed a phrase into each.

The "list of places named Christmas" search returned over 60 million results. The "list of places named Phoenix" search returned slightly over 11 million results.

Annja decided to start with the later.

The very first result was an entry under the title "list of places named for the Phoenix." Clicking on it, she found two short lists: one for places in the United States named Phoenix and one for places in other countries with the same name.

Annja dismissed the first list automatically. As tempting as places like Phoenix, Arizona, and Phoenix, Maryland, sounded, she highly doubted that Hitler would have gotten within fifty miles of the US mainland in 1945.

That left her with a list of nine other possibilities, from Vacoas-Phoenix, Mauritius, to Camp Phoenix in Kabul, Afghanistan. She was immediately able to scratch off Camp Phoenix, followed quickly by Phoenix Park in Dublin, Ireland; the Phoenix Concert Theater in Toronto, Canada; Phoenix, British, Columbia; The Phoenix, an opera house in Venice, Italy; and the Phoenix Cinema in London, England.

Three possibilities remained: Vacoas-Phoenix on Mauritius, Phoenix in the Durban township of South Africa, and the Phoenix Islands in Kiribati.

Annja called up an online atlas and put a map of Mauritius on the screen for the three of them to see.

Mauritius, actually the Republic of Mauritius, was an island nation in the Indian Ocean about 1,200 miles off the coast of Africa. The nearest large land mass was Madagascar.

The fact that it was an island excited Annja at first, since *Insel Wolf* meant Island of the Wolf or Wolf Island, but it didn't seem to go anywhere. Drawing a line straight east of Mauritius put them smack in the middle of the Indian Ocean, and there wasn't any-

where within four hundred miles that could even re-
motely be called Christmas.

They turned their attention to South Africa next.
That Phoenix was an Indian settlement that officially
became a township in 1976. Prior to that it had been
associated with the Phoenix Settlement in nearby
Durban, founded by Mohandas Ghandi in 1904 and
used by him as a base for his nonviolent protests on
behalf of Muslim Indians in South Africa.

"Ghandi and Hitler?" Paul said. "I'm not seeing
that one."

Annja and Garin agreed.

They turned their attention at last to the Phoenix
Islands in Kiribati. The map told them that the Phoenix Islands were a small chain of islands in the central Pacific Ocean, just east of the Gilbert Islands.
There wasn't much to them—six atolls and a couple
of sunken reefs.

But then came the surprise.

"Look! Christmas!" Paul said, pointing at the
screen.

Northeast of the Phoenix Islands was another island named Kiritimati. Under the name, in parenthe-
sis, was the subtitle "Christmas Island."

Annja stared. "East of Phoenix…"

"…and southwest of Christmas," Garin finished
for her.

Eyeballing it, Paul stuck his finger on a spot in the
middle of the Pacific Ocean.

This map showed nothing but water.

"We need a better map," Annja said and hurriedly

searched for one. She was able to locate a much more detailed version relatively quickly and threw that up on the screen for everyone to see.

This time, when they followed the directions as closely as possible, they ended up with the tip of Annja's finger sitting on a small rock of an island at the exact location the message suggested.

It might not have a name on the map, but everyone in that room knew exactly what it was called.

*Insel Wolf.*

They had found the location of Hitler's final headquarters!

# 19

They caught a few hours of sleep and were back at it early the next morning. Annja could feel the pace taking a toll on her both physically and mentally, but she didn't dare let up. They were already two days into their new deadline, and they were most likely going to lose a third by flying halfway around the world to reach their destination. Paul summed up what they were all thinking over breakfast.

"Couldn't he have built this thing a little closer to home?"

Annja laughed. She had to agree; it was most definitely in the middle of nowhere, though she supposed that was the point. When the whole world wanted you dead, it was probably best to find a nice deep hole to hide in, and Hitler had certainly seemed to do just that.

While the island's location might have been advantageous for his needs, it certainly created a bit of a problem for Annja and her allies. It was roughly 800 miles from Samoa and just shy of 750 miles from

Tahiti, the two nearest staging points. That was a lot of open ocean, she thought.

"So how do we do this?" Paul asked, staring at the map Annja had spread out on the table.

"Fly into Tahiti and rent a boat, I guess."

Paul seemed skeptical. "Do any of us know anything at all about boating across the open ocean? Because I can tell you right up front that I don't."

Annja didn't either. She'd mostly had her feet firmly planted on the ground—or somewhere under it—for the last several years. The longest she'd ever spent near the open ocean was the time it took to fly from the United States to Australia, and even then she'd been 30,000 feet above sea level.

"I do," Garin said quietly, surprising them both. "A number of years ago I made a solo journey around the world in my sailboat."

Annja hadn't known that. Of course, when it came to Garin, a "number of years ago" might mean he made the trip a century or more in the past, but if that was the case, it only made the feat more impressive in her eyes. She liked to be alone, but she didn't think she could manage the two months or more that it would take to circumnavigate the globe. Her respect for his abilities went up a notch.

"That settles it, then," Annja said. "We fly into Tahiti and then rent a boat. We make the journey to the island, find whatever the heck is hidden there, and then get Doug out of this jerk's clutches once and for all."

*When put like that, it all sounds so easy.* But Annja knew the reality was going to be much different.

In order to get there, they were going to have to fly to Los Angeles, refuel, and then continue on to Papeete, Tahiti. Annja did the calculations in her head. The flight from Munich to Los Angeles would take approximately thirteen hours. One hour to refuel. Another eight and a half hours from Los Angeles to Papeete.

Practically an entire day of flight time.

From there, they would have to cross nearly 750 miles of ocean to reach the island. Figure an average speed of 30 knots and that added another sixteen, maybe seventeen hours of travel.

If they left right now, they wouldn't arrive for at least a day and a half.

The ticking of the clock might just be their downfall. The kidnapper had given her a seven-day deadline. This was already day two. With a day and half of travel time, they would be down to roughly three days to find Hitler's secret headquarters on the island and report back to the kidnapper.

There were so many things that could go wrong, from flight problems to weather delays, that Annja just wanted to scream in frustration.

Still, they had to try.

She turned to Garin. "How soon can the plane be ready?"

"Fifteen minutes after I call and give the crew the destination."

"Tahiti by way of Los Angeles. The faster they can get us there, the better."

"Got it." Garin pulled out his cell phone and turned away to make the call.

"Don't worry, Annja," Paul said. "We'll make it in time."

She just hoped he was right.

THEY ARRIVED AT the Munich International Airport an hour later. Their driver took them directly to the hangar where several of Garin's jets were stored. Boarding the same plane that had taken them from Miami to Munich a week earlier, they prepared for the flight in the opposite direction now.

Not wanting the crew to know where they were headed, and being an accomplished pilot in his own right, Garin decided to fly the plane himself, dismissing the crew and giving them the next week off. Annja knew he could do it; whatever mystical process had extended his life had also given him extraordinary stamina. She'd seen him go days without sleep before. With that detail taken care of, Annja and Paul settled into the comfort and luxury of the passenger cabin.

The first part of the flight was used to nail down some of the finer details of the adventure ahead of them. Annja used the onboard satellite phone to hunt down a charter boat they could use once they arrived in Tahiti while Paul connected to the internet and dug up as much information on the nation of Kiribati so that they would know what to expect when they arrived there.

By the time they were halfway across the Atlantic, both issues had been dealt with satisfactorily and the two of them were eating lunch, having prepared it in the planc's well-stocked galley.

"I wanted to thank you," Annja said, between bites of her filet mignon.

"Thank me for what?"

"Saving my life last night."

Paul looked up from his sea bass. "He was going to shoot you."

It was said so matter-of-factly that Paul could have been talking about filling a hole in his garden rather than the death of another human being, thug or not.

"You don't seem all that torn up about it," Annja said.

Paul put down his fork. "Of course I'm torn up, Annja. I killed a man. Even in self-defense that's a difficult burden to carry. But I'd be damned if I sat around and did nothing while he gunned you down in cold blood!"

*Ah, so he does feel something, after all,* she thought.

Annja inwardly sighed with relief. She had been starting to have her doubts, and a Paul who wasn't upset by the taking of a human life was a Paul she didn't know and didn't want to know.

Since taking up the sword she'd been challenged by some of the most ruthless people on the planet, ones who would think as much about taking her down where she stood as they would crushing a mosquito between their palms. She'd had to defend herself and others through the use of the sword, and sometimes the results weren't pretty. Like the guy she'd been forced to kill the night before.

While she put on a hard face and got through it, the truth was that she regretted each and every man or woman she'd been forced to kill. Not enough that she'd do it differently if she had the chance to do it over again, but that wasn't the point anyway. She'd been protecting either herself or some other innocent each time she'd killed, and she felt justified in what she had done. Even so, killing was hard; it left an indelible mark on her soul that never quite went away and she didn't wish that on anyone.

Least of all the man she thought she might be falling for.

"You'll get no argument from me," she told him. "But I still appreciate what you did."

He smiled at her and Annja felt him let go of some of the tension he'd been holding a moment before.

Still, she wondered about something.

"Have you been carrying that gun with you the whole time we've been together?"

He met her gaze, and she thought she saw a bit of anger flare in his eyes. It was there and gone so quickly, however, that she couldn't be sure.

*Probably my imagination,* she thought.

That belief was reinforced when Paul smiled at her. "Do I look like the type who regularly carries a gun around with him?"

Before she could answer, he went on. "Besides, how would I have gotten it into the country past Customs and all that, if I was? No, Garin gave it to me while you were, ah, indisposed for a few minutes, before we went to Paris. He said not to trouble you about it but to keep it handy in case it was needed. I'd learned to shoot while I was covering the Sudanese civil war a couple of years ago for the magazine, so I didn't see it as a big deal."

That sounded like something Garin would do, so she dropped it. There was no sense arguing about it. Paul obviously knew how to handle a weapon, and if she was honest with herself she would admit that his ability was more reassuring to her than anything else.

Who knew what might be waiting for them in the South Pacific? Knowing he could handle himself would let her focus on more important things, like finding Hitler's last bolt-hole.

Paul surprised her with a question of his own.

"Have you given any thought to what you're going to do if this guy doesn't let Doug live?"

*What will I do? There's no question what I will do,* she thought. *I will hunt the guy to the ends of the earth and make him pay for it.*

She didn't say anything like that to Paul, though. She wasn't sure he would understand. Instead, she kept it simple.

"Let's just hope it doesn't come to that," she said. "If it does, I suppose I'll cross that bridge when the time comes."

The rest of the flight passed without incident and

they landed in Los Angeles on schedule. After making sure that their resupply and refueling was underway, Garin caught a couple of hours of sleep in the rear cabin so that he would be refreshed for the final leg of the journey ahead.

That couldn't come soon enough for Annja, and she was practically frothing with impatience by the time Garin was given clearance from the tower for them to get underway.

*Next stop, Tahiti*, she told herself as the blue waters of the Pacific rolled out beneath the aircraft and they took to the skies once more.

# 20

"What do you mean you can't let us have the boat?"

Annja, Garin and Paul stood in the charter company's office in the Tahitian capital of Papeete. Outside, it was a bright, sunny day with temperatures in the mid-80s, but since the clerk's statement moments ago the temperature inside the room had gotten decidedly icy.

"I'm very sorry, ma'am, but as I said, you can't take just the boat. You have to take the crew as well. They are the ones who will drive the boat."

"But we don't need a crew," Annja argued. Pointing at Garin, who stood a few feet behind her, she said, "Our captain is an accomplished sailor. He will drive the boat."

They'd arrived late the night before and gotten several hours of sleep in an airport hotel before rising early and heading out to the wharf where they were to pick up their charter.

That's when things went a little awry.

The Polynesian clerk, little more than a teenager really, looked at Garin, then very quickly turned back to Annja and shook his head. "The crew must go with the boat. That is the boss's rule."

Annja started to protest for the third time, but Garin gently pulled her aside and stepped in front of the counter. He put both hands on it and leaned forward, intimidating with his size but not overtly so.

"Is your boss here?"

The clerk shook his head.

"Can you call him on the phone?"

The clerk nodded.

Garin waited for him to do so, but the clerk just stood there looking at him.

Garin sighed. "Can you call him now, please?"

"Oh, yes, sir. Just a second please."

The clerk picked up the phone, dialed a number and spoke in rapid-fire Tahitian to whoever picked up at the other end. He listened, then handed the phone to Garin.

Annja's companion didn't beat around the bush. "I will pay you three times the fee we've already negotiated if you'll let me charter the boat without the crew."

There was a pause and then Garin said, "Thank you. A pleasure doing business with you," before handing the phone back to the clerk.

The clerk listened again, agreed with whatever was said and hung up. He looked up at Garin and smiled tentatively.

"If you give me a moment, I will prepare the paperwork."

"Please," Garin said, "by all means."

The crisis averted, Annja took a deep breath and tried to relax.

*Losing it now isn't going to help anyone, least of all Doug,* she reminded herself. *Keep it together.*

When the details were completed and Garin had paid for the charter, the clerk, Teva, took them out to the dock to see their boat, the *Reliant*.

According to the paperwork, she was a Harmony 47 sailing cruiser, built in the Ponchin Yachts shipyard. It was forty-seven feet in length with a deep keel and a fully battened main sail that would provide a rich sailing experience.

Or, at least, that's what the brochure said. Annja just hoped the thing was as fast as it looked.

The 75-horsepower engine was powered by fifty-five gallons of diesel fuel carried in the lower diesel tank, and they had arranged to have an extra twenty-five gallons of fuel stored in the holding tank for emergency use. They were also carrying fifty gallons of fresh water.

The boat had three double cabins, a cabin with two single berths, two toilets, two showers and even a dinghy powered by a 5-horsepower outboard motor that they could use to get to shore once they arrived.

All in all, it appeared that it would suit their needs rather nicely and Annja was pleased with her selection. Garin, too, seemed to be happy with it; at least he was smiling as he looked over the engines, sails and rigging, if that was any indication.

Teva had already stocked the boat with their requested items—a box of assorted tools, rope and a

few high-powered handheld flashlights in addition
to water, food and diving equipment—so they were
able to get underway as soon as he turned over the
keys. Annja and Paul sat on padded benches on either
side of the cockpit as Garin stood behind the wheel,
deftly easing them out of their berth, then turning
them toward the open sea.

The first several hours passed without incident.
The weather was clear, the sea calm, and there was
a strong wind. Garin got the sails up and had the
boat practically flying across the water at a ferocious
thirty-two knots, a slightly faster pace than Annja
had originally estimated. The warm sun and the salt
spray lulled her into a relaxed state and she could almost forget what they were there for.

Almost.

By midafternoon, however, dark clouds could be
seen gathering on the horizon, and the radar was
warning of a sizable storm headed in their direction.
Garin gathered them to discuss the situation.

"We've got two choices ahead of us," he told Paul
and Annja. "We can try to find an island to use as
shelter and wait out the storm or we can try to push
through and hope we don't get hit with the brunt of it."

"What's the radar say?" Paul asked.

"At the moment, if the wind holds steady, it looks
like the main thrust of the storm will miss us."

"But that can change, right?" Annja asked.

Garin nodded. "At a moment's notice."

"How much farther do we have to go before

reaching Wolf Island?" she asked. If they were close enough, she was inclined to just make a run for it.

Garin grabbed a chart out of a nearby drawer and rolled it out on the tabletop. He looked at it, and then pointed to a spot northwest of Tahiti, close to the Line Islands.

"We're here," he said. "That puts us about three-quarters of the way to our destination. We could take shelter here, on the leeward side of one of these smaller islands. Drop anchor, batten down the hatches, and just ride it out. "

"Or?" Paul asked.

"Or we can run north along this route," Garin said, tracing a line on the map with his finger, "as fast as we can and hope we stay ahead of the storm."

*If there was ever a time I wished I had a crystal ball.*

But she didn't have one, which meant she was going to have to rely on her gut. And right now her gut was telling her to push onward and not let the storm slow them.

"What do you think our chances are?" she asked, wanting someone else's opinion on the topic so that she wasn't relying on her desire to be right rather than the facts at hand.

"It's hard to say," Garin replied. "If the wind stays steady and the storm doesn't change course, then I'd put them at sixty-five, maybe seventy percent in favor of outracing the weather. If the wind dies down or the storm changes course, then all bets are off."

*We're running out of time.*

She turned to Paul. "Any ideas?"

He shook his head. "I know next to nothing about sailing and even less about tropical storms, so I'll go along with whatever the two of you decide."

That was all Annja needed to hear.

"We go for it," she announced.

The decision made, they dug in and made preparations for the race to come.

Garin handed out life jackets—just to be safe, he said—and they pulled them over their heads and buckled them tightly about their waists. Then, and only then, did they begin securing what they could, not wanting to lose anything important if the weather got worse later on. When that was finished, they turned their attention to hoisting the jib, wanting to catch as much of the wind as physically possible to help them outrun the storm.

For a while things went pretty well. The heavy winds combined with the added sail helped to boost their speed another few knots, making Annja feel like an America's Cup racer as they shot forward across the water. Their speed was exhilarating and the knowledge that they were closing in on their destination with every passing moment helped ease her anxiety somewhat.

Provided things stayed as they were, they would reach the island in less than three hours.

As it turned out, that was wishful thinking.

Just over an hour later the weather began to change. The radar showed that the storm had shifted course and was certain to cross their path, probably within the next thirty minutes.

It didn't take long for the seas around them to begin getting rougher, the swells growing in size and frequency, but the boat handled them with deft efficiency, much to Annja's relief. Garin didn't appear concerned by the inclement weather, so Annja tried not to let it bother her, either. She figured she wouldn't panic until he did.

It didn't occur to her that Garin might be worried but keeping a poker face so as not to concern his companions.

Annja stayed with Garin for a bit, watching him manage the situation with a deft hand. He worked the boat like the master sailor that he was, pulling every inch of forward momentum out of her, unwilling to admit defeat even as the storm grew around them.

When she became tired of that, Annja went below to find something to keep her mind occupied. She sat at the table and calculated their current position, marking it on the map for later reference. When she was done with that, she stared at the radar for a while, noting the shaded mass that marked the main thrust of the storm that was closing in on their position from the east. She tried to calculate how long until they might be within its grip, but she wasn't adept enough at reading the Doppler data to figure it out and eventually gave up.

She turned her attention at that point to helping Paul secure anything that wasn't bolted to the deck and was in the midst of doing that when she felt a change come over the boat. For a moment she couldn't identify what it was and then it came to her.

They were slowing.

She dropped what she was doing, turned and rushed back up on deck. Paul followed closely on her heels.

The sight that greeted them when they emerged from the companionway stole the voice right out of Annja's throat.

The sky had lost its openness and had closed around them like a vice; the white clouds were now a deep gray interspersed with a green tinge that made everything look wrong in the odd-colored light.

Annja had seen sky like that once before on a trip to Alabama. It had been just before a pair of twisters came rolling through town, destroying everything in their paths. She could still remember the silence that had seemed to grip the town in the seconds before the twisters struck.

She realized that the same silence enveloped the boat now.

Annja looked up and saw that the sails were hanging limp, the wind having mysteriously dissipated just moments before. The only thing pushing the boat forward at this point was their earlier momentum and that was bleeding away quickly against the resistance of the water. Even the water seemed to have turned against them, going from brilliant blue to a flat, angry-looking gray, the color of a battleship.

She knew in that instant that they'd made a mistake.

They should have looked for shelter.

Garin's urgent shout cut through her mental fog.

"We've got to get those sheets in!" he shouted. "Annja, take the helm! Paul, with me!"

Annja did as she was told, rushing to his side and taking the ship's wheel in her hands. She barely had a grip on it before Garin rushed forward, snatching the crank handle from its storage place and dragging Paul with him as he went. Annja could feel the water pulling at the boat, fighting the rudder and trying to turn it. She tightened her grip on the wheel, keeping it steady, trying to give them time to do what they needed to do.

Garin slammed the crank into position on the mast winch and began winding it as rapidly as he could. For a moment nothing happened and Annja worried that the winch was broken—*did we check that before leaving?*—but then the jib began to come down, lowering itself a bit more with every revolution of the crank. Once it was low enough, Paul began gathering it around the bottom of the mast, lashing it into place. It wasn't the best way of storing it, but time was of the essence and it would do for now.

They had just finished with the jib and were turning their attention to the mainsail when the sky was split with lightning and rain began to pour down on them. The temperature dropped fifteen degrees in the space of a heartbeat as a cold wind blew in along the forefront of the storm, making everyone's job that much harder. Annja gripped the wheel tightly in her hands, doing what she could to keep the boat on course, as Garin and Paul fought to get the mainsail down and stowed away before the storm could rip it to shreds.

A crash of thunder and a flash of lightning told Annja that they had lost the race.

# 21

The storm fell upon them like a vengeful ghost, determined to wrap them in its arms and drag them down into the depths.

The swells were ten feet high and growing by the moment. Annja tried to keep the boat at a forty-five-degree angle to the oncoming waves, knowing that if she let the boat turn too far to one side or the other and come broadside to the waves, the force of the water would capsize them. If that happened, it would all be over but the dying.

The *Reliant* rode up one side of a swell, hung in the air before crashing back down, only to repeat the process when the next swell arrived. Waves crashed over the bow, the water rushed across the deck and swept aside anything in its path that wasn't tied down while dousing them in its icy spray. Afraid that they might be the next to go, Garin broke out the safety lines and made sure that they were all clipped into one. If they were swept overboard, the rope could be used to haul them back onto the deck.

At last they got the sail stored. Garin returned to

the wheel, ordering both Annja and Paul belowdecks for safety. Annja tried to protest, but Garin would have none of it.

"There's nothing you can do out here," he shouted over the noise of the storm as he tried to get the engines started to keep them gaining headway against the storm. "Get below. Use the radio to report our present position to the charter company, just in case."

*Just in case of what?* she wanted to know, but didn't ask. Truth be told, she was afraid to hear it spoken aloud. Sometimes ignorance really was bliss.

In the main cabin she flipped on the radio, picked up the microphone and tried to raise the charter company in Papeete. Ten minutes later she was still trying. When she grew frustrated, Paul took over, first trying to reach the charter company, then reaching out to any vessel that might be in range.

No one answered.

It was as if the storm had swallowed them whole.

They had just given up when the companionway hatch opened and Garin stumbled through it, forcing it shut against the wind behind him.

Annja stared at him and then said, "Who's driving the boat?"

Garin came down the steps and dropped exhausted into a chair. "No one. We can't get enough power out of the engine to make headway against this storm, so I've shut them down so we don't burn them out and I deployed the sea anchor. That will give us enough drag to keep our bow to the waves and prevent us from capsizing. Beyond that, there's nothing we can do. We're simply going to have to ride this one out and wait for the storm to pass."

Waiting proved to be harder than it sounded, however, with the wind howling, the thunder booming and the boat bobbing and rocking every which way on the rough seas. Every creak and groan had them glancing around, wondering if the boat was going to hold.

As the storm raged around them, the minutes ticked past slowly.

When they hadn't sunk or sprung a leak after the first half hour, Garin excused himself to go get some rest, leaving Annja and Paul alone in the galley. They talked quietly for a time and then they, too, decided it was best if they got some rest. They retired to Annja's cabin together and lay awake for a time in each other's arms, listening to the storm.

Eventually, Annja slept.

ANNJA JERKED AWAKE. She lay in bed in her cabin for a moment, trying to figure out what had awoken her. The boat seemed quiet, the sound of the rain striking the deck above almost soothing after the roaring thunder earlier.

She put out her hand, felt the space next to her and was surprised to find it empty.

"Paul?" she said into the darkness.

There was no answer.

The bed was still warm, which indicated he hadn't been up for long.

*Probably just using the bathroom*, she thought.

But when he didn't come back after a few minutes, an uneasy feeling began to unfurl in her gut.

*Relax*, she told herself. *You were probably just keeping him awake with all your tossing and turning. He's most likely in his own cabin right now, trying to get some sleep.*

But something still didn't feel right.

She got out of bed, grabbed a set of dry clothes from her bag and quickly dressed. When she was finished she pulled on her shoes, opened the door to her cabin and quietly stepped out into the companionway. Her cabin was adjacent to Paul's in the elevated area at the rear of the boat while Garin had chosen the large cabin in the forepeak. Annja stepped over and knocked on Paul's door.

"Paul? Are you in there?" she asked quietly.

There was no answer.

She opened the door and flicked on the light.

The bed was empty and didn't appear to have been slept in.

*Where the heck was he?*

A cool draft tickled the back of her neck and she turned, peering up the companionway to the hatch above. A clatter reached her ears, and she realized that the hatch door was banging open and shut in the wind above her.

*Was that what had awoken her? Could Paul be out on deck?*

The boat was still rocking strongly, a sign that the seas around them hadn't calmed all the way yet, and she could hear the rain still coming down steadily.

*What reason could he have for being out on deck in weather like this?*

It didn't make any sense.

Annja went back to her room, grabbed the rain slicker she'd left hanging on the back of the door and returned to the companionway. Holding on to the railing, she climbed up to the hatch and pushed it open, peering out into the night.

The boat's running lights were on, giving her just enough illumination to see that the cockpit was empty. Paul was not there.

Growing more concerned, she stepped out onto the deck, fishing for the flashlight stored in the compartment just outside the hatch. The boat was bobbing up and down in the swells, but she could see well enough with the help of the light to know that there was no one on deck.

*Where on earth was Paul?*

She turned away, intending to go below, but stopped when she heard something on the edge of the wind. She paused, listening, and after a moment heard it again.

It sounded like a yell, a very faint one, but a yell nonetheless.

She carefully stepped out onto the deck and rushed toward the bow of the boat, shining her flashlight into the dark water around her. The wind whipped and whistled in her ears, making it hard to sort out individual sounds, and when she didn't see anything in the beam of her light she began to think that she had imagined the cry after all.

But that uneasy feeling persisted, it grew, in fact, into full-fledged concern, and she gave the water around her another slow and steady search with the flashlight.

As the *Reliant* dipped into the trough of another big swell, she spotted something rising toward the peak of a wave a few dozen yards away.

Annja rushed to the rail and shone the light in that direction. She cursed the waves as she waited for them to align themselves, but as the boat topped the next swell and started down the other side she caught a flash of yellow where she'd seen the object seconds before.

It was a rain slicker just like the one she was wearing and had come from the ship's stores.

"Paul!" she shouted.

Nothing but the wind came back to her.

Fear seized her heart in its iron grip. She didn't know how it had happened, but he had to have come out on deck and been knocked overboard. If she hadn't come out looking for him when she had...

"Hang on! I'm coming!"

She turned, searching frantically for the life preserver that she'd seen lashed to the hull earlier.

It was nowhere to be found.

"Hang on!" she shouted again over her shoulder. She had no idea if Paul could hear her, but on the off chance that he could, she wanted him to know that he wasn't alone.

Garin suddenly emerged from the companionway, blinking sleep out of his eyes, a life jacket in his hands.

"What's going on?"

"It's Paul! He's fallen overboard!"

That woke him up quickly. He handed her the life jacket and told her to put it on. Then he scanned the water around them, cursing all the while. When he had himself under control he said, "It's going to take me a few moments to raise the anchor and get the engine started."

"We don't have a few minutes," Annja said. "If he's out there in that storm, he could be dead by then. I'm going after him!"

"Annja, that's suicide. The waves will drag you under. Just let me…"

She didn't hear the rest, for she had already headed for the bow of the boat. She stripped off her rain slicker, not wanting it to drag her down, then climbed up on the rail and dived overboard.

While the ocean wasn't the raging tyrant it had been earlier, the seas were still quite rough. She fought her way to the surface, pulled the cord to inflate her life jacket, then struck out swimming in the direction that she'd last seen Paul.

It was slow going. The waves fought her at every turn, as if they understood her objective and were doing everything in their power to keep her from accomplishing it. She'd swim forward ten yards, then get pushed back five by the next swell, so she was constantly trying to regain ground that she'd just lost. Even with the life jacket, she was constantly being swept under by waves crashing over her head. If she hadn't been in excellent physical condition, it would have been nearly impossible to make it through.

Complicating things was the fact that it was pitch-black out on the water, with no moon to light the way. If it hadn't been for the waterproof flashlight in her hand, she wouldn't have been able to see anything. As it was, she would reach the top of a swell and quickly flash the light about, looking for Paul, before she would be swept downward into the next trough between waves.

At one point she came up to the top of a wave and thought she spotted a large shape against the darkness of the storm a few dozen yards away. A chill ran up her spine at the sight as she worried that she'd somehow gotten turned around and what she'd seen was the *Reliant* trying to make its way toward her. If so, she was drifting farther and farther away from it with every push of the sea and she began to panic, thinking that she'd swum away from Paul instead of toward him.

Frantic, she looked back over her shoulder and was relieved to see the running lights of the *Reliant* right where she expected them to be. Confused, she turned back around and swung her light in the direction she thought she'd seen it in, only to come up empty.

The object was either gone or it hadn't really been there in the first place.

With no time to worry about it or investigate it further, she put it out of her mind and kept swimming forward, searching for Paul.

After what felt like hours, she spotted something floating off to her right. It was at the very limit of her flashlight's beam, but she decided to take a chance on it and swam hard in that direction, not wanting the waves to pull it out of reach before she could get there. Drawing closer, she could see that it had a flashing red light attached to it. Annja's life jacket had a similar light. It was automatically activated when the light got wet and served as a beacon for rescuers.

Annja swam harder.

At last she could make out Paul's form floating in the water ahead of her. He was on his back and he didn't appear to be moving at all. Now seriously worried, she used the last of her strength to make her way through the surging water to his side.

One look and her worst fears were realized. Paul lay unmoving.

# 22

"No, no, no!" Annja cried as she pulled him in close. She got her arms around him from behind and used the front of her life jacket to keep his head up and out of the water.

She looked around, trying to find Garin and the *Reliant*, but she could barely see her hand in front of her face. She shouted for help several times, but soon gave up, wanting to preserve her strength as she figured she was going to need it.

Now that she had found Paul, the adrenaline that had driven her began to wear off, and Annja realized just how tired she was. Fighting the waves had taken almost all of her strength, and it was all she could do to simply hold on to Paul's body and keep the two of them afloat as they were tossed about by the waves.

The usually warm water was cold from the storm and that worked against her as well, sapping what little strength she had left. She locked her hands together, determined to hold on to Paul for as long as she could and praying that Garin got there soon. If he didn't, there wouldn't be one but two bodies that he was going to have to fish out of the water.

Leaning her head back against the inflated back of the life jacket, she shouted into the night again.

"Here, Garin! We're over here!"

The weather seemed to mock her, the rain deadening her cries before they were whisked away on the wind, never to be heard again.

Aware of every passing second and the additional danger they posed for Paul, Annja tried to use the flashlight to signal her location, but when she lifted her arm over her head the flashlight slipped from her numb fingers and slowly sank out of sight.

*So this is it,* she thought. *This is how it ends. Adrift in the middle of the ocean with no around to see me go.*

If she'd been a different sort of person, she might have given up right then and there. Might have released her hold on Paul and let them both slip beneath the surface, following the light down into the depths. But it was precisely because she was such a fighter that she held on against what seemed to be worsening odds, determined to keep struggling right to the very end.

And well that she did, for seconds after the light sank out of sight a massive shape slid into view just a few yards away and the beam of a floodlight suddenly blinded her.

"Hold on!" Garin called.

It was a sure sign that she was at the limits of her

strength when she couldn't even shout back at him, just nod wearily.

Garin brought the boat in as close as he dared and then waited for the next swell to carry Annja and Paul a few feet closer to him. When it did, he reached out with a grappling hook and slipped it over Annja's arm, keeping them from drifting away as the sea swelled beneath them.

Foot by foot he dragged them over until they bumped against the hull of the boat. Reaching down, Garin grabbed Paul and hauled him up on deck, then did the same to Annja.

He tried to put her down on her feet but her legs collapsed out from under her, too weak and cold to support her weight. That was fine with her; she was happy to just lie there on the deck while Garin tended to Paul.

"He's not breathing," Garin said, kneeling over the unconscious man. He turned Paul's head to one side, made sure his throat was clear and started CPR. Garin began with two breaths strong enough to move the chest up and down and then started an alternating series of chest compressions and breathing.

*Breathe, Paul, breathe,* Annja begged silently as Garin continued his ministrations.

Compressions and breaths. Compressions and breaths.

*Come on!*

Paul lay there unresponsive.

*Please don't let this all have been for nothing.*

Garin finished the latest set of compressions and

was getting ready to give Paul another round of breaths when the journalist suddenly coughed up a lungful of water and began choking on whatever was left in his system. Garin held on to him and rolled him over on his side, letting the water drain out as Paul hacked and spit.

When he was convinced the other man was breathing again on his own, Garin eased Paul back down and turned to Annja.

"We need to get you both downstairs and into dry clothes. Can you walk?"

Annja nodded, then struggled to her feet as Garin helped Paul do the same. Between the two of them they got Paul belowdecks and into his cabin. Garin helped support him while Annja stripped off his wet clothing and then together they helped him get into bed.

While they were doing that, Garin casually asked, "What were you doing out on deck anyway, Paul?"

The journalist mumbled something about trying to get pictures of the storm.

That made sense to Annja—Paul was a freelancer and therefore always thinking about the next project he could pitch—but Garin didn't seem satisfied. He lingered in the doorway and seemed about to say something else before Annja scowled at him, shooed him out the door and followed in his wake.

Back at the table in the galley, Annja asked, "What was all that about?"

"What was what about?"

"Interrogating the guy who almost drowned."

She knew "interrogating" was a bit strong, but she was feeling protective of the man she'd just risked her life to save.

"Aren't you curious about what your sweetheart was doing out on deck in the middle of the night?"

"Of course I am," she replied. "But I can wait until he's had some rest before I ask him."

"Yes, but by then he'll have had plenty of time to come up with an answer."

Annja couldn't believe what she was hearing. "Come up with an answer? What, do you think he was lying?"

"I don't know what to think."

"Get real, Garin. We're in the middle of nowhere. What else would he have been doing?"

Garin looked away, frustrated. "I don't know. Maybe he told someone else about the treasure and he was signaling to them when we weren't looking."

Annja's thoughts flashed to the dark shape she thought she'd seen sliding through the water near them, but then she pushed it aside, convinced that she'd been imagining things.

*We're out here alone, and it was nothing more than a stupid accident*, she reminded herself, and said the same thing to Garin.

"All right, all right," he said. "I'll leave it alone for now, but I'm telling you…"

A long grinding sound filled the boat, interrupting him. Both Annja and Garin grabbed the table in front of them as the boat collided with something hard on the port side.

"What on earth?" Annja asked.

Garin wasn't waiting around to give an answer; he was already climbing up the companionway, flashlight in hand.

Annja followed.

Back out on deck they found that the rain had finally stopped and the sky was starting to clear, with a bit of moonlight now showing through the rents in the clouds. The seas were still choppy, but not as bad as they had been earlier, allowing both Annja and Garin to make out the dark shape of the coral outcropping that the *Reliant* had just scraped past.

"Where did that come from?" Garin exclaimed, even as he rushed back to the cockpit and started the engines again.

Looking ahead, Annja could see more of the reef poking above the water, and she began to call out directions to Garin as he worked the wheel, guiding the *Reliant* around and through the maze of coral and rock.

They had been at it for only a couple of minutes when Annja spotted something large looming ahead of them. She peered through the semidarkness, trying to make out what it was.

The clouds momentarily moved away from the moon, giving her a decent view.

"Look!" she shouted, pointing.

An island was a few hundred yards ahead of them. They could see its tropical foliage and sheer cliffs emerge from the darkness as they drew closer. Pure chance had kept them from wrecking on the rocky outer reef that surrounded the island, and now that they were inside its range Garin decided it would be best if they found a place to drop anchor and wait out the remainder of the night, continuing on in the morning.

Annja agreed.

They made a slow circuit of the island, seeing nothing for long moments but sheer cliffs rising right out of the surf.

*It's not going to be easy climbing those,* Annja thought.

But then, about three-quarters of the way around the island, she spotted the entrance to a narrow inlet between two large pillars of stone. It looked deep enough to accommodate the boat, so Garin steered toward it, passing between the cliffs for several minutes until they emerged into a sheltered cove that seemed the perfect place to wait out the rest of the night.

Annja switched on the electric windlass, dropping the anchor to secure the boat, while Garin shut down the engines. Satisfied that they'd done what they could for the night, they retired to their cabins to get some sleep.

# 23

When Annja got up the next morning, she found Garin and Paul sitting at the galley table enjoying a breakfast of fresh fruit and coffee. Annja grabbed a cup of her own and slid in next to Paul.

"Are you doing all right?" she asked.

"Yeah, I'm good," Paul said. "And thanks. I wouldn't be here without you, I'm told."

Annja waved his thanks away, but Paul persisted.

"No, really, I appreciate what you did, both of you," he said, looking from one to the other. "It was stupid of me to endanger the mission like that. I shouldn't have been out there in the first place."

"What were you doing, anyway?" Annja asked, reaching for an orange and peeling it.

"Trying to get pictures of the storm."

Garin opened his mouth to say something, but Paul held up a hand, stopping him. "I know. You don't have to tell me. It was a dumb idea. I didn't think it through to be honest."

Annja agreed that it had been dumb, but she'd also made her own share of mistakes in the past and didn't hold it against him. Everyone had survived; that was the important thing.

Still, she was curious. "So what happened exactly?"

Paul sighed. "I was leaning on the boom, using it to stabilize one of my shots, when it shifted beneath my weight and swung outward, dumping me into the water. Even then I would have been okay if a wave hadn't come along right at that moment and carried me away from the boat. No matter how hard I swam, I couldn't seem to get back to it."

"And your camera?" Garin asked.

"I lost it when I fell overboard," Paul told him. "No doubt it's at the bottom of the sea by now."

"Well, I'm sure you can buy another one, heck, another hundred, with your share of the treasure when we get back home."

Paul smiled. "That's true, isn't it?"

The thought seemed to make him feel better and that made Annja happy.

"Speaking of treasure, how soon until we leave?" she asked. "Unless the storm blew us radically off course it can't be that much farther to Wolf Island, can it?"

Garin got up and poured himself another cup of coffee. "Oh, I don't think it's very far at all," he said, "but I'm surprised you want to leave so quickly."

"We're on a deadline, remember?" Annja said, perplexed by his laissez-faire attitude. He didn't seem to be in a hurry to go anywhere even though every min-

ute they stayed here was another minute wasted in
their search for the lost Nazi headquarters.

Garin shrugged in response. "Hey, I get it. We can
leave anytime that you're ready, really. I just figured
that you'd want to check out the Nazi U-boat moored
in the lagoon outside before we went anywhere, but
if you don't want to…"

Annja blinked at him in surprise. "U-boat?" she
asked.

Garin nodded. "I think it's U-648," he said with a
near-expressionless face. "But I might be reading the
number on the conning tower wrong. It is faded a bit
from being in the sun so long, after all."

Annja sat there, at a loss for words as she tried to
process what he'd just said. When it finally sank in,
she jumped up and headed over to the companionway leading above, practically falling on her face in
her haste to get up the steps.

Behind and below her, she heard Garin chuckle.

*If he's pulling my leg, I'm going to gut him like
a fish*, she thought as she stepped out onto the deck
and looked around.

Garin wasn't kidding.

Less than fifty yards away a World War II German
U-boat lay moored against the rotting remains of a
wooden pier jutting from the white sand beach just
beyond. The boat was rusted and its paint job faded
from being in the water and sun for so long, but the
red-and-black swastika painted on the conning tower
could still be faintly seen.

Annja couldn't believe what she was seeing.

A U-boat, short for *Unterseeboot*, or undersea boat, was a German military submarine used to disrupt both Allied fleet activities and commercial shipping, especially resupply, during World Wars I and II. The Germans had the largest submarine fleet in the world at the time and made spectacular use of it during the Battle of the Atlantic in WWII, so much so that it was the only time that Winston Churchill had ever contemplated the need for Great Britain to surrender.

Organized into "wolf packs" or groups of U-boats working together to attack a common target, the U-boat commanders became the bane of Allied shipping after the fall of France, operating out of multiple bases on the French coastline and having easy access to the North Atlantic, the English Channel, and the Mediterranean. After the United States entered the war, the U-boats ranged from the Europe to the coast of the Americas, from the Caribbean and the Gulf of Mexico to the waters of the Arctic. It wasn't until the United States, in conjunction with its British allies, gained superiority in the air later in the war that the situation began to change. Without the air cover previously provided by the Luftwaffe, and limited by the time they could spend below the surface as a result of their weak batteries, the U-boats were forced to spend more and more of their time on the surface. This made them vulnerable to Allied airplanes as well as the increasingly sophisticated submarine-hunting tactics that were developing at the time.

Gradually the tide had turned against them and the

U-boats and their commanders were picked off in increasingly higher numbers as the war was brought to a close. Of the forty thousand men who went to war as part of the German U-boat fleet, thirty thousand of them were to die in their iron coffins, earning them the record for the greatest number of losses in any combat unit in the history of war.

It was a humbling statistic.

It had often been rumored that a number of high-ranking Nazis had used the last of the U-boats to flee for the safety of Argentina, Bolivia and Uruguay, countries with no extradition treaties with the United States and Great Britain, but it had never been proved.

Seeing the boat docked in the middle of the South Pacific gave some credence to those rumors. It also suggested that Annja and her companions had at last reached their destination.

Somehow, in the midst of the craziness of the previous night's storm, they'd managed to find *Inles Wolf* without even realizing it!

She was still staring at the vessel in amazement when the other two came up the steps and joined her on the deck.

"Will you look at that!" Paul exclaimed when he turned and saw the U-boat for the first time.

Garin, of course, didn't say anything; he was too busy standing there with a smug look on his face.

Annja turned and punched him on the arm.

"Ow! What was that for?"

"For not waking me up the moment you saw it, you idiot!"

Rubbing his arm, Garin said, "After last night, I thought you deserved a rest."

She had needed the sleep, but she wasn't going to admit that to him. Instead, she said, "Did you check the GPS? Are we at the proper location?"

"Do you know what the odds are of that U-boat being here if this wasn't *Inles Wolf*?" Garin shot back.

"I don't care about the odds. Did you or didn't you check the GPS?"

"Yes, I checked it. We're in the right location, as near as I can tell."

That was a relief.

Annja smiled. "Okay, who wants to go look at the U-boat?"

THEY HAD NO idea what condition the boat would be in after all this time, so they gathered a few supplies and loaded them aboard the dinghy before lowering it into the water. Annja and Paul sat up front, holding on to the gunwale, while Garin moved to the rear of the boat and fired up the outboard motor. After that, it only took a few minutes to cross the lagoon to the hulk of the submarine.

Unlike modern submarines with their rounded hulls and bulbous front ends, the U-boat had a sharp-edged front that cut through the water like a knife and a sleek wedge-shaped body that resembled a shark more than anything else. Even after decades of in-activity, the boat still looked dangerous and Annja couldn't imagine what it had to have felt like for the merchantmen who were the vessel's typical prey to look out across the water and see one of these monsters rise from the depths to attack.

They approached from the side, so Annja was able to clearly see the conning tower, with its periscope and snorkel, as well as both the deck gun in front of it and the antiaircraft gun in its swivel mount behind.

Annja mentally reviewed what she knew about U-boats as they drew closer. The average boat was roughly 220 feet long and displaced about 700 tons of water. It carried a crew of 35 men, was loaded with 12 torpedoes, and could remain beneath the surface for a little more than two hours on fully charged batteries.

This boat had docked with its bow pointed toward the entrance to the cove, most likely so that it could put to sea quickly if it was discovered. That told Annja that the lagoon was probably much deeper than she expected, given how much room it took to maneuver a boat of this size.

She wondered what had happened to it and why it was still here so many years after the war. Surely the captain and crew would have wanted to go home at some point, if they were still capable? Perhaps the boat had run out of fuel. Or was no longer seaworthy due to battle damage that they couldn't be seen from the surface.

Just looking at the thing she had a hundred more questions, and she hoped that they'd find some answers once they got aboard.

Garin brought the dinghy alongside the dock on the side opposite the U-boat. Paul hopped out, testing the strength of the pier. When it seemed that the wood was solid enough to bear their weight, Paul grabbed the mooring line from Annja and tied the boat to one of the pier's support poles. Once it was secure, Garin helped Annja onto the dock, passed the duffel bag full of tools up to her, then jumped out himself.

They crossed the dock and stepped up onto the wooden deck of the U-boat. It had rotted through in a few places, but for the most part was still intact. "The hatch is this way," Annja said, leading the two men toward the conning tower. She skirted the deck gun and mounted the steps on the other side of the conning tower to enter the central section. A hatch lay in the middle of the floor, leading down into the ship.

Unsurprisingly, not only was the hatch closed but it looked as though it had been rusted shut for a long time.

*Still, one has to try*, Annja thought.

She bent, grabbed the wheel that opened the hatch and did her best to turn it.

It didn't move.

"Give it a try, guys," Annja said.

She stepped back, letting Garin and Paul take her place. They grabbed hold of the wheel on opposite sides and leaned their weight into it. Annja could see the muscles in their arms bulging, but the wheel didn't move.

"All right, don't give yourselves hernias," Annja said. "Step back."

When they had complied, she took an aerosol can of nut and bolt loosener out of the duffel bag at her feet and sprayed it liberally over the point on the underside of the wheel where it met the crank shaft. She waited a few minutes, then took an oversized wrench from the bag. Lifting the tool over her head, she brought it smashing down against the wheel of the hatch. She did that half a dozen times, alternating spraying it and hitting it with the wrench.

Satisfied, she stepped back and inclined her head at the hatch again.

The men got the message. Situating themselves on either side of the hatch, they tried again.

Nothing.

Annja stepped in and went through the whole routine a second time, then signaled Garin and Paul to give it their best shot.

The wheel still didn't turn.

"Come on, you son-of-a-gun," she said, stepping forward once more.

The spray had to have finally had enough time to work some of the rust loose, for when the men tried, the wheel moved an inch to the left before getting stuck.

"Yes!" Annja cried.

Now they knew that it would open if they just kept working at it. Ten minutes later they were able to turn the wheel fully and unlock the hatch.

"Ready?" Paul asked, and at his companions' nods he pulled back on the hatch, opening it.

Foul air rushed out of the opening, causing them to turn their heads for a moment, but it dissipated quickly. Annja traded her spray can and her wrench for a high-powered flashlight and shone it into the interior of the boat.

At the bottom of the ladder, a human skull stared back at them through the light.

# 24

"Hello, what have we here?" Annja said, upon seeing the skull. It wasn't the first time she'd encountered human remains during her work and it certainly wouldn't be the last. She moved the beam of the light around slowly, noting there were quite a few more bones at the bottom of the ladder. The ladder itself looked stable; they should be able to get to the bottom without a problem.

What was waiting for them down there might be another story, though.

*Stop the nonsense,* she scolded herself. *This sub's been locked up as tight as a drum for decades. If anything was waiting down there for you, it's long dead.*

She ignored the little voice that chimed, *"That's what I'm afraid of!"* back at her.

They tied the hatch in the open position, so that it couldn't fall and accidentally seal them in. When they had finished, Annja turned to the others. "I'll go down first and have—"

"No," Garin interrupted. "I'll go."

Annja rounded on him, annoyed. "Are you suggesting that there's something down there that I won't be able handle?"

Garin looked at her with so little expression that Annja was sure that he was holding back laughter. That suspicion only grew when it took him several seconds to get his response out.

At last he said, "Nothing of the sort, actually. I outweigh both of you. If the ladder is going to break, it is most likely going to do so under my weight and not yours. If you go down first and the ladder breaks when I follow you, that means there will be at least two of us stuck down there. If I go down first and the ladder breaks, only one of us gets stuck, leaving the two of you to find a way to get me out."

Annja felt her cheeks heating up at Garin's perfectly reasonable explanation, and she did her best to ignore the sensation.

"Right. I knew that," she said, turning away so she didn't see the smirk trying to break free on Garin's face.

Garin took hold of the rails on either side of the ladder and stepped down onto the second crossbar, testing to see if it would hold his weight.

When it did, he began his descent. He eased down, one crossbar at a time, until he reached the bottom, then stepped onto the interior deck of the submarine, doing his best not to step on the bones of the skeleton that were lying at his feet.

"I'm good," he called up the others. "Send Paul down next."

Once Paul reached the bottom, Annja started her

descent, and soon the three of them were standing in the central control room taking a look around.

The first thing that Annja noticed was that the compartment was cramped. She'd expected it to be, it was a submarine after all, but it was even smaller than she expected. There was a heavy bulkhead at each end of the compartment, with a hatch in the center leading to either end of the boat. In the center were large cylindrical tubes that no doubt housed the optics for the periscope. Around them were crammed multiple work stations for the command crew. The port side held the main helm controls, the main vent controls, what looked to Annja like a bilge pump and a large tank of some kind, possibly for drinking water. On the starboard side was an exposed motor, most likely for the periscope, the compass and attack computer, and the ladder up to the conning tower.

She and her companions nearly filled the space; Annja couldn't imagine what it would have been like with six to eight men working in here at the same time. She was very glad that she wasn't claustrophobic, for if she had been, she doubted that she could have gone any farther.

The skeleton lying at the base of the ladder wasn't the only one; Annja counted two more. There was also a fair amount of evidence that a fight of some kind had taken place. There were broken gauges, what looked like bullet holes in the bulkheads, and even a soot-blackened area where the navigator's table should have stood.

She supposed a fire could have caused the damage she was seeing, but that didn't explain the bullet holes. Had the soldiers fought among themselves and accidentally caused a fire? Had the three dead men been trapped by the flames or were they dead, possibly from the smoke, before the fire broke out?

WITHOUT A PROPER lab in which to analyze the remains, she would never know.

That made the archaeologist in her twitch in discomfort.

She bent next to the nearest skeleton and looked closely. She could see small bits and pieces of cloth between and under several of the bones and realized that it was all that was left of the man's uniform. It looked as if he'd died in his chair, doing his duty.

Paul interrupted her thoughts.

"Why did they leave the bodies here?"

She turned and frowned at Paul, not sure if she'd heard him correctly. "What was that?"

"Why weren't the bodies given a proper burial?" he asked. "Wasn't that the custom back then?"

It was. Honoring the dead was one of the customs that transcended cultural and physical boundaries.

Which made Paul's question all the more curious.

So why not now? Why not here? What had happened to the crew that was so bad that it kept them from tending to their own? she wondered.

That was the question of the day, it seemed.

"I don't know," she told Paul. "Maybe they were the last survivors and there was no one left to take care of them when it was their time to go."

It was as good an explanation as any, she supposed, but it made the presence of the skeletons even more upsetting than before.

What was so deadly that it killed all three men at the same time, right where they were?

Plague was the first thought that popped into her head.

It wasn't a very comforting one.

Paul had to have been thinking something similar because he stepped away from the skeleton he'd been examining, and said, "You know, this might not be such a good idea. Maybe we should go."

But Annja shook her head. "We can't leave. We don't know what we are looking for, and this is a pretty big island to search blindly. If we're going to meet the deadline, we need to find a clue as to where to begin looking for Hitler's hideaway. The best place to find something like that is on this boat."

She couldn't help but add, "Besides, if they did have something like bubonic plague, you can rest assured that you've contracted it already."

The stricken look that crossed Paul's face in response to her comment told her it probably wasn't as funny as she thought it was.

She considered what she knew about U-boats, trying to remember where the captain's cabin, if it could even be called that, was on the boat.

Forward of the control room? Aft?

She couldn't recall.

In the absence of clear direction, she mentally flipped a coin and when it came up tails, chose aft.

Walking to the hatch in the bulkhead at the rear of the room, Annja examined the flywheel in the center. Unlike the wheel on the hatch above, this one was free of rust and in good shape. She dug her trusty can of bolt loosener out of the duffel hanging over her shoulder and gave the flywheel a few sprays before giving it an experimental turn.

It didn't budge.

She peered at the flywheel, using her light and getting in close, but it looked just fine. There was no rust that she could see, nothing gumming up the works.

It should open.

Unless it was locked or jammed from the other side.

Oddly unsettled by the notion but not sure why, Annja turned and moved to the other end of the compartment. Garin was trying to open the opposite hatch, with about as much success as she'd had with hers.

This one, too, seemed to be locked or jammed from the opposite side.

"Are there any other hatches topside that we can use?" Paul asked.

Annja shook her head. "The conning tower hatch is the only real entrance to the submarine."

"What do you mean 'real entrance'?" Garin asked.

"I mean an entrance that the crew normally uses. That doesn't mean that it's the only way into the ship, just that it's the one that sane people use. For instance, technically speaking, if you were small enough and the doors on both ends were open, I suppose you

could climb through either the forward or aft torpedo tubes and get in that way, but even I'm not crazy
enough to try that."

"So we're dead in the water?"

"I didn't say that." Garin's question had gotten her
thinking about the other ways into the boat and one
big one stuck out in her mind.

"We could try the escape hatch."

"What's that?" Paul asked.

"It's an emergency hatch built into the floor of the
forward torpedo room. It was designed to allow the
men in that compartment to escape the boat in the
event of an emergency."

"Did it work?"

Annja shrugged. "Not really. The difference in
pressurization between the air inside the boat and
the water outside meant that the hatch couldn't be
opened until the hatch compartment was flooded.
The guys trying to escape would have to climb inside,
calmly wait for the chamber to flood, and then open
the hatch before swimming for the surface. When
your boat is headed for the ocean floor, it's awfully
hard to stay calm enough to do something like that.
Never mind the fact that if you do pull it off and get
the hatch open, it might already be too deep for it to
make any difference and you drown on the way up."

"And you think we can use this to get inside that
part of the boat?" Garin asked.

"Possibly. If I can get the outer hatch open and if

the hatch mechanism still works well enough to flood the interior chamber, then yes, we might be able to."

She thought about it for a few seconds and then said, "Yeah, I think it's worth a try."

# 25

Annja knew that the number of successful escapes from a sinking submarine using the hatch she'd just described were few and far between. Normally that might have given her pause, but in this instance she didn't think it really mattered. After all, she wasn't trying to get out of a sinking sub, she was trying to get inside one. One that was still tied to a dock, no less. That should make all the difference in the world.

Still, to be as safe as possible, they decided that Annja would wear a scuba tank during the attempt and would carry the small underwater cutting torch from the *Reliant*'s emergency tool kit. That way, if something went wrong with the hatch and she found herself trapped in the compartment, she would have air to breathe while she cut through the hatch in order to get free.

Having decided on their next step, the trio returned to the *Reliant* to gather the necessary tools. The lagoon water was warm—a pleasant change from the icy Alpine lake that was the site of her last dive— and so there was no need for special equipment like a dry suit and its associated layers of clothing. For this dive, all Annja would need was her wet suit, her scuba gear, her light and a small cutting torch.

By late morning they were back in the dinghy and motoring to the submarine for the second time that day. Instead of tying off at the dock on the other side from the boat, however, this time Garin brought them in close, right up next to the bow of the warship. He shut down the outboard motor and had Paul drop the anchor over the side to keep them from drifting.

Annja checked her tank and regulator, then pulled on her mask and flippers. She sat on the edge of the boat with her back to the water and, with a thumbs-up to Garin, fell over backward into the lagoon.

The water was clear and visibility was good. She swam over to the hull of the submarine and followed it forward until she reached the mouths of the forward torpedo tubes. Using that as her reference point, she dived deeper, under the keel, then began shining her light across the hull, looking for the hatch leading into the escape trunk.

It didn't take her long; the hatch was partially open, which made it fairly easy to see along the smooth curve of the hull. She swam over to it and shone her light through the hatch into the compartment, checking to be sure some denizen of the deep hadn't decided to take up residence there. The space was empty, so she wouldn't have to chase out a moray eel or any barracuda. The interior hatch leading from the escape trunk into the ship proper seemed to be closed, which was a good sign that the forward compartment she hoped to enter was still airtight.

She spent several minutes clearing as much of the growth from the hinges as she could, and pushed the hatch back and forth to be certain it would move. It was a bit stiff at first, but after several repetitions it seemed to move a little easier.

Annja grabbed hold of the hatch's inner handle and slipped into the escape trunk. She pulled the hatch shut behind her as she did so and shoved the lever that pulled the hatch closed.

The escape trunk had been designed to hold four seated men at the same time. Annja had plenty of room around her but had to remain in a crouch or she'd bang her head against the hatch above her.

Now came the real test.

After spending so many decades moored in the same spot, Annja knew the charge on the submarine's batteries had long since failed, so she didn't bother trying the controls to power the drain. Instead she shone her light against the inner chamber wall to the left of the control panel until she found the hand crank that served as the backup control system. She had to hit it with her dive light several times before it would move, but at last she got it to turn. She spun the crank clockwise as far as it would go and then locked it into place.

She waited.

After a few seconds Annja felt the water begin to flow down her body, draining out of the escape trunk as the bladder she'd just activated forced air into the trunk, increasing the pressure and pushing the water out through the drains beneath her feet.

When the water had drained completely, Annja removed her regulator and tested the air.

The wave of dizziness that washed over her in the seconds before she got her regulator back into her mouth and took a gulp of clean oxygen told her that the air inside the trunk was anything but breathable.

*That's fine,* she thought. *I'll just stay on the regulator while I check things out.*

Now that the air pressure inside the trunk matched the air pressure inside the submarine, she should be able to open the inner hatch without flooding the entire ship in the process.

She crossed her fingers, made a quick plea to whoever might be listening, and then reached up and grabbed the flywheel in the center of the hatch above her head.

Unlike the others she'd encountered so far, this one spun easily. She gave it a few hard cranks and then, when the wheel wouldn't move any farther, pushed upward on the hatch.

It fell open with a bang.

She was in!

Annja stood up and, in doing so, brought her head and shoulders out of the escape trunk and into the forward torpedo room. She was relieved to see that the compartment had remained watertight even after all this time. There was air in the chamber as well, but she knew that it would more than likely be stagnant, too. Until they could open the inner hatch and allow some fresh air to flow down the conning tower hatch and into the rest of the boat, she was going to have to keep breathing from her tank.

Putting her hands on the floor next to the hatch, she boosted herself out of the escape trunk and into the torpedo room. She left the hatch open behind her, wanting to be sure she had at least one avenue of escape if she couldn't get the interior hatch leading to the control room open from this side. Worrying about the outer hatch was bad enough; she didn't want to be concerned that the inner one wouldn't open.

Annja looked around.

To the rear of the compartment were three sets of bunk beds, which she guessed had to have been the accommodations for the junior ratings aboard. Next to those and closer to her was the torpedo loading rack, which held two torpedoes. The angled loading hatches for the four aft-facing torpedo tubes were next, while overhead hung a hoist used to maneuver the torpedoes from their storage space below the decking up onto the rack. There was a bulkhead hatch blocking off this compartment from the next. When she tried the flywheel, it spun without resistance and she was able to move aft, toward the control room where the others were waiting.

Passing through that first bulkhead, the next compartment in line was another wardroom of sorts, with two sets of bunks on either side of the aisle. As she flashed her light across the beds, she saw that she was no longer alone.

Three of the four bunks were occupied.

She started, surprised, her breath echoing in her ears through the regulator, but then she relaxed when she got a closer look at the beds' occupants. As with the sailors in the control room, these men weren't going anywhere. They were little more than skeletons in gray uniforms, the flesh having long since decayed, but the clothing they wore was far better preserved than that worn by their companions in the control room.

Annja noticed something sticking up from the body in one of the lower bunks. She reached out and carefully pulled it from the rib cage that had kept it in place for so many years.

It was an arrow with a wooden shaft and fletching made from the dark feathers of some kind of tropical bird. The broken remains of a bone tip were still tied to the other end. The rest was probably still stuck somewhere in the man's skeleton.

Despite her earlier thoughts about plague, she realized that the answer was much simpler. These men hadn't died of some mysterious illness at all, but rather at the hands of men just like themselves. She didn't know what they'd done to deserve death, if they'd done anything at all, but somehow the crew had made some deadly enemies upon arrival and had paid the ultimate price for those transgressions.

There was a mystery to be solved here, more than one, actually, but now was not the time. Annja pressed on, knowing the others were waiting for her.

The next bulkhead led to another wardroom, this one with bunks on the right and a small table on the left. There was a little more space in this compartment than in the previous one, but not much.

*Officers' quarters,* she thought.

Annja knew she was closing in on the middle of the boat, and a check of her air supply showed that she still had about half a tank left. If things continued at the pace they were going, she would have plenty.

Beyond the wardroom, she found the radio and sound detection rooms on the right and a single bunk with a curtain in front of it on the left.

That curtain—and the fact that the bunk was opposite the two most important stations on the boat—told her that it was the captain's bunk. The location allowed him to be kept abreast of new orders or new contacts as soon as they came in while the curtain served as the only bit of privacy that the man had. It wasn't much, but on a boat of this size it probably felt like heaven to be able to close yourself off, even for just a few minutes, from everyone else.

This was the first place that she intended to search for an answer to what had happened to the boat and its crew, but first she had to open the bulkhead hatch and let her companions, as well as some fresh air, into the boat.

The bulkhead at the front of this section of the hull was the one leading into the control room. From this side it was easy to see that it had been locked tight. Given the signs of a struggle in the control room, as well as the body of what could only have been an injured member of the crew in the senior petty officer's wardroom behind her, Annja could only believe that the boat and its crew had come under attack at some point in the past by person or persons unknown but most likely indigenous to this island.

Which begged the question, what had happened to the rest of the crew?

She pounded on the hatch with the underside of her fist to let Garin and Paul know that she was all right and then set to work releasing the lever that locked the gears that allowed the flywheel to turn. It had gotten stuck fast, and it took her a good five minutes to work it free, but at last the bit of steel retracted and she was able to spin the flywheel without resistance.

When she opened the hatch she found Garin and Paul standing on the other side in the control room, waiting.

"Everything all right?" Paul asked.

She nodded and gave him a thumbs-up, to his obvious relief.

She stepped into the control room, where fresh air was now circulating thanks to the open hatch in the conning tower. She pulled her regulator out of her mouth and shut off the air flow coming from her scuba tank, then slipped free of the straps. The tank was heavy when it wasn't in the water, and she was glad she didn't have to move around in the cramped quarters with it strapped to her back any longer.

They had to wait several minutes for the air in the forward section of the boat to be refreshed with what was coming in through the open hatch, and that gave Annja time to explain what she'd found on her trip through the interior. She told them about the bodies she'd found in the rear wardroom and of her belief that the crew might have been attacked at one point by natives and gave them the arrow she'd removed from the skeleton as evidence of her theory.

The close confines of the submarine were making Paul uncomfortable, so he climbed back up into the conning tower to wait for them while Annja headed to the captain's quarters and Garin went forward to take a look at the bodies.

In the drawers beneath the captain's bunk Annja found a few sets of uniforms, a toiletries kit and a leather-bound journal. Picking up the journal, she retreated to the next wardroom, sat down at the small table there and began leafing through the book, looking for anything that might point them in the direction of the base.

It had to be here somewhere.

# 26

The journal was written in German but fortunately the author had a fine hand and the letters stood out crisp and clear even after all this time.

Annja flipped to the front of the book and read the first entry, dated late January 1943.

January 29, 1943
Four days from port. Have just two torpedoes remaining. Crew is on limited rations due to the amount of time we've been at sea, but their spirits are still high from our latest kill and I am confident we can make the return journey without mishap.

Her grasp of German was limited and a bit rustier than she would have liked, but she was still able to understand the majority of what she read and could infer the rest when she wasn't positive of the exact meaning.

The entry went on, giving a detailed report of an encounter with a solo Allied aircraft, British in origin, that had tried to depth charge them into oblivion earlier in the day. It was fascinating reading, but not something that was going to help them with their task.

Annja flipped ahead several pages and dipped into another entry, this one from November 8, 1944.

Have delivered a second load of construction materials to the island. The soldiers were happy to see us. We brought with us fresh staples for the kitchen and news of the war, even if it was a month or more out of date. The crew has a fever, the result of the sudden change from the cold of the North Atlantic to the heat and humidity of the tropics. Spirits remain high and the camp doctor told me that it should pass soon.

Annja nodded to herself. The dates fit with one of the key facts that she already knew, namely that Hitler had ordered the base built long before he'd entrusted the knowledge of its existence to his so-called friend and ally Martin Bormann.

She turned several more pages and then read another entry, this one dated late January 1945.

Arrived to find the pier finally complete. Being able to offload the supplies without using the boat's launch allowed the crew to finish in half the usual time, which was greeted with cheers all around. Delivered 400 kilos of flour, 200 kilos of salted meat, plus assorted carpentry tools.

Dined with the base commandant, Colonel Schnell, in the main facility and was highly impressed with what they have accomplished in just the short time since our last visit. Schnell must be working the crews night and day to accomplish so much, but it looks like the facility will be completed on time, much to our joint relief.

Rumor has it that M.B. will be arriving in late April to supervise the preparation for our leader's arrival and if it is not finished by that point heads are sure to roll.

There were several more entries of a similar nature, noting the delivery of various supplies and commenting on the continued progress, but nothing that indicated where the base actually might be.

Still wondering what had happened to the boat and its crew, Annja turned to the last few entries, noting that they were much closer to one another chronologically. In fact, they were all dated the same afternoon, March 30, 1945.

1400 hours
Limped into port with our batteries all but depleted and with barely any fuel left in the tanks. We survived the depth charge attack 48 hours earlier, but just barely.

Tried to raise those at the base via radio to no avail. The usual reception party was absent from the pier as well.

Have sent Doerner and Fritz to the base to get extra hands to help us offload the supplies. With the engines damaged in the latest attack, we will need to make significant repairs. I fear we will not be going anywhere soon.

1640 hours
Sentries claim to have seen movement in the trees, but when a search party was sent out there was no sign that anyone had been there. Am uncertain whether the sentries actually saw something or simply let the shadows confuse them after so long aboard ship.

One thing is clear. Doerner and Fritz have not returned and I fear for their safety.

1830 hours
Shortly after nightfall the boat came under attack from an unknown number of natives. The sentries were killed and the enemy was in the process of boarding the boat before they were discovered. Four of the crew died in defense of the conning tower, but their sacrifice gave the rest of us time to take cover inside the forward and aft compartments and seal the hatches behind us.

I have ten seamen with me in the forward compartments, three of whom are sufficiently wounded that I don't expect them to make it through the night. Have received reports that Sergeant Gorman and five others are holed up

in the engine room at the other end of the boat,
but are almost out of ammunition. Am awaiting
reinforcements from the base but fear the worst
may have happened. Have already destroyed the
code book and the Enigma device just in case.

2245 hours
The natives are trying to set fire to the boat!
Have decided to try and get my men out while
our attackers are otherwise occupied and before
we die of smoke inhalation.

My plan is to send them out four at a time
through the escape hatch, with myself and Lieutenant Pieske being the last to abandon ship.

The men have been instructed to swim for
the south side of the cove and rendezvous there
for the hike inland to the base.

That was it; after that, there weren't any other entries in the logbook. If the captain and his men had
made it out, they hadn't come back in the years since.

Annja cursed in frustration. The boat had turned
out to be a waste of time after all, for they were no
closer to finding the location of the headquarters now
than they had been when they arrived on the island.
The captain's comments suggested that the base was
inland somewhere, but any reasonable person would
have deduced the same. What she really needed—a
map or at least a list of landmarks—was nowhere to
be found.

And the clock was still ticking.

Garin found her there a few moments later.

"Anything?"

She shook her head. "A few references to the facility or the base, but that's all. Nothing that can help us find the place."

"I'm not surprised."

"Why's that?"

"If anything, U-boat commanders were practical people. They had to be, to survive in one of these tin cans for any length of time. He knew where the base was and its location wouldn't make a difference to his time at sea, so why keep note of it in the war diary?"

As much as she hated to admit it, Garin's logic made sense.

"So how do you propose we find this thing?" Annja asked.

"The same way we've found any other artifact we've ever gone looking for—with our heads. You're thinking about the clock and not about the job at hand," he said, smiling to take the sting out of his remark. "Forget about Doug for a minute and just think about the base. It was supposed to be Hitler's secret hideaway, right? A place where he could bide his time and come up with a new strategy but also one that would keep him safe should the Allies come looking for him."

"Yes, I would think that would be the case."

"So if you were him, where would you put your super-secret headquarters?"

"Not on an island in the middle of the South Pacific," Annja retorted.

Garin waved the comment away. "I could have come up with a hundred better places, too, but that's not the point. He built it here. This U-boat tells us that if nothing else. So put yourself in his shoes. What would he need to do it right?"

Annja thought about it and then ticked off a few points with the tips of her fingers. "It would have to be someplace that couldn't be seen from the air in order to keep it from being discovered by Allied aircraft as they continued to fight Japan here in the South Pacific. It would need to have a sizable water source of its own, to sustain him and his flunkies for any length of time. And it would need to be somewhere that they could defend easily just in case worse came to worst and they were discovered despite their efforts otherwise."

"Okay. So where do we find someplace like that on this island?"

Annja never got the chance to answer.

At that very moment, Paul called to them from outside.

"You guys need to come out here. Like, right now."

# 27

Annja stood beside Garin and Paul feeling a strange sense of déjà vu as she stared at the tribesmen lined up on the dock, standing in groups on either side of the conning tower. It was almost as if the events described in the captain's journal were playing themselves out all over again seventy years later.

Except this time, she was the one in the crosshairs.

There were roughly twenty tribesmen in all. They were short and stocky, well muscled, with dark hair and a deep Polynesian cast to their skin and features. They were armed with an assortment of spears, clubs, and bows, all of which were currently pointed at Annja and her companions. Many of the men had intricate tattoos on their faces and chests, reminding Annja of Maori tribesmen she had met in the past.

None of them looked particularly happy.

There was no way for Annja, Garin or Paul to go for their weapons. The minute they did so, all three of them would become human pincushions.

Option one was out.

Given that sealing themselves aboard the U-boat

had done nothing to save the U-boat commander and his men, Annja decided that option two was out as well.

That left option three. She smiled broadly, waved at the tribesmen, and said, "Hi there," in the friendliest voice she could muster.

The tribesmen stared at her without saying anything.

Annja was suddenly overcome with the urge to say, "Take me to your leader" but wisely clamped her mouth shut before it could slip out.

She didn't think her sense of humor would be appreciated.

Garin whispered to her. "What are you doing?"

She ignored him, her eyes on the men in front of her.

The largest of the tribesmen standing on the pier stepped forward. He said something in a language that Annja didn't understand, staring up at them as he did so.

Annja shrugged in response, having no idea what he'd said.

That seemed to anger him, for he said something in a more forceful tone and with a wave of his spear indicated that the three of them should come down from the conning tower.

Annja wasn't so sure that was a good idea, but she didn't see that they had much choice.

"Annja, his arm! Look at his left arm!" Garin whispered.

She did so and at first wasn't sure what Garin was

referring to. So he had biceps as big around as her thigh, so what? But then he waved his spear at them again, this time a bit more impatiently than the last, and Annja saw what had gotten Garin excited.

Around his biceps was a faded red armband bearing a white circle with a swastika in the center!

On a whim Annja addressed the leader in German. "Do you understand me?" she asked.

The weapons that had been pointed at Garin and Paul were suddenly shifted in her direction and the tribesmen began whispering to one another in an agitated manner.

It wasn't quite the response she'd been hoping for.

Before she could say anything more, the man with the armband barked out a command to the others. The group to the left of the conning tower moved in closer and with their weapons made it clear that Annja and the others were to come down.

When Annja hesitated, one of them jabbed at her with his spear.

That prompted Garin to step forward to defend her, which only served to further rile the tribesmen. Several of them were shouting and brandishing their weapons now, and it looked as if things were about to get seriously out of control.

Thinking quickly, Annja held her arms over her head and said, "Okay, okay. Relax. We'll come with you." As before, she said it in German.

At least the leader understood, for he barked out another order and those closest to them backed off, giving them room to come down from the conning tower and onto the deck.

No sooner had they done so than the tribesmen moved in, grabbing their arms and pulling them down to their knees. Spears and arrows were thrust in their faces with what could only have been an order not to move as one of the warriors stepped forward and bound their hands behind their backs.

"I think you're making them angry," Garin said, which only served to get him cuffed on the side of the head by the nearest tribesmen.

Annja gave him her best "trust me" expression, but she wasn't sure that he understood. After all, it wasn't so long ago that trust was a scarce commodity between them.

Once their hands were secure, the same tribesmen patted them down. He did a better job than Stuggart's guards had in Paris, for he found both Garin's and Paul's weapons. Both of them were handed to the leader, who glanced at them and threw them into the lagoon. The tribesmen dragged them to their feet and led them off the boat and onto the pier. Several of the other men disappeared into the U-boat and returned moments later carrying the captain's journal, as well as Annja's scuba equipment and the duffel bag of tools that they'd brought with them.

The rope holding the hatch was cut, allowing it to slam shut with a bang. Apparently satisfied that he'd taken care of everything that needed to be taken care of, the leader turned on his heel and began walking down the pier in the direction of the jungle, shouting an order over his shoulder as he went.

It didn't take much to figure out what that order had been, for the other tribesmen moved in on the three captives, dragging them to their feet and pushing them in the same direction.

*Guess they want us to follow him,* Annja thought as moved forward.

Behind her, Garin and Paul followed suit.

THE TRIBESMEN MARCHED them across the beach and into the jungle, following a path that Annja couldn't see amid the deep undergrowth, but that they seemed to have no trouble finding. They moved deeper into the interior with every step they took, and soon the sound of the crashing surf was lost far behind them. Anytime Annja or the others tried to speak, they were quickly whacked in the head by the nearest tribesman and they soon learned to keep their mouths shut.

They'd been walking for about two hours, heading north the entire time, when the leader called for a short break. Annja, Garin and Paul were forced to the ground with the tribesmen standing in a circle around them. Water jugs were produced and passed around, and even the prisoners were allowed to drink. All too quickly they were pulled back to their feet and the hike began anew, but this time they headed northeast.

Shortly thereafter Annja noticed that the trail was growing steeper, and it was clear that they were now climbing upward.

She tried to keep track of where they were going,

but soon the physical effort took its toll and it was all she could do to keep trudging along, following the tribesman in front of her, and doing her best to stay on her feet. All the activity over the past week had sapped her usual reserves, and she found herself on shaky legs when they stopped for another water break several hours later.

This time the tribesmen were a little more lax in watching the prisoners, and they were able to sit close and whisper to one another. From Annja's perspective, it was almost as if the tribesmen knew that the physical exertions of the past hours had done more to effectively quell any thoughts of escape than their weapons or presence could.

"Who do you think these guys are?" Paul asked quietly.

Annja kept her face pointed downward so none of the tribesmen would see her lips moving as she said, "Indigenous islanders would be my guess."

"And that guy with the Nazi armband? What do you think that is for?"

Annja shrugged.

The truth was that she had two different thoughts on that armband. On one hand was the possibility that, back in the day, the tribesmen had been influenced by the men who had come to the island to build Hitler's headquarters. The Germans had worn the armbands and so now the leader of the tribesmen wore one, too. On the other hand, perhaps the tribesmen had slaughtered the Germans, who they saw as invaders of their land, and the current leader now wore the armband as a symbol of his ancestors' power and prestige in conquering them.

In her view, it was fifty-fifty, either way.

Another few gulps of water, five minutes more of rest, then they were being pulled to their feet for what turned out to be the final leg of their journey.

They trudged upward for another hour until all of a sudden they broke free of the undergrowth and found themselves standing on a promontory high above the island, looking out over the open caldera of the extinct volcano that formed the center of the island.

The view was spectacular.

In practically every direction the blue-green waters of the open ocean stretched out to the horizon, reaffirming just how isolated this particular spot on the planet actually was. Directly ahead of them, the gaping mouth of the volcano stretched for nearly a mile. The far side was lower, so they could see where the jungle began again on the opposite slope and then ran downward all the way to the cliffs.

Annja was looking out over the ocean, enjoying the cool breeze that was a welcome change from the steaming heat of the jungle through which they'd just come, when all of the sudden Paul said in amazement, "Well, I'll be…"

Annja looked at him, then followed his line of sight to where he was staring at a spot about a third of the way around the rim.

For a minute she didn't see what it was that had surprised him so, but then it came into focus as she was able to separate the cold gray of the steel from the lighter gray of the stone.

Someone had bolted a primitive elevator to the inside of the caldera.

# 28

Suddenly Annja understood.

Instead of spending the time and energy, never mind the expense, to excavate an entire underground network of tunnels and passages to serve as the final headquarters of the Third Reich, Hitler had ordered his men to make use of the existing passages and caves. Inside the cone of the volcano, a perfect place had been created thanks to lava eruptions hundreds, if not thousands, of years ago.

The Nazi base was not above ground at all, but below, in the deep tunnels and chambers nature had already provided at the heart of the volcano!

Annja had to admit that it was a brilliant move.

The base would be all but invisible to everything but the most direct fly-over, and even then the pilot would have to have absolutely superior vision to make out anything moving along the inside slope of the caldera. Any smoke or steam generated by the work the crews were doing underground during the construction phase would have simply been dismissed as a natural by-product of a slumbering volcano. And if the Allies had found the location before the war ended, routing the Nazis out of it would have been akin to driving the Japanese out of the tunnels beneath Mount Suribachi on Iwo Jima, a task that had cost nearly 7,000 American and over 20,000 Japanese lives.

Just as on Iwo Jima, the pumice stone that formed the cone of the volcano would have been easy to dig through and, when mixed with water, formed a kind of natural cement that would have allowed the crews to create smooth walls, floors and ceilings inside their sanctuary.

If Hitler had ever made it this far, it would have taken years to roust him out, Annja realized. Thank heavens he hadn't.

The leader led the way around the edge of the volcano and over to the elevator platforms. There were adjacent to each other, so one group could be going up while the other was going down. Each basket could hold three men comfortably, four in an emergency. Since one of the baskets was already on the ground below, Annja had plenty of time to watch how it operated before it was her turn to board.

Each elevator consisted of an iron basket attached to a steel cable that ran through a pulley system bolted to the inside of the caldera wall and to the control system inside the basket. Crank the handle counterclockwise and the basket would descend as the cable slowly let itself out. Let go of the crank and the cable was automatically locked in place by a complicated system of interconnected gears. Turn the crank in the opposite direction and the elevator went back up again. A second cable system raised or lowered it from outside the basket, allowing it to be brought back up again without someone riding inside.

The one disadvantage was that it was slow—it took nearly twenty minutes for the basket to make the trip down and back up again—but Annja had no doubt that it had been expressly designed with this lack of speed in mind to make it even more difficult for an invading force to reach the men holed up there.

The man with the armband went down first, alone. When the basket came back up, Garin was escorted inside and two of the tribesmen descended with him. The process was repeated for Paul and then for Annja.

The descent went slowly, giving Annja plenty of time to study the controls in case she needed to make use of them later. It was clear to her that the system could be easily sabotaged; breaking off the gears would keep them from locking, at which point it would take remarkable strength to crank the basket all the way to the top or keep it from rushing down uncontrolled to the bottom.

They descended to a ledge about three-quarters of the way down the side of the caldera. A tunnel had been carved into the rock at that point and, after disembarking, Annja was led inside and down a series of connecting passageways, each one lit by what looked to be oil-burning lamps hung on the walls, to a closed set of double doors in front of which Garin, Paul and the rest of their captors were waiting.

One of the tribesmen cut her bonds. Garin and Paul

were rubbing circulation back into their freed limbs. As she was being cut free she glanced at Garin, to see if he wanted to turn the tables on their captors, but he subtly shook his head. *Let's see how this plays out*, his eyes seemed to say, and she nodded her agreement.

No sooner had she been cut free than the doors were pushed open and the group entered a wide audience chamber with a raised dais at the other end.

As they walked toward the dais, Annja looked around, trying to take it all in.

Two oversized Nazi banners, like those that hung on either side of the Olympic flame at the Summer Games in Berlin just before the start of World War II, decorated the walls on either side of the dais. They had to be thirty feet high, stretching completely from floor to ceiling. In front of them, fires burning in two gold braziers with eagle wings jutting from either side lit that end of the room, illuminating the man who sat on the dais lazily watching them approach.

He was old; that was the first thing she noticed about him. What was left of his hair was stark white and hung limply across his mostly pale scalp. His skin was wrinkled and marked by liver spots in quite a few places. But his eyes—his bright blue eyes—burned brilliantly and revealed the intelligence that still lingered within the man's mind.

The black uniform he wore, nearly identical to the one she and the others had seen hanging in Hans Stuggart's office back in Paris, looked as though it had been carefully tended for many years, but the silver Death's Head insignia he wore on his collar tabs shone as bright as newly minted quarters.

Two native guards stood at the foot of the dais on either side, and it was no surprise to Annja to find that they, too, had armbands like that worn by their captor. Clearly it was a sign of status in this community, and it made sense that the men who had been chosen to guard their leader would have the honor, if you could call it that, of wearing it.

If she was honest, just the sight of it being used so openly made Annja retch. She wondered if the natives had any real concept of the depravities that the symbol stood for.

Lining either side of the room, from the entryway to the foot of the dais, were more tribespeople. Most of them were men, but there was a fair number of women and children mingling in the crowd, as well.

They had been talking and chattering among themselves when the doors first opened, but as they got a closer look at the visitors they fell silent one by one. Soon the only sound in the room was the echo of the group's footsteps as Annja and the others crossed the room to stop and stand in front of the dais.

Their captor bowed low, then launched into an explanation that was given in rapid-fire German with a Polynesian accent, a strange sound if Annja ever heard one. She couldn't follow all of it, but from what she gathered, he was explaining how he had found them by the lagoon, taken them captive and brought them directly there.

When the guard finished, the old man in the SS

uniform struggled to his feet. He took a few steps forward so that he was standing in front of his throne, then spoke in a voice that was surprisingly strong for so frail-looking a man.

"Who sent you to kill me?" he asked in German.

Annja's mouth dropped open in surprise. It was perhaps the last thing on earth that she expected him to ask. Kill him? The very idea was preposterous. They didn't even know who he was.

Annja did have her suspicions, though.

She glanced at Garin, whose German was far better than her own, but when he remained stubbornly silent she thought it best to at least say something. The man on the dais in the uniform of an SS colonel didn't look as if he had a lot of patience, and it probably wouldn't help their cause any if they angered him.

But before she could say anything at all, Paul suddenly pushed his way forward.

The guards in front of the throne stiffened, preparing to cut him down should he make a move for the throne, but Paul stopped just a few steps in front of Annja. She watched as he kept his gaze firmly on the man in front of him, snapped his heels together, and thrust out his hand in a perfectly executed Nazi salute.

"Seig Heil!" he shouted in a German accent that matched the colonel's own.

Annja stared.

Their captor had to have been as surprised as she was, for it took him that long to react. He started forward, one ham fist raised, but the colonel held up a hand, stopping him.

He stared at Paul, who was still standing there, as stiff as a statue with his right arm extended at forty-five degrees in front of him, and then slowly nodded.

Paul brought his arm down but stood rigidly at attention.

*I hope he knows what he's doing*, Annja thought. *This is a dangerous game he's playing.*

But for Paul, this was far from a game, as Annja found out in the next few seconds.

"Speak," the colonel told him.

Paul relaxed into parade rest and then bowed his head momentarily in a gesture of respect to the man standing in front of him.

Annja's stomach suddenly twisted. What was going on here?

"Colonel," Paul began, "I am SS Sturmbannfürher Paul Krugmann. My father was SS Oberführer Heinz Kahler, former commandant of the Flossenburg Prison Camp and later a member of our leader's personal staff from the time he was at Wolfsschanze to the final days in the bunker in Berlin."

The colonel backed up and sat down on his throne. "Go on."

"After the war my father escaped to Spain and later emigrated to America where he changed our family name. What he did not lose, however, was his belief in our leader's plan for the Reich, and he devoted his life to teaching me all he knew so that I might carry out the last order the Fürher issued to him before dismissing him from the bunker on April 28, 1945."

Annja felt the blood drain from her face as she listened to what Paul was saying. She'd thought at first that he was creating an elaborate charade to try to get them out of the situation they found themselves in, but his words dripped with sincerity and had the unmistakable ring of truth to them. Paul had come here for one purpose and one purpose only—to have the conversation he was now having with the man in front of them.

The man Annja suspected was Colonel Schnell, the commander of the last headquarters built for Adolf Hitler and the legitimate heir to the Fourth Reich.

# 29

To make things worse, Paul wasn't yet finished.

"Our leader told my father of the base being constructed on Wolf Island and of the gold stored there. He was ordered to retrieve the gold and put it to use to rebuild the Party so that it could once again take its rightful place as the dominant political force in the Fatherland.

"But my father was injured during his escape to Spain and lost the use of his legs. Confined to a wheelchair for the rest of his life, he had to wait until I reached the proper age to carry on in his stead. He began to teach me about what to do once I recovered the gold, but the one thing he didn't relay to me was the location of Wolf Island.

"Four years ago my father succumbed to an unexpected stroke, leaving him a mindless husk, the location of the gold forever lost in the quagmire that his mind had become. That was when I conceived my plan to get this woman to help me find it!"

When Paul turned and pointed at her, Annja's world turned sideways and tipped over. She felt as if she was falling from a tremendous height and the fall went on and on and on as he laid the truth of his duplicity bare for all to see.

"Annja Creed is perhaps the world's foremost expert on finding objects and artifacts believed to be lost forever in the sands of time. She was the one person in all the world who had a spitting chance at finding the aircraft containing the letter in which our leader passed on the location of this facility to his trusted confidante Martin Bormann. The one person with an ego big enough to believe that she could find that letter and break that code when others had been trying and failing for decades."

Annja swallowed bile as she realized the import of what Paul was saying.

He was admitting that he'd led her on from the very start, that he had orchestrated this whole thing to get her to do his dirty work for him, that he had made sure that she wouldn't think of calling it quits no matter how tough things got because…*because he'd been the one who had kidnapped Doug in the first place!*

Annja was in motion before she consciously thought about it, charging toward Paul with single-minded determination, her gaze locked on his smirking face as she reached into the otherwhere for her sword…

As she rushed past the leader of the tribesmen, she never saw him turn, never saw the fist that suddenly exploded against the side of her head, stunning her before she could get her sword to fully materialize.

She collapsed in a heap on the floor, fighting for consciousness, while her attacker kicked her several times in the ribs for good measure.

She could hear Paul still talking, could hear Garin's roar of rage at the treatment she was being subjected to, but it was all distant, as if it were happening to someone far away. Even the pain from the blows barely registered as her pain-fogged mind tried to come to grips with the fact that her friend's kidnapper had been right there all along.

Traveling with her.

Dining with her.

Sharing a bed with her.

She was barely aware of it as she vomited all over the floor.

When she came back to herself, Paul was still talking to Colonel Schnell. She lay where she was, not caring that she could smell the stink of her own vomit, and she listened to what he was saying, already planning what she was going to do about it.

"Even now, my men are waiting offshore with the equipment needed to remove the gold from this bunker and transport it, and you, back to the Fatherland, where our plans can at long last be put in motion."

"Why should I go with you?" the colonel asked.

That comment stopped Paul in his tracks. "I'm sorry?"

"Why should I go with you?" Colonel Schnell repeated. "I am content here. I have my subjects, my kingdom, my gold. What do I need you for?"

Annja had known Paul long enough to recognize when he was thinking furiously.

Now was the time to interrupt.

"He's lying, Colonel Schnell," she called out, from her position on the floor. "Don't listen to him."

Paul turned and glared at her with such a hate-filled expression that she wondered how she had ever believed he cared for her.

She didn't let it stop her though.

"He just wants the gold for himself. You are completely irrelevant to his plans."

She was aware of Paul walking toward her, but she didn't bother to look at him, keeping her attention on the colonel. He looked back and forth between her and Paul, and Annja knew that she had cast a little doubt in his mind. Now if she could widen that gulf...

She was so intent on the old Nazi on the throne that she didn't see the younger one she'd come here with draw back his foot. Annja was caught completely by surprise as Paul's booted foot sent her into oblivion.

WHEN ANNJA CAME back to consciousness, she found herself lying facedown on a cold stone floor. Her face throbbed painfully, and she knew the left side of it was badly swollen because she could barely open that eye.

She pushed herself upright and immediately regretted it as a wave of dizziness washed over her. She put her palms flat on the floor beside her and waited for it to pass.

"You might want to stay lying down with your face

on the floor," she heard Garin say. "The cold will help bring the swelling down."

"That bad, huh?" she asked, as she turned her head to try to find him.

If the bars between them were any indication, she was sitting in a cell with Garin occupying the one next to her. Of Paul there was no sign.

"At a guess I'd say he cracked your cheekbone, maybe even the bone around your eye socket. It's gonna hurt like a son of a gun for a while."

*Good,* she thought. The pain would remind her of what a fool she'd been.

"Where are we?"

Garin shrugged. "In a cell on one of the lower levels. The complex is pretty large, from what I could see as they dragged us down here. It's not surprising, since they've had more than seventy years to work on it."

Annja used the bars at the front of her cell to pull herself upright. Her head spun for a minute, making her wonder about a concussion, but she was going to have to get used to it if she was going to get them out of here.

"You don't seem too worried about things," Annja said to him.

"Why should I be? You're going to draw your sword and get us out of here, hopefully sooner rather than later, and given what he's done I wouldn't bet on Krugmann living to see the sun come up tomorrow."

Annja shook her head. "I can't kill him."

Garin grunted. "Please don't give me any of that

crap about taking an innocent life. That man is far from innocent, in fact..."

She waved her hand, interrupting him. "It's not that. I'd kill him in a heartbeat and sleep like a baby afterward if it weren't for one thing."

"What's that?"

"We still don't know where Doug is."

Garin was quiet for a moment.

Annja knew just what he was thinking.

"I know what you're going to say," she said.

"You do?"

"Come on, Garin. We've known each other long enough to be able to anticipate a few things. You're thinking that Doug has been dead for days, maybe since the last phone call I made. But I can't assume that. If he is alive, I'll be condemning him to death if I take Krugmann out before I've had a chance to question the man."

*Funny how he was Paul before this and now he's Krugmann. Now there's a coping mechanism if I ever saw one*, she thought.

"It's your call. I'll back you either way."

Annja felt tears welling in her eyes at Garin's unqualified support. She'd certainly had her differences with this man in the past, but right now in this place and at this time there wasn't anyone she'd rather have by her side.

She was too honest with herself not to understand that she was valuing the very thing that she had always disliked about him, which was his utter ruthlessness. Garin wouldn't hesitate when the time came and right now she was finding that very reassuring. Later, she'd deal with what that meant—ethically— for her; right now, they had to get out of this place and rescue Doug.

If he was still alive.

*Don't think like that*, she scolded herself. *He's alive. You know he is.*

But if he wasn't, she was going to be sure to make Krugmann pay.

"So what…"

She didn't get any further.

The steel door on the other side of the room opened suddenly and a squad of islanders—she decided then and there that's what she was going to call them, for lack of a better name—came into the room, accompanied by the large warrior who had originally taken them captive.

"Garin?" Annja asked, wondering if now was the time for them to take their chance at getting away.

He had to have been thinking the same thing. "Your call," he replied, backing away from the door to his cell as the islanders walked over to it.

*Five against two,* Annja thought, *those are pretty good odds.*

But before she could do anything, the leader pointed at Garin and said something in his own language.

At his command, two of the islanders took the long pole-like objects that they were holding and jabbed them through the bars of Garin's cell. He managed to twist away from the first one but the second caught him square on the thigh. There was a flash and the crack of electrical current, and Garin was suddenly on the floor shaking as if he'd just stepped on a live wire.

Annja looked up to find the leader looking back at her.

"Are you going to come quietly or do I have to shock you, too?" the leader asked her in German.

Not knowing what that kind of current would do to her already fragile equilibrium, Annja decided going along with them was the best course of action for the time being. She raised her hands over her head and waited as they unlocked the door to her cell and waved her forward.

# 30

They led her down several passages and up at least two long winding ramps before coming to a door with a lock on it. The leader produced a large iron key from a chain around his neck that she hadn't noticed before and inserted it into the lock, giving it a hard turn to the left.

The lock clicked loudly and the door popped open.

The leader pushed it open the rest of the way and said, "They're waiting for you inside."

Annja didn't move. "Who's waiting?"

Her captor eyed her but didn't say anything more.

"I'm not going anywhere until..."

Her captor said something in his native tongue and the two islanders carrying the shock sticks started to turn toward her.

"All right, all right," Annja said, holding up her hands. "I'm going. There's no need to get huffy."

She walked forward until she crossed the threshold of the door her captor had just opened. He reached out to pull it closed behind her, and as he did so he said, "Watch his left foot" under his breath.

Annja was so surprised that she stood there, dumb-struck, and her chance to ask him what the heck he was talking about passed, as the door slammed shut behind her.

*Watch his left foot? Whose left foot?* she wondered. *And why is he warning me?*

She tried the door, assuming that it would be locked but knowing she had to try it anyway. The hum of many people talking at once reached her ears and she turned, looking down a passageway. It ran straight ahead of her for a dozen or more yards, then opened into a well-lit space. From where she stood, it appeared to have a sand rather than a stone floor. The sound of the crowd came from there.

Intrigued, Annja headed in that direction.

The sound grew louder as she reached the end of the tunnel and passed into the room beyond to find herself standing under the open sky, the moon brilliant and the stars twinkling high above. The amphitheater, for that's what it was, was circular in shape and about as wide as the skating rink back in Central Park. The walls rose about fifteen feet, above which rows of seats filled the space, reminding her of a gladiatorial arena. Even as she thought that, she realized that her earlier assumption was right; the floor was made of sand that looked to be several inches deep and was so reminiscent of the beach sand from the lagoon that Annja wouldn't have been surprised to learn that it had come from there.

The rows of spectator seats were full of islanders—men, women, children even—and they were all staring down at her now as if she were a bug under a microscope. She could see things changing hands between some of them and guessed that they were taking bets in whatever passed as the local currency.

That told her that she wasn't going to be alone in this arena for long.

She walked into the center of the arena and turned slowly in a circle, taking it all in. She found a shaded spectator platform with a large throne-like seat in the center directly over the tunnel through which she entered, and as she looked it over she saw a door at the back open and Colonel Schnell enter. He took a seat on the throne and then, and only then, did his entourage follow him, including several island women who gathered around his chair, fawning over him.

*No wonder the old coot doesn't want to go anywhere*, Annja thought. *He is treated like a king here.*

She was still watching him with distaste when the door at the back of the booth opened again. Krugmann entered and took up a position standing near the railing to the left of the colonel's chair.

He had an anticipatory look on his face that didn't make Annja feel comfortable at all.

He was up to something, that was for sure.

Colonel Schnell stood and raised his hands, instantly quieting the crowd around him.

"Pretty good trick," Annja said into the silence. "What are you going to do for an encore?"

It was lame, and she knew it, but it was better than just standing there waiting for something to happen to her. At least this way she'd get the last word in.

Schnell looked down at her the way a picnicker might examine an ant before stomping on it. Ignoring her remark, he addressed her in German, saying, "I have been told by the major that you are an enemy of the Reich. Is that true?"

Annja looked at him for a long moment and carefully answered in the same language. "It's hard to be an enemy of something that hasn't existed since long before I was born, don't you think?"

Krugmann spoke up. "See what I mean, Colonel? An insolent and far-from-ideal attitude."

Schnell looked over at him and Krugmann closed his mouth with a snap.

*So there isn't a lot of love between them yet,* Annja thought. She might be able to use that to her advantage. But first she needed to know what they wanted from her.

Schnell turned back to address Annja once more. "Is it still your contention that Major Kahler is lying about his reasons for being here?"

It took Annja a moment to realize that he was talking about Paul. Apparently he had decided to revert to his father's name, as if that made his actions somehow less despicable. Annja intended to disabuse him of that notion as soon as possible.

*Focus on the problem at hand,* she reminded herself.

"Of course he's lying," she replied. "That's all liars do is lie."

"Normally I wouldn't give someone outside the Party a moment's thought, but you have intrigued me."

*Be still my heart.*

"Because of that, I'm going to give you the opportunity to prove yourself truthful."

Annja laughed. "Bring on the polygraph machine then," she told him.

The colonel paused and stared at her, clearly not knowing what on earth she was talking about, and Annja felt a smile spread across her face in response. *Keep wondering old man, keep wondering.*

The colonel continued.

"Defeat your opponent, and I will consider what you say about Major Kahler. Lose, and you won't have to worry about his opinion, or mine or anyone else's for that matter. Do you understand?"

*Yes, psycho, I understand.*

Annja nodded.

*"Lasst die Spiele beginnen!"*

"Let the games begin," she translated beneath her breath.

The sound of a steel door closing drew her attention, and she turned to see the biggest islander she'd yet seen walk into the arena.

In his hand he held a nail-studded club.

Annja, of course, was unarmed.

*Gotta love a fair fight,* she thought, and then ran forward to confront him.

# 31

The islanders in the stands cheered as their hero entered the arena. He didn't acknowledge their cheers in any way but simply lumbered straight at Annja as she moved forward to greet him, although she suspected that they had two different concepts of just who the winner of this battle was going to be.

The islander ran straight at her, swinging his club at the last moment in an attempt to wipe her out with one crushing blow.

Annja ducked underneath the blow, letting the club pass harmlessly over her head as she rushed in and delivered a powerful kick to the inside of his knee.

Normally that would be enough to hyperextend the knee joint, causing the leg to collapse under its own weight.

This time it had about as much success as kicking a tree trunk. Maybe less.

Annja spun, intending to follow through by coming back in and attacking the other leg, but her opponent was much quicker for his size than she had expected. He was already lashing out with a backhand that caught her square in the chest, lifting her off her feet and dumping her in the sand a few yards away.

*Wow, that hurt!* Annja thought, as she struggled to her feet.

She heard the whistling sound of the club coming her way, and she threw herself to the side, narrowly avoiding getting knocked into next week.

She rolled when she hit, putting some distance between herself and her opponent. When she got back to her feet, she had a handful of the sand lining the floor clutched in her left hand.

The islander was already moving in, bringing the club whistling downward again, and this time Annja timed the blow, noting how long it took for him to recover and lash out again. When he was still in the middle of recovering from that second blow, Annja darted in and threw the sand in his face.

He pulled his head back, but the damage was already done. Momentarily blinded, he swung the club he was holding around him in a circle, trying to trip her up. She jumped lightly over it and twisted her body into a spinning crescent kick that she brought slamming toward his collarbone.

The blow never landed.

The islander dropped the club, grabbed her foot in midair and yanked her toward him, intending to smother her in his grasp.

Anticipating that very move, Annja let him draw her closer and then lashed out, trying to smash the side of her hand into the soft, unprotected flesh of his throat, only to have him drop his chin at the last moment, deflecting the blow.

They went around and around like that with neither of them gaining the upper hand but causing a number of minor injuries along the way.

Annja knew she could draw her sword at any time, but doing so would reveal her secret not only to all of the islanders sitting in the stands but also to Krugmann and Schnell. That was something she wanted to avoid at all costs, for there would be little doubt that they would use all of the resources at their disposal to try to take the sword from her at that point and use it for their own nefarious ends.

So instead of simply skewering the big guy where he stood, Annja was going to have to whittle away at him piece by piece until she could deliver the final blow that sent him to the ground.

She was moving away from another of his strikes when she remembered what her captor had said at the entrance to the arena.

*Watch his left foot.*

She did so and what she saw was so obvious that she was surprised she needed anyone to point it out to her.

Every time the islander prepared himself for a strike, he pivoted on his left foot, anchoring it in place to give him as much torque as possible.

Annja knew she could use that to her advantage.

*Thank you, whatever your name is,* she thought.

They circled each other warily again, Annja biding her time and the island warrior doing the same.

Krugmann shouted something from the stands, and the islander used the temporary distraction to rush at Annja again.

Rather than skipping backward out of reach, which had been her modus operandi for the entire fight, Annja did the exact opposite, rushing forward and kicking that unsupported leg with everything she had.

It folded like a house of cards.

The warrior dropped to one knee, leaving his face and head unprotected.

Annja chose that moment to leap into the air, spinning at the apex of her leap, and lashing out with a perfectly executed heel kick that struck the warrior in the side of the temple.

"Timber!" she wanted to shout as the mountain of a man crashed forward to lie unmoving on the arena floor.

The crowd shouted and cried out.

Panting, she turned and saw the surprised expression on both Krugmann's face and Schnell's.

"Guess I'm telling the truth," Annja called up to Schnell. "Maybe it's time you put Krugmann to the same test."

Whatever Schnell was going to say in return was interrupted as the door to his observation platform burst open and four men with submachine guns in their hands crowded into the narrow space and held their guns on everyone in there, including Schnell.

To the gunmen's surprise, but not Annja's, the old Nazi let his displeasure be known. "What is the meaning of this?" he shouted at the newcomers.

Krugmann answered for them with a very smug smile on his face. "This, dear Colonel, is a military coup. If you do as you are told, no one has to get hurt, least of all you."

"What do you want?"

"The gold, of course," Krugmann said.

"I'm not giving you anything," Schnell replied.

Krugmann drew the gun at his hip and shot the old man in the foot.

Schnell screamed.

"Oh, shut up,!" Krugmann said. "Get over here before I put the next bullet in your head."

Schnell snapped his mouth shut and hobbled over to Krugmann, who passed him over to one of his men.

As Schnell was being led out of the observation booth at gunpoint, Krugmann nodded at one of the men who stood behind him with a submachine gun. That man withdrew a walkie-talkie from his pocket and radioed someone else. Seconds later the door her first opponent had entered through swung open and three of Krugmann's men entered the arena.

All of them were armed with a club or some form of bladed weapon, and they used them to laconically salute Annja.

Krugmann laughed at the sight. "I'm surprised at you, Annja. I thought for sure you would figure it out long before this. Every time I thought you had, you ended up surprising me with your blind ignorance. Which is really too bad, as I assumed you'd be a better opponent than that."

"Come on down here and I'll show you just how

good I am," Annja shouted, without taking her eyes off the three men standing on the other side of the arena.

"Sorry, dear, but I don't have time to waste on such petty problems. While you lie dying there in the sand, I want you to think about the fact that not one, but two of your friends are now in my custody. I'm going to enjoy using them in new and interesting ways."

With that parting remark, Krugmann left the observation deck.

Down below, on the arena sand, Annja watched her opponents move in.

# 32

With Krugmann and Schnell no longer around, Annja decided it was time to even the odds somewhat.

Reaching into the otherwhere, she drew her sword, watching in satisfaction as it appeared whole and fully formed in her hand just a second later.

Whatever was left of the once boisterous audience went deathly quiet.

Feeling far more confident, Annja moved in to face her attackers.

The three men split up as they got closer, moving to surround her and make it so she couldn't keep her eyes on all three of them at once. They were playing a cautious game, and that made her think they'd heard a bit about her prowess with a blade.

Annja, of course, had no intention of doing anything of the sort. Rather than wait for them to surround her, Annja picked one of her attackers and charged directly at him, hoping to put him down before the other attackers had a chance to move in on her unprotected back.

As she leaped forward, her attacker tried to backpedal and give time for his allies to close in on Annja from behind.

Unfortunately for him, he'd never trained on sand and didn't know how to move in it gracefully. The heel of his shoe caught in the sand behind him, tripping him up. As he flailed his arms for balance, Annja rushed forward and skewered him through the chest.

When she pulled the blade out, he gave a shuddering little sigh and collapsed to the ground to move no more.

The ferocity of her attack gave the other two men pause, but only for a moment. Clearly they thought they were better than the man who had been killed, so they moved in with confidence, weapons at the ready, determined to complete their assignment.

That confidence, and the way it made them view Annja as an opponent not worthy of their attention, would prove to be their undoing.

Annja waited for one of the men to move in close, trying to draw her into an attack and thereby give the other man a chance to strike at her unprotected rear.

It was a simple plan and might even have worked if Annja didn't have a plan of her own.

She played along with what they were doing, pretending not to know that they were playing a game of cat and mouse with her. When the man in front of her began backpedaling to get away from her, just as her previous attacker had done, Annja abruptly spun and charged the man behind her.

He had been expecting to rush forward and attack her from behind and therefore actually took several more steps in her direction before he realized that she wasn't moving away from him as expected. That she was, in fact, rushing directly at him screaming at the top of her lungs.

The killer tried to stop his forward momentum but it was already too late. Annja rushed him, they had a short but decisive exchange of blows, and then she was turning away to face her third and final opponent while his buddy lay bleeding to death in the warm sand behind her.

This time Annja moved to the center of the arena and stood there, waiting.

*If you want a piece of me, you're going to have to come get it,* she thought.

Her opponent hesitated, but only for a moment. Apparently his fear of punishment at Krugmann's hands was more daunting than the idea of dying right then and there, for he advanced on her slowly and carefully, exchanging blow after blow but taking no chances.

Annja bided her time, waiting for an opening, until she realized that the thug in front of her was deliberately stalling, no doubt to let Krugmann get away.

The thought of that man escaping the hand of justice was almost too much to bear.

*Enough of this!* Annja thought.

They struck and parried, struck and parried, then Annja pretended to lose her balance and stumbled backward.

When the man overreached in an effort to pin her down, Annja trapped his sword with her own and then flung it away, disarming him and leaving him defenseless.

"Look, I'm just following…"

Annja lunged forward, driving her sword through the man's shoulder. He screamed and fell backward, with Annja tearing the blade out as he fell.

She quickly straddled him and pressed the edge of the blade against his throat. "I want some answers and I want them now!"

Five minutes later, Annja moved cautiously through the tunnels, trying to find her way back to where she and Garin had been kept prisoner. She did her best to avoid running into any islanders, and the one time she couldn't she left the young man in a darkened corner after a swift blow to his head with the flat of her sword.

After several minutes of stumbling around in the tunnels, she found the room she was looking for.

Garin, however, was no longer there.

"They took him away," a voice said from behind her in German. Annja whirled to find the colonel's right-hand man standing there, the one who had taken them prisoner at the submarine.

"What do you mean they took him away?"

"Just what I said. Shortly after you entered the arena, the dark one's men came and took him away. One of them said something about returning to the boat, but that was all that I overheard."

Annja was confused. "Why are you helping me?"

The islander shrugged. "Is it not said that the enemy of my enemy is my friend?"

Annja answered that with a folk saying of her own. "Yes, but it is also said that you should keep your friends close and your enemies closer."

The islander smiled. "It would seem that you are going to have to decide to trust me on nothing more than the wisdom of our elders."

*Fat chance of that, buddy,* she thought.

Annja tried to push past him, but he reached out and stopped her.

"Listen to me a moment. I believe that I can help you."

"Help me? I'm not even sure I can trust you."

"My people have been controlled by others for far too long. Now we may finally act. You have given us that chance, we will give something to you."

*Ah. So the islanders weren't willing participants in all of this after all. At least they hadn't started out that way.*

"And you think that if you help me, I will help you free your people from the yoke of this man and those who support him?"

"Yes," he answered simply.

She would, too; that's just the kind of person she was.

But first Garin, and then Doug.

"You've got a deal."

She showed him how to shake on it, then asked him to take her to the elevator back to the top of the caldera. She was convinced that Krugmann would return to the boat he had talked about to get reinforcements and to begin loading the gold as his men removed it from its mountain hideaway. If she could get aboard that boat, she could rescue Garin and possibly discover where Krugmann was keeping Doug.

After that, who knew? First things first.

As she headed through the underground tunnels with her co-conspirator in the lead, Annja asked, "What do I call you?"

He glanced back at her and grinned. "My name is Matahi."

"Okay. And you can call me Annja."

His grin widened.

Several times along the journey they passed other islanders, and each time Matahi had a quick conversation with them, no doubt to invent some reason the colonel's prisoner was roaming around free.

At last, when she thought she couldn't take any more of this underground passage, they emerged onto the ledge where the elevator hung.

Neither basket was there, more proof that Krugmann had not remained within the facility but had, in fact, returned to the top of the caldera. Since he was most familiar with how the elevator worked, Annja let Matahi call one of the cars down while she tried to work out a plan for what to do when they caught up with Krugmann.

Unfortunately she was pretty much out of ideas— at least productive ones—in that regard.

It took nearly twenty minutes for the car to reach them. When it did, Annja and Matahi climbed in and then shut the gate behind them. Matahi took control of the crank and began to wind it, starting the elevator car on its long ride up to the top of the caldera.

Annja spent the time worrying about Garin and wondering if Doug was still alive.

They heard the bullet ricochet off the side of the basket before they heard the report of the shot, but the latter was only a second or two behind.

They looked around frantically, trying to spot who was shooting at them.

"Look! There!" Matahi shouted.

About a hundred yards above them, the second car was on its way down. In the basket were two men, both of whom were leaning over the side and pointing rifles toward Annja and her companion.

"What do we do?" Matahi asked.

"Duck!"

He did as he was told just as a pair of shots whizzed by.

They were in trouble and Annja knew it. As long as the other basket was allowed to descend or ascend, then the men in it could fire at them at will until they killed them.

If they wanted to survive, they had to take out those riflemen.

There was only one problem.

Neither Matahi nor Annja had any kind of weapon with which to return fire.

They were going to have to do it the hard way.

"How quickly can you get us level with them?" Annja asked.

Matahi looked at her like she'd just lost her mind.

"Level? Won't that make it easier for them to shoot us?"

"Not if I can dissuade them."

"And how are you going to manage that?" he asked her.

"Let me worry about that. For now, just get us up there!"

Shaking his head at the craziness of the idea but doing it anyway, Matahi crouched lower in the basket and focused on turning the crank, resuming their upward motion.

While he did that, Annja tried to figure out what it was going to take to get the basket rocking back and forth far enough that she could get close to the other one.

Thankfully, the men in the second basket were terrible shots. The bullets missed, sailing off into the distance or bouncing off the nearby rock and showering them with stone fragments.

As the firing continued, Annja walked back and forth from one side of the basket to the other, using her weight to get it to start swinging like a pendulum.

"What are you doing?" Matahi asked in a shaky voice, letting go of the crank to grab tightly to the sides of the basket. There were no safety belts, and it was a long way down to the bottom.

A long way—yes, but a relatively short trip should a person fall.

Annja glanced at him, but didn't stop her motion. "I'm making us a more difficult target for them to hit."

"They won't have to hit us if you make us fall out. Stop that."

Annja shook her head and kept up her steady motion. "We have to take out that other basket or they can just sit there and fire at us until we're finally hit."

Matahi's eyes grew wide. "You are insane."

"No, I just want to live."

"You've got a crazy way of showing it," the islander replied, but he kept cranking the handle and moving them slowly up the inside of the volcano.

As they got higher and the other basket came lower, the gunshots were starting to come closer. Matahi suffered a cut to his cheek when a bullet caused some fragments of rock to explode from the cliff face beside him. If the basket hadn't been moving side to side, the shooter probably would have taken them both out by now.

Annja ducked lower but kept moving back and forth.

It wouldn't be long now.

Finally the baskets were at the point where they were almost parallel to each other. Their fate would be decided in the next few minutes, Annja knew, and she prepared herself for what was to come.

She was only going to get one chance at this.

Annja waited until they were swinging away from the second basket to quickly explain her plan to Matahi. "When the basket swings the other way, there will be a moment at the farthest edge of our swing when we will be perfectly lined up with the other basket. That will be our moment to act. No matter what happens, keep the basket swinging. Got it?"

The islander nodded, clearly scared out of his wits by the swaying of the cage but determined to handle it and be of use to her. Annja admired his bravery; a person had to be a little insane to attempt what she was about to do, but frankly she didn't see any way around it. They'd been lucky so far, but this close the gunmen really couldn't miss unless they were complete incompetents. That still might be the case, but she wasn't betting on it.

The cage completed its swing to the outside and started heading back in the other direction. Annja crouched behind the side wall and watched the other cage as they rapidly swung toward it.

*Wait for it*, she told herself, *steady...*

Bullets were bouncing off the side of the cage now, the shooter in the other basket firing straight at them at this point. Annja gritted her teeth and ordered herself to resist the urge to duck for she needed to be ready to move.

*Steady...*

Annja's cage was headed toward the other at full speed, and the shooter finally decided that discretion was the better part of valor and ducked behind the walls of his own cage. If the two collided, he didn't want to be knocked over the side.

It was exactly the move Annja had been counting on.

The cage reached the farthest point of its swing. For a moment it hung there, directly opposite the other. Annja jumped to her feet, snatched her sword from the otherwhere and slashed at the cables holding the other cage up.

She felt the shock of connection before she heard the loud crack of the cables giving way.

For just an instant she was poised there, sword outstretched, staring into the eyes of the shooter as he crouched next to his partner near the crank, the rifle in his hands pointed directly at her.

His finger twitched on the trigger.

The cage started its swing back in the other direction, pulling her a fraction of an inch to the side as the bullet whipped through her hair without striking anything solid, fortunately not blowing her head to smithereens.

Then they were headed back in the other direction, and Annja released the sword. She watched as the other basket began to tilt downward, the cable holding it in place no longer in one piece. Annja could see the shooter and his partner grabbing for the side of the cage, not quite understanding yet that they weren't falling out of it but that it was falling along with them.

Annja stared as they dropped out of sight.

She turned and found Matahi peering at her in horror.

"What did you do?" he gasped.

"Taught them that shooting at us is a very bad idea."

She glanced over the side of the cage in the direction the other had fallen and then amended her statement. "Make that *was* a very bad idea."

Matahi grunted.

She was about to say something in her defense when there was a loud bang from above her head and one side of the cage suddenly dipped downward.

Annja instinctively grabbed the main cable over their heads with one hand and Matahi's arm with the other just as the basket dropped out from beneath under their feet!

# 33

Annja hung there, hundreds of feet above the ground, holding on to Matahi with one hand and to the cable above her head with the other.

Below her, her new friend screamed in fear and kicked his legs as if looking for support where none existed. If he kept it up, she was going to drop him.

"Hey, knock it off!" she said.

He kept screaming and moving about.

"Matahi! Knock it off, Matahi, or you're going to make me drop you!"

That seemed to get through to him for he suddenly started repeating something in his native language, over and over again. Annja couldn't understand him, but she figured it was something along the lines of "Don't drop me!"

If he held still, she probably wouldn't.

Probably.

"Stop kicking and squirming around!"

At last he stopped moving.

They were still swaying from side to side just as they'd been before the cage had come apart around them, which was just making matters worse, but there wasn't anything they could do about that now.

Annja knew there was no way she was going to be able to support Matahi's weight for long. Not like this, at any rate. They needed to get off this cable.

But how?

She glanced above her head and could see that they were still about a hundred, maybe a hundred and fifty feet from the top. That was a long way to go, but it was doable at least. She'd climbed higher before.

*Yeah, but not right after fighting four big men in hand-to-hand combat and holding a large man's weight with only one hand.*

She told her inner voice to shut up and, surprisingly, it did.

This was not the time for negative thoughts.

She could feel her shoulders already burning from the pull being exerted on them in both directions. She didn't have much time; she needed to figure this out and figure it out fast.

She let herself drift in a slow circle and looked at the nearby wall of the caldera. It was pitted with fissures and cracks, just the kind of things that could serve as hand- and footholds for an experienced climber. She'd climbed harder faces than that.

*Yeah, but not without a rope,* her inner voice piped up.

*Quiet, you!* she told it. *It's not like I've got a choice here. I've free climbed a steep slope or two before. I can do this one.*

But could Matahi?

That she didn't know.

"Matahi, can you hear me?"

"Yes," came the shaky reply.

"We need to get off this rope and onto the rock wall beside us."

His fingers tightened around her wrist. "What? What are you talking about?"

"I can't hold you much longer, and I doubt I can hold on long enough for you to climb up and over me to shimmy up the rope. So we need to climb up the inside of the wall."

"That's crazy!"

"Crazy or not, it's the only chance we've got."

"But…"

She'd had enough. "Shut up and listen to me or we're both going to die!"

Matahi shut his mouth with a snap.

"You need to kick your legs toward the wall so we start swinging toward it. That way you can grab hold of it when we get closer."

"Kick my legs?"

"Yes, but gently."

He made a couple of tentative motions that got them moving slightly, but not enough.

"Harder, Matahi. A little harder."

He did as he was told, and after a few minutes they were swinging almost all the way to the wall. Annja could see that the area they were facing had some bomber climbing holds that she could grab to get her off the rope.

But she couldn't do anything until she let go of Matahi.

"When we get close to the wall, I want you to grab on to it and hang on."

"I can't do that!"

"Yes, you can. Just reach out and grab something with your free hand when we get close."

To his credit, he tried. They swung close to the wall and he reached out and touched the rock, but couldn't get his hand wrapped around anything and they swung back again with him flailing about.

Annja gritted her teeth and did everything she could to hold on to him, but she could feel his weight dragging her farther down the cable she was holding on to.

"We're running out of time, Matahi. I can't hold us much longer. You have to grab the wall and hold on to it this time."

He didn't reply, but when she looked down she could see that he was flexing the fingers of his free hand, getting ready to make another try.

They were still swinging to and fro, and it was a simple matter now to nudge them close enough for him to reach out a second time.

"Got it!" he called out at the same time she felt some resistance to her swing.

"Okay, find a foothold for your feet. When you've got something secure enough to hold you, let go of my arm."

"I can't do that."

"Of course you can," she told him.

If he didn't let go soon, there was nothing she was going to be able to save him. It was as simple as that.

"On the count of three, okay?"

She didn't wait for his reply.

"One…"

"Two…"

"Three!"

To her immense relief she felt the weight come off her left arm as the islander clung to the face of the cliff instead.

Now it was her turn.

She swung toward the rock face and quickly chose a handhold before she swung back out again. Keeping her gaze fixed firmly on that spot, she waited for the cable to send her back in that direction on the reverse side of the swing, mentally counting in her head.

*One…two…three…*

She threw herself against the wall, jamming her hand inside the crack she'd seen on the first swing and twisting it to one side, using the pressure of her fist against the interior of the space to hold her there for the few seconds it took for her feet to find a corresponding perch.

At last she was secure against the rock, using her legs to support her to give her aching arms a rest. She put her forehead against the stone and breathed a sigh of relief.

That had been a little too close for comfort.

*It's not over yet,* she reminded herself. *You still have to climb to the top.*

"You still with me, Matahi?"

All she got was a grunt from below her, but that told her he was still alive, at least, and that was good enough.

"We need to start climbing while we still have the strength. One hold at a time, okay? Find a spot for your right hand, then your left, then do the same for your feet. It's not a race. Take your time and make sure each hold is secure, understand?"

Then another thought occurred to her.

"No matter what you do, don't look down."

Having exhausted all of her advice, she began to make her own ascent. There was nothing more she could do for her companion; he was going to make it or he wasn't. It was as simple as that.

*Reach up with the right hand and find a hold,* she urged herself. *Do the same with the left. Move the right foot to a new location. Do the same with the left. One small movement at a time, over and over again.*

She didn't think about where she was or how much farther she had to go. She couldn't afford the distraction. All it would take was one wrong move, one loose grip, and it would be so long Nelly.

Doug still needed her. Now Garin needed her, too.

There was no way she was falling off this volcano!

After what felt like hours of inching upward one hand- or foothold at a time, Annja reached up over her head and felt nothing but air. She looked up and discovered the lip of the caldera just inches away.

*Don't get hasty now,* she reminded herself. *Plenty of climbers have been injured on those last few moves where they thought they were in the clear.*

Making certain she had solid holds, she pulled herself up and over the edge. When she had her feet up, she rolled away from the drop and lay there on her back, staring into the sky for several minutes as the shakes she'd been resisting for so long suddenly took hold of her and racked her frame.

When the fear had passed, she eased herself back over to the edge and peered down the cliff face. At first she didn't see Matahi and she feared the worst. Had he fallen off and she hadn't noticed?

Then she spotted him less than twenty feet from the top, moving slowly and cautiously as she'd been doing. She wanted to encourage him but didn't want to break his concentration, so she just silently cheered him on and was ready to help him over the top when he reached it.

Together they lay on their backs and worked to calm their beating hearts.

Matahi mumbled something in his native language.

"What was that?" she asked.

He repeated himself, this time in German. "Shoot me if I ever want to do something as stupid as that again."

Annja laughed. "Gladly."

She pushed to her feet and swung her arms about, making sure they had good circulation so that the lactic acid buildup would dissolve faster and they'd cramp less.

Matahi looked up at her.

"Where are you going?"

"To save my friends, remember?"

He was silent for a time, then said, "I knew there was a reason we did that crazy stunt. I just couldn't remember what it was."

"Well, if you can get me down to the beach, I promise you won't have to help me any farther."

Matahi smiled. "That's a deal."

# 34

After the confrontation on the elevators and the climb up the inside of the volcano, the hike through the jungle was anticlimactic. Matahi led her to safety with unerring accuracy.

Twice they stopped to refresh themselves from the stalks of certain plants that her companion pulled up and cut open. Annja was glad he was there; she would have been dying of thirst by the time they made it to the lagoon if she had to do this alone.

Dawn was only starting to creep over the horizon when they reached the trees sheltering the beach. Annja could see the hulk of the U-boat and beyond that, anchored in the cove, was the *Reliant*.

But they weren't the only two boats out there.

A massive yacht was now moored a few yards away from the *Reliant*. It flew a Swiss registration flag and had five decks plus a large helipad on the aft section of the upper deck. It had its running lights on, and in the moonlight it was easy to see the ship's name, *Redemption*, was painted in red on the side.

*Figures.*

She could see a handful of guards patrolling the decks, but this far out in the Pacific she expected that discipline would be lax. She should be able to sneak aboard without too much trouble. Then it was just a matter of locating Garin, getting him off the boat, and locating Krugmann so that she could find out where Doug was being held.

Nothing to it.

She turned to Matahi and put out her hand.

"Thank you. I couldn't have gotten this far without you."

He shook her hand. "You will be all right from here?"

"Yes," she lied, not really having any idea but not wanting to endanger him any further.

"All right then, I will return to tend to my people. Good luck to you, Annja Creed."

And then, like a ghost, he was gone, disappearing into the jungle behind her.

Annja waited a few minutes and then made her way down to the water's edge. She stayed in a crouch, in case there was a sentry on the beach that she hadn't seen, but the view seemed clear and she didn't run into anyone before she reached the lagoon. She guessed that the yacht was about fifty yards offshore, which would be a good swim but not a particularly trying one.

She sat on the sand, took off her shoes and left them near the pier. She eased into the water, not wanting to make any more noise than absolutely necessary, and then gently began swimming in the direction of the yacht. The water was cool but not cold, and thanks to the protected nature of the lagoon it was as flat as a sheet. She swam first to the *Reliant*, which was moored closer to shore than the *Redemption*, and hung on the side for a moment, listening. It didn't sound as if anyone was aboard so she swam around to the diver's platform at the back and pulled herself onto it.

She knelt there, listening, making sure that she was alone. Satisfied that there was no one else aboard, she crossed the cockpit to the companionway and slipped down into the darkness of the lower deck.

Knowing how easily sound carried across the water, she kept her motions small and moved slowly where and when she could. It had been hours since she'd eaten, so she got some food out of the refrigerator and ate a couple of quick sandwiches, gulping them down with a glass of water. The food revitalized her, gave her the energy she knew she would need for the next step of her plan.

She went back up on deck, this time carrying Garin's binoculars, and spent some time studying the activity across the lagoon aboard the *Redemption*.

She made out four guards, two on the top deck and one each on the second and third decks. They were carrying automatic rifles, but she couldn't tell what make from this distance. They appeared to be wearing some kind of uniform, as well, but it was hard to tell exactly what.

A glance at the battery-powered clock in the cockpit told her that it was coming up on 4:00 a.m. The sun would be up in another two hours. She needed to get aboard the yacht, find Garin and get him out before the sun came up at 6:30. She wasn't sure she could do it. Given the size of the boat, it might take her that long just to search two decks. Hopefully she'd get lucky sooner rather than later.

Hopefully both Garin and Doug were still alive.

She put the binoculars away and changed into a bathing suit. Grabbing an extra set of swim fins from the locker on deck, she slipped them on and lowered herself into the water at the rear of the boat. She set out swimming for the yacht, using the fins to give her more power underwater without the noise that kicking her feet on the surface would have made.

Ten minutes later, she reached her destination.

It looked much bigger from her current vantage point down at the waterline. She'd hoped to be able to just pull herself over the side, but the boat rode much higher in the water than she'd expected and the railing was several feet out of reach. She began to make a slow circuit of the craft, looking for another option she could use to get aboard. She finally found what she needed on the port side aft. The launch ramp had a cigarette boat currently stored on it, but there was plenty of room for her to pull herself out of the water and walk up the ramp to the lower deck.

Annja moved as quietly as she could, not wanting to call attention to herself until it was absolutely necessary, at which point she intended to make as much noise as possible to help cover her escape with Garin.

She began quietly opening doors and checking the rooms beyond, not knowing where Krugmann was keeping his captive. Why he hadn't just killed Garin earlier Annja didn't know. She supposed it was because Krugmann had decided, from all he'd seen during their time together, that Garin was wealthy and perhaps he could ransom him to someone, his family or the board of directors of one of his multinational corporations.

Perhaps Krugmann was hedging his bets in case she defeated his henchmen. Was Garin merely being used as bait?

That was a distinct possibility, too.

The third room she checked happened to be the engine room, and she saw that it had a map of the boat hung on the bulkhead. She spent a few minutes memorizing the layout of the boat as best she could. Who knew when that information might come in handy?

She had just opened the door across from the engine room when she heard voices coming in her direction. She slipped into the dark room and pushed the door most of the way closed, leaving only a little crack through which she could watch and listen.

The guards stopped in the middle of the passageway, outside the room in which Annja was hiding. One of them produced a pack of cigarettes, European by the look of them, and passed both a cigarette and a lighter to his buddy. They lit up and stood around, either on break or just not caring that they might get caught. They spoke in English, but Annja couldn't pinpoint their accent, which meant they could be from anywhere.

Most of what they discussed was inconsequential to Annja—the latest football scores (British football, not American), the shift they'd been assigned to for the next week, and how glad they were that they didn't have to shadow that stupid sailboat they'd been following through terrible weather for the past couple of days. Annja was aware of the ticking clock and was getting ready to step out and give them the action they'd complained they were lacking, when one of them told the other that the boss had returned to the boat with two prisoners in tow. One had been placed in the suite next to the owner's while the other had been tossed into the storage closet on deck two. They seemed to find that funny, given just how many empty suites and other accommodations were available on a boat that size, but the boss wanted him locked in a closet so locked in a closet he would be.

The men finished their cigarettes and moved on. Annja gave them a few minutes and then slipped out of the room and returned to the engine room next door. She went straight to the diagram of the boat, found the storage closet she thought they were talking about and worked out a path to get to it that didn't leave her too exposed.

She moved to the rear of the boat and climbed the steps to the deck above, hiding for a few minutes in a shadowed alcove until the guard passed by. She knew from watching their routine from the *Reliant* that she had six and a half minutes before the guard completed his sweep and returned to the same spot. She pulled open the door to the interior hallway and quickly but quietly padded along on her bare feet, counting doors as she went.

Reaching it, she tried the handle.

It was locked, which wasn't unexpected.

"Garin? Are you in there?" she whispered through the door. She paused and then heard a muffled reply from within. She couldn't tell what the person was saying, but there was definitely someone inside.

"If you can hear me, get back from the door. I'm going to break it open, and I don't want you to get hurt in the process."

She gave him a moment and then reached into the otherwhere for her sword. She inserted the point between the doorjamb and the door itself, then levered it down and out.

The door popped open with a crack.

She glanced at her watch.

Three and a half minutes to go.

She opened the door and stepped inside. It was a linen closet. Shelves lined the walls, and she could see labels that said Double, Economy, King and Queen, as well as others noting a particular pattern or emblem on the towels they contained.

Pressed up against the far wall, only his upper body visible in the light, was a man in dirty clothes with a hood over his head.

Annja hurried over to him and pulled off the hood.

Doug Morrell sat there blinking with his hands and feet tied together and a gag tied around his mouth.

"Doug!" Annja couldn't believe it.

He tried to say something, but the gag wouldn't let him.

Annja fought with the knot for a second and then managed to get it free.

Doug cleared his throat, spit up a bloody wad of phlegm, and then said in a voice that sounded as if it hadn't been used in a while, "You've got to get out of here! It's a trap!"

# 35

"A trap?" Annja said. "For whom?"

"For you!"

Doug tried to stand up, but his feet were still tied together and he would have toppled over if Annja hadn't caught him.

"Hang on," she said. She bent and used the sword to slash through his bonds. She did the same with those on his hands and wrists before helping him to his feet, taking care with his injured hand.

He looked to be in fairly decent shape for a man who had been held prisoner for more than two weeks. His face was bruised and three of his fingers were broken, but it appeared that they were feeding him regularly and had tended to his injuries.

Annja was so glad to see him that she did something she very rarely did.

She pulled him close and gave him a big hug.

Doug squirmed and tried to get free, which only went to show her just how agitated he actually was.

"I'm serious," he said. "You have to leave. This whole thing has been a setup to get you here. He said something about wanting the sword, which, at a guess, I'd say is the one you are holding in your hands. What the heck are you doing with a sword anyway?"

Yep, that was Doug all right. Nonstop talk that jumped from subject to subject. It was good to have him back. Now all she had to do was get him off the boat.

But it wasn't going to be that easy.

"He wants the sword, huh? He'll have to come and get it, then."

A voice spoke from the doorway behind her.

"Don't mind if I do."

It was followed immediately by a soft spitting sound and a quick little jab in her neck.

Annja spun.

Paul Krugmann stood in the doorway of the closet, a dart gun in one hand.

Annja reached up and found the dart embedded in her neck.

She opened her mouth to say something, but the darkness claimed her before she could utter a word.

THREE HOURS LATER, Annja came to with a pounding headache and an awful taste in her mouth.

"Here, drink this," a voice said, and a glass of water was placed against her lips.

Suddenly realizing how thirsty she was, Annja tried to guzzle it down.

"Easy, easy now," the voice said, pulling the glass away. "Those tranqs play havoc on a person's stomach. You don't want to be spitting it all up again right away."

She turned her head to see Garin standing there with the glass of water.

"More?"

"Please," she croaked.

He gave her some and then let her take the glass herself.

Annja looked around, saw Doug sitting on a couch nearby and asked, "Where are we?"

"Locked up in a stateroom aboard Krugmann's yacht. Son of a gun is probably as rich as I am, given the size of this thing."

"He wants more than the gold we already found for him."

Garin leaned in so that Doug couldn't overhear. "I can guess. He wants the sword, too."

"Yeah. Well, he can't have it."

No one was taking that sword away from her while she was still alive, that was for sure.

"So he noticed. He thought he had you dead to rights in that closet, what with you standing there sword in hand and everything. As soon as those tranqs hit your system though, the sword vanished right in front of him as if it had never been there. Boy, was he angry."

Garin smiled at the memory.

"Good," Annja said. "Serves him right."

Garin walked away to stare out the window at Wolf Island. "Yes and no. Good because he doesn't have the sword yet. Bad because he's unlikely to give up until he gets it."

"We'll just have to disabuse him of that notion, won't we?"

Garin nodded, but didn't say anything more.

When Annja felt a little better, she went over and talked to Doug a bit, asking how he was feeling and if he wanted to talk about what had happened. None of the story was particularly original as it turned out.

He'd been heading to where he'd parked his car down the street from his office when a plain white van pulled up and asked if he could help with directions. Doug had stopped, the doors to the van opened and he'd found himself being hustled inside before he could even call for help. His captors had kept him in a safe house for a few days and then flown him halfway around the world, where they had finally boarded the boat to come here.

That was all he'd seen or heard until his kidnapper had busted in a few hours ago, talking about a magical sword and what he could do if he had it in his control. Then he questioned Doug about it. Doug was punched around a bit when he told the man that he had no idea what he was talking about. That's when his captor had mentioned Annja's name and locked Doug in the storage closet, believing she would come for him.

Which, as it turned out, he was right about.

Now they were all stuck.

"We're not stuck. Trust me on that one," she told him, approaching the door and trying the handle.

Locked, as Garin had said.

But she wasn't Garin.

"Hey!" she shouted, startling the other two in the room. "I want to talk with Krugmann!"

She kept it up for five minutes until someone came to the door, told her to pipe down and promised that he'd tell the boss that she wanted to talk.

Not too long after that the door was unlocked and a pair of guards stood outside. One pointed at Annja and said, "You, out. The major wants to see you."

"Now, hold on," Garin began, stepping in front of Annja and blocking the way. "She's not going anywhere alone."

The guards laughed. "Well, I guess it's a good thing for us that he wants all of you, then."

Garin nodded as if he'd gotten them to change their plans and followed Annja and Doug out the door.

The guards took them up another level and out to the bow, where there was a large open area that was sometimes used as a tennis court and sometimes as Krugmann's personal training and practice area.

Krugmann was there, dressed in a white fencing suit, a blade in his hand. Schnell was there as well, sitting in the shade under a sun umbrella, a fruity-looking drink in his hand. He was still dressed in his ancient SS uniform, with his foot bandaged, and looking decidedly out of place on the modern ship.

The guards dragged Garin and Doug over to some folding chairs on the other side of the training area, and pushed Annja out in the center where Krugmann was.

"Annja," Paul said with a smile. "How good of you to join us."

"Whatever, Krugmann. I'm not in the mood for your games."

Paul chuckled. "Oh, but what fun those games have been these past few weeks. I must say, seeing you in action tonight was even more amazing than I imagined. I mean that with all sincerity. I stuck around, you know, to watch the fight with my men. You cannot imagine my complete surprise when that sword appeared from thin air."

Annja didn't say anything.

That didn't seem to matter to Paul, who apparently wanted to gloat about how he had manipulated her.

"I had heard the rumors that you had an almost mystical way of finding lost cities and hidden treasures. But I must admit I was more than a bit skeptical that you could pull it off. I needed to be sure that you had just the right motivation to keep pushing you forward."

Paul smirked. "That's where I ran into some problems, you see. You don't have any family. Don't have any friends, either, not real ones. No one that I could snatch off the street and threaten in order to get you to do what needed to be done. No one except that pathetic individual seated over there."

He pointed to Doug.

"I didn't think it would work. Why would she care about him? I asked myself, and all of my answers were lacking. But I went through with the plan anyway. If it didn't work, I knew I could always fall back on threatening a child or, even better, a whole school of them, to get you to cooperate.

"But to my utter surprise my plan worked even better than I thought possible. You were like a mother bear protecting her cubs. And the way you went after the task at hand? Such focus! Such dedication! I applaud you."

And he did too, putting his épée under his arm and giving a couple of little claps in her direction.

"How'd you do it?" Annja asked. It was the one question she wanted an answer to. She thought she knew how it was done, but she didn't want to guess, she wanted answers.

"Do what, exactly?"

"Make the calls to me when you were sitting right there beside me the whole time. It wasn't you, was it? Just one of your flunkies?"

"Oh, the first time it was me, all right. After our afternoon escapade you wanted to clean up before dinner and that gave me plenty of time to make the call once I knew my team had picked up the bait back in New York. The sound of your voice when you realized it was all true…"

Annja took a step toward him, her anger burning red hot.

He eyed her from his standing position and suddenly she knew that was exactly what he wanted, for her to call the sword and attack. He stood on the balls of his feet, practically vibrating with anticipation.

She stopped and threw out another question to distract him.

"And the diver in the Alps? Was that you, too?"

"No, someone I hired to do the job. I thought I

might be able to continue from there on my own but, as it happened, that wasn't the case and I was actually quite pleased it worked out that way after all."

Annja nodded. That was what she had expected.

"And the night of the storm? You were signaling this boat, weren't you?"

She remembered the dark shape that she'd thought she saw gliding by in the midst of the storm. She hadn't thought much about it at the time, but now, in hindsight…

"That was my one mistake," Krugmann admitted. "As you suspect, I was out on deck, signaling my team, when that stupid boom swung free and knocked me right off the boat. I found it deliciously ironic later to think that if it hadn't been for you and Garin, I would have drowned before finding the island. Fortunate that you both were there, wasn't it?"

"Yeah," Annja answered dryly. "Very fortunate."

"So here we are at last," Paul said. "At the end of our journey together."

"Is it now?" Annja said.

Paul smiled, but there was nothing friendly in the expression. "I want that sword."

Annja didn't bother to pretend she didn't know what he was talking about. He'd seen. Once that particular secret was out of the bag there was no stuffing it back in again.

"You can't have it."

"Even if it costs your two friends over there their lives?"

Annja didn't blink. "Even then."

There was no way she was giving up the sword to a monster like the one standing in front of her. Garin knew that. Doug, well, she'd done what she could. Almost made it, too.

Krugmann snapped his fingers and the guards pulled out their guns and pointed them at Garin's and Doug's heads.

Garin didn't say anything but Doug shot a tremulous, "Annja? What's going on?" in her direction.

She didn't even look.

Paul eyed her for several long minutes and then waved his hand again.

The guns were withdrawn.

"You really would sacrifice your friends to keep that blade from me, wouldn't you?"

"Yes," she said.

"It must be some special blade."

"It is."

Again, there was no use denying it.

Paul sauntered over.

"May I see it?"

"No."

"Why not?"

"Because it's not a toy to be trifled with."

He laughed. "Come, come, let's at least be honest with each other, Annja. You used the sword to pop the lock on a linen closet. If that's not trifling with it, then I don't know what is."

"That was my using the sword to save the life of an innocent. That is never a trifling matter."

"Hmph."

Paul walked around her, watching her, enjoying his power over her. Annja knew that was what he was doing so she stayed perfectly still, not letting him rile her a second time.

Eventually he'd grow tired of his game.

It didn't take long.

"I'll tell you what. I propose a little contest. Just you and me. The stakes will be your lives."

*Here it comes,* she thought. *Wait for it. Let him think it is his idea.*

"Yes, let's you and me have a little contest. Your swordmanship against mine. Winner takes all."

"What does that mean?"

"If I beat you, you relinquish the sword to me. If you beat me, I let the three of you go free."

Annja couldn't lose, not really. Besting Paul would mean another threat to the world eliminated. If she herself was bested, the sword would vanish back into the otherwhere, never to be drawn again.

Or, at least, she thought that was the case.

*So don't lose,* her inner voice told her.

Good advice. It isn't as if she had a choice, anyway. Not really.

"Agreed."

Paul chortled, long and lustily. "At last we get to the good stuff," he said with glee.

# 36

Annja turned her back, and when she turned around again she had her sword in hand.

Paul's eyes widened, as did those of the aged Nazi seated behind him.

*That's another snake that needs dealing with,* she thought. But for now she'd take them one at a time.

Paul snapped his fingers, and one of his flunkies walked over with a custom-made sword case. He laid it on the table, undid the clasps and opened it. He stepped back out of the way once he had done so.

Paul walked over and drew a gleaming katana from within the case. He swished it through the air a few times, getting a feel for it, and then walked back toward Annja.

"The only rules for this match," he said, "are that there aren't any rules!"

On the last word he spun and leaped into the air, the leap designed to hide the direction of the sword strike after he switched the blade from one hand to the other.

It was an impressive move. It might have worked

on a lesser opponent. But Annja had been carrying her blade for a long time now, and she had learned to trust its instincts. She expected treachery from Paul, and so when he lashed out, fully expecting to end the fight with a single blow, Annja's blade was there to meet his own.

As their swords locked against each other with the two of them eye to eye, Annja did the one thing she'd been wanting to do since yesterday afternoon.

She spit in his face.

The look of outrage that crossed his features as she laughed and spun away was worth all the gold in Hitler's little hideaway.

"You'll have to do much better than that if you want to beat me, Paul," she goaded him from the other side of the practice area.

He wiped his face and came after her with a vengeance.

He attacked her with ferocious energy, sending strike after strike in her direction. Slashes and thrusts and cuts and jabs, he did everything he could to simply overpower her defenses with brute strength.

Annja deflected them all.

She was like a dervish herself, spinning and turning, jumping and leaping, using the blade in a purely defensive fashion to keep Paul from scoring a blow. He wanted to kill her, it was in his eyes if not his hands, and she could not, would not, allow him to succeed.

Far more than her life was at stake.

Despite Paul's savage attacks, it was Annja who

drew first blood. As he spun away from a series of brutal strikes, her blade seemed to dance on its own, slipping between the blows like a striking snake and leaving a thin cut along his cheek.

He stopped, stepped back.

He brought his other hand to his face and felt the blood there.

The rage that overcame him when he realized he'd been struck was like a demon untamed. He lifted his head and screamed at the sky, one long ululating shriek.

If Annja had been thinking clearly, she would have simply lunged forward and thrust her sword up to its hilt in his chest, but his strange behavior had her momentarily stymied and by the time she had her wits about her, he was on guard once more.

"First blood to you," he said, and saluted her with his sword.

In the next instant the blade came down and his other hand rose.

Annja threw herself to the side.

The one-shot derringer hidden in the sleeve of his fencing jacket went off with a bang, the bullet slashing through the air quicker than any sword blade.

Fortunately for Annja, Paul's treachery was nothing new, and she was on guard for the slightest move. Her instant decision to throw herself to the side saved her life, for the shot from the derringer lashed across the outside of her thigh rather than finding a home in her chest as had been intended.

She hit the ground, rolled and came back up again,

finding that the leg hurt like hell but would still bear her weight.

But for how long?

Paul hadn't moved since he fired the shot, and as Annja regained her feet he smiled across the practice area at the blood running down her leg.

"Second blood to me."

He tossed the derringer aside and rushed forward again, brandishing his sword.

Annja met him halfway.

Slash and parry. Cut and jab. Around and around they went, neither of them gaining any significant advantage, their blades ringing as though they had voices of their own as they came in contact with each other.

They broke apart, both of them breathing heavily now. Sweat mixed with blood on Paul's face, giving his features an almost demonic cast. Annja was favoring her left leg, the blood flowing a little more freely from all the exertion.

The adversaries slowly circled each other, watching, waiting, looking for that perfect moment to strike.

This time Annja struck first, dropping into a very low back stance, her blade lashing out at Krugmann's knees. He in turn leaped upward, jumping over her blade and bringing his own down in a dazzling slash that embedded the tip of the blade in the wood of the deck. If Annja had still been there, she would have been carved in two.

But she wasn't, having spun away before her sword

had even finished its horizontal cut, knowing that she'd already missed.

They closed with each other again, blades ringing. Annja was concentrating so much on making sure his blade didn't touch her skin that when they came in close, their blades locked together once more, she didn't see his haymaker come swinging in past her defenses.

His fist smashed into the same spot where his boot had landed the previous day.

Pain exploded across Annja's face, momentarily blinding her, and in that moment, as brief as it was, Paul struck.

His sword lashed out, point first, and only Garin's scream of "Left" allowed Annja to know the strike was coming.

Trusting Garin implicitly, something she would deny vociferously if anyone ever suggested it in casual conversation, she twisted away as fast as she could.

Rather than skewer her lung, the blade carved a furrow across her rib cage but did not sink home.

Annja shook the pain and the tears out of her eyes, saw Paul coming in with another attack and threw herself out of the way of that one, too.

She rolled as she came out of it, twisting her shoulder in the midst of the somersault so that she came back up in a crouch. Facing her opponent, she parried his strikes before he could force her back again.

Annja was feeling the pain of her injuries now, was aware that she was starting to slow from the blood loss and knew that she had to end the contest quickly or face the very real chance that she might not survive.

She exaggerated her weakness, dragging her leg behind her even more than she had been seconds before. When Paul came in again with another flashing dervish of strikes, Annja parried them all but let them look a little bit sloppy, a little slower than usual.

He grinned at her through their blades and took the bait, driving in hard again, obviously thinking that at last he could overwhelm her effective defenses.

Paul pushed her back beneath the tenacity of his onslaught, trying to beat her into submission. As he came in with a horizontal strike designed to cut her in two, Annja let go of her blade and tossed it straight up into the air, the sun glinting off the plain, unadorned hilt. As the blade went up, Annja went down, dropping below the slash of Paul's sword, falling backward in a limbo-like maneuver to give room for the blade to pass by.

As Paul's eye went up, watching her sword, the follow-up to his own strike forgotten in that instant, Annja caused the sword to vanish into the otherwhere.

In the space of the next heartbeat, she caused it to reappear in her hand, the hand that was already in midswing with a perfectly timed blow targeted at Paul's midsection just below the rib cage.

He realized his mistake too late.

His gaze dropped in the split second before Annja's sword found its target.

He tried to counter, tried to bring his blade down

to intercept her strike, tried to get his torso out of the way of the incoming blow, but it was too little too late.

Annja's sword cut him open from one side to the other.

Paul died with a surprised expression on his face, as if he couldn't believe that he'd been bested by the woman he'd duped so cleverly for so long.

Annja stood over him, breathing heavily.

Looking down, she muttered, "Good riddance."

# 37

When their leader was cut down by her bladesword, Annja was relieved that the rest of the thugs aboard the yacht showed their true colors and surrendered like the cowards that they were. Only Colonel Schnell displayed a bit of fight, but he was just one man, and a ninety-five-year-old one at that, and he was quickly subdued and disarmed when he tried to use one of the guard's guns before they surrendered.

The aircraft Annja and her team had lifted out of the lake was seized by the government in Berlin. Brandt's and Adler's remains were retrieved from the lake and also returned to Germany for appropriate burial.

The gold was identified as belonging to the Hungarian National Bank, as Annja had suspected. The bank, of course, laid claim to it as soon as word of its existence leaked, and was backed up by the court ruling that quickly followed. Annja did receive a five percent finder's fee, which she promptly donated, not wanting to profit from something the Nazis had once stolen. In her subsequent conversations with the media, she didn't mention Wolf Island or the gold that she suspected was hidden there, and neither did Garin. Krugmann's boat, with his body aboard, had been quietly scuttled in deep water off Wolf Island, so no explanations were needed on that score, either.

That was how Annja wanted it and this time Garin was inclined to go along with her.

Matahi and his people were free of outside influence for the first time in more than seventy years. Both Annja and Garin thought they deserved every chance to restore the way of life they'd known before the Nazis had turned up.

One day she might return, she thought, just to explore the base fully, but as far as she was concerned the gold—which might or might not be there—could stay lost.

There was too much blood on it already.

\* \* \* \* \*

# COMING SOON FROM

**GOLD EAGLE**®

## Available September 1, 2015

### GOLD EAGLE EXECUTIONER®
**SYRIAN RESCUE** – *Don Pendleton*
Tasked with rescuing UN diplomats lost in the Syrian desert, Mack Bolan is in a deadly race against time—and against fighters willing to make the ultimate sacrifice.

### GOLD EAGLE SUPERBOLAN®
**LETHAL RISK** – *Don Pendleton*
A search-and-rescue mission to recover a high-ranking defector in China leads Mack Bolan to a government-sanctioned organ-harvesting facility.

### GOLD EAGLE DEATHLANDS®
**CHILD OF SLAUGHTER** – *James Axler*
When Doc is kidnapped by a band of marauders in what was once Nebraska, Ryan and the companions join forces with a beautiful but deadly woman with an agenda of her own...

### GOLD EAGLE ROGUE ANGEL™
**THE MORTALITY PRINCIPLE** – *Alex Archer*
In Prague researching the legend of the Golem, archaeologist Annja Creed uncovers a string of murders that seems linked to the creature. And Annja is the next target...

# JAMES AXLER
# DEATHLANDS®

**The saga that asks "What if a global nuclear war comes to pass?" and delivers gripping adventure and suspense in the grim postapocalyptic USA.**

Set in the ruins of America one hundred years after a nuclear war devastated the world, a group of warrior survivalists, led by the intrepid Ryan Cawdor, search for a better future. In their struggle, the group is driven to persevere—even resorting to the secret devices created by the mistrusted "whitecoats" of prewar science.

Since the nukecaust, the American dream has been reduced to a daily fight for survival. In the hellish landscape of Deathlands, few dare to dream of a better tomorrow. But Ryan Cawdor and his companions press on, driven by the need for a future less treacherous than the present.

**Available wherever Gold Eagle®**
**books and ebooks are sold.**

GOLD
EAGLE®

GEDL2015